Mr K Released

Mr K Released

MATÉI VISNIEC

TRANSLATED BY JOZEFINA KOMPORALY

LONDON   NEW YORK   CALCUTTA

Seagull Books, 2019

Originally published in Romanian as *Domnul K. eliberat*, 2010
© Matéi Visniec, 2010

First published in English translation by Seagull Books, 2019
English translation © Jozefina Komporaly, 2019

ISBN   978 0 8574 2 648 2

British Library Cataloguing-in-Publication Data
A catalogue record for this book is available from the British Library

Typeset by Seagull Books, Calcutta, India
Printed and bound by WordsWorth India, New Delhi, India

1

One fine day, Kosef J found himself released from prison. It all started with the rattling of the chains that secured the two locks on the lift. Then the doors at the very end of the corridor were flung open. Lastly, there was some muttered swearing followed by the creaking of the breakfast trolley. But only when the two elderly prison guards walked past Kosef J's cell without even breaking stride did he realize that something unusual was about to happen.

In the first few minutes Kosef J was deeply confused and somewhat offended. This was the first time that Franz Hoss and his deputy, Fabius, passed by his cell as if he, Kosef J, wasn't even inside. He could tell that, as usual, the flaps of the slots for the food trays were being opened one by one, and that all the other familiar noises punctuated the very particular ritual of breakfast time. Old Franz Hoss kept on howling and smashing against the metal doors. Fabius, at the end of his rope, as always, carried on mumbling and complaining about the prisoners' stench.

This was followed by about five minutes of silence. Only a few stifled splashes and the rattling of someone choking on his food broke the silence.

Kosef J jumped out of bed and dashed to the door. He pressed his temple to the cold metal frame and listened. He felt queasy. All the other prisoners were having breakfast.

All the other forty-nine prisoners in the other forty-nine cells were eating, while he, the fiftieth in the fiftieth cell, had been completely ignored for some mysterious reason. This was the moment when old Hoss reappeared at the end of the corridor.

The old prison guard had an unmistakable walk. He shuffled, and his steel toe plates kept scraping the concrete floor while the soles of his boots were scratching along the floor like sandpaper. Kosef J could hear these boots head towards his cell, as if they were two strange, slightly crippled, but nonetheless menacing animals. 'Good God,' Kosef J said to himself, 'I hope this isn't going to turn nasty.' He stepped back, sat down on the edge of his bed and tried to hold his breath for a few seconds.

Franz Hoss opened the door, slid to a halt on the threshold, and said with a smile on his face: 'Good morning, Mr Kosef J!'

'What?' Kosef J started and rose to his feet involuntarily.

Franz Hoss entered the cell and began to examine its walls. He walked up and down, shaking his head a few times in disapproval. He placed both of his palms on the wall and waited carefully, as if he wanted to measure the dampness in that particular spot. Then he let out a sigh, and sat down on the edge of the bed.

'The weather is set to take a turn for the worse,' the old guard announced with sadness. 'Yes, it is indeed,' he added, scratching his beard.

Kosef J thought he was dreaming. First of all, he could scarcely believe that old Franz was capable of showing such an unusual side to himself: tired and—as a result—

calm, sad, and—due to the sadness—also very warm and human. Moreover, it seemed inconceivable to him that the rancorous guard would be capable of such a relaxed and even chatty tone, a tone that practically encouraged conversation.

'This rain is killing me,' Kosef J seemed to hear, as if in a dream. 'It never used to rain like this.'

'What?' Kosef J muttered again, startled. This was his second shocked 'what', and he felt a little ashamed of being unable to cope with the conversation.

'No, no,' old Franz responded immediately, slightly invigorated. 'We've obviously never had rain like this before.'

A terrible thought, unfolding at breakneck speed, started to blossom in the prisoner's mind. 'Maybe they want to kill me, maybe they are all mad, maybe my mother is here to see me,' Kosef J heard himself thinking, and for a moment he was convinced that he must have been thinking out loud. But no, he certainly hadn't been thinking out loud, because old Franz remained seated on the edge of his bed and scratched his beard from time to time.

'It's already November and soon it will be December,' Franz Hoss mused and stared into Kosef J's eyes, as if he wanted to read the other's thoughts.

'But it didn't rain in September,' Kosef J said suddenly, astonished at hearing himself speak.

'What do you mean it didn't rain?' the guard snapped.

'It didn't rain,' Kosef J insisted.

'What do you mean it didn't rain?' the guard yelled, in a blunt yet still cordial tone.

'It didn't rain,' Kosef J insisted, sure of himself. He would have liked to have added 'simply', but didn't, considering that he had already gone too far. Nevertheless, he felt overwhelmed by happiness. He had managed to squeeze in no fewer than two 'what's, which meant that he'd had the courage to contradict the old guard twice. 'Now,' Kosef said to himself, 'he's welcome to go ahead and hit me.'

But Franz Hoss didn't hit him. Instead, he lowered his gaze to the floor, with the expression of a man worn out by toil and advanced age. All of a sudden, Kosef J felt sorry for the old prison guard. He almost regretted his insistence on 'it didn't rain'. What was the point of troubling an old and possibly ill man?

Then the sound of jumbled words coming from the corridor caught his attention. Somebody was dragging himself along the row of doors. 'It's Fabius,' Kosef J realized, and an unpleasant thought stuck in his mind.

'It's Fabius,' the old guard confirmed, as if he had heard the prisoner's private thoughts and wanted to reassure him.

'Good morning, Mr Kosef J,' Fabius said as he appeared at the wide open door.

Kosef J nodded and stared into nothingness. Ultimately, prison guards could get away with whatever they liked. If the two old men felt like greeting him in this cordial way, there was no stopping them. By the same token, if the two guards wanted to beat the living daylights out of him and after each blow wish him 'good morning, Mr Kosef J,' no one would have been able to stop them.

On this particular morning, however, deputy Fabius and his boss, Franz Hoss, seemed to have no such perverse

4

intentions. Fabius continued to lean against the doorframe, looking bewildered, as if he wanted to enter but was too embarrassed to do so. A few moments of silence followed. Fabius fished out a pack of cigarettes and weighed it in his palm before handing it to Franz Hoss. The old guard pulled out a cigarette with an expression of profound gratitude.

'Would you care for a cigarette, Mr Kosef J?'

Kosef J registered the question and felt as if he was in the grip of a hurricane with his head submerged under water. Something baffling was unwinding, something extremely unpleasant like a waking nightmare.

'It's better this way,' he could hear Fabius's voice.

The two guards lit their cigarettes and Kosef J realized that Fabius was about to put the pack back into his pocket. His bafflement must have been interpreted as a refusal.

'No, no,' Kosef J hastened, 'I want one, too.'

'Smoking is a curse,' Fabius observed, holding out the pack of cigarettes. 'Especially when it's humid.'

'I agree,' Franz Hoss confirmed.

'Do you?' Fabius turned to his boss, smiling.

'I do indeed!' Franz Hoss endorsed his colleague, and Kosef J caught a glimpse of a fantastic image: the two guards smiling at one another in full agreement, which clearly made them both happy.

'Really good,' Kosef J said pointing at the cigarette, mainly because he felt obliged to share this moment of harmony.

'I have more,' Fabius responded. 'Do let me know if you want another.'

The cell quickly filled up with smoke. The cigarette made Kosef J even dizzier and his legs started trembling. His heart was pumping faster and faster, yet still carried insufficient amounts of blood to his brain. This triggered a staccato beat, as if someone had been frantically chopping onions in a kitchen. Kosef J wondered whether his heartbeat couldn't be heard *a little* too loudly in the cell. He would have liked to sit down on the edge of the bed, at least for a minute, but was unsure how to ask for permission.

Franz Hoss giggled. Fabius took two steps forward, stopped in front of Kosef J and patted him protectively on the shoulder. A second later all three were sitting on the edge of bed, smoking. Kosef J couldn't recall ever having felt so relaxed and so *protected*. In fact, he would have preferred to die, to make this sensation last or to hold on to it forever.

2

The first thing Kosef J noticed when he woke up was his cell door left ajar. He sat up and looked around carefully. The objects in the cell appeared in a blur, yet he did his best to identify them. A terrible fear nestled in his throat when he realized how late it was. The light seeping through the narrow cell window indicated lunchtime. Kosef J jumped to his feet and rushed to the wall with the window. He hooked his hands into the bars and, propping himself up on his knees, managed to lift his chin above the lower edge of the window.

The inmates were working in the prison's kitchen garden.

Kosef J got down from the window and rubbed his palms together, disheartened. Finally, his brain decided to kickstart. If the detainees were working in the prison's kitchen garden that meant, yes that meant that it was *Sunday*. Because it was only on Sundays, during recreation hours, that the detainees were allowed to work in the prison's kitchen garden. Kosef J came instantly to grips with the entire anomaly of this morning. He remembered vividly that he *did not get* breakfast. Then he realized that he was now excluded from garden work as well, a work that the detainees loved because they were allowed to eat green beans and peas.

'This isn't right,' Kosef J said to himself. The smell of cheap cigarettes in his cell made him sick. His whole mouth was a wound, his lips were burning, and on the tip of his tongue he could detect a few loose leaves of bitter tobacco. Yet he was allowed to sleep straight through Sunday morning, something that had never happened before. The latter thought brought some calm to him, together with the feeling of being well rested. He had never felt so well rested and so lucid before. And he had never felt a greater urge to work in the kitchen garden.

He walked to the door left ajar and surveyed the part of the corridor within view. The entire floor was deadly silent. Utterly perplexed, Kosef J waited for a few minutes in front of the door left in such a careless state. He didn't have the slightest idea what he was supposed to do or not to do. After a while he decided to open the door a little further, so he could get a better look at the corridor. He stretched his arm out and pushed the door gently. He found it beyond belief that the door didn't display any resistance. He got to look down the corridor, like he wanted, but he couldn't see it in its entirety. After a while, he decided to open the door properly and try to take in the *whole* corridor.

The corridor was deserted. At its end, the door leading to the lift was left ajar, too. Kosef J thought that after all, if things were the way they were, he could perhaps allow himself a short walk on the corridor. He slid past the walls, looking into the other cells. Nobody, nowhere. He got to the end of the corridor, where the lift was. Once there, he stopped, changed his mind and turned around. He found himself in his cell again, more confused than ever. Once more, he clenched the bars on his window and gazed outside.

The detainees were still working briskly in the prison's kitchen garden. It was a sunny day and some had taken their shirts off.

Kosef J experienced a sense of envy, even begrudgement. His stomach gave clear signs of unease. A skipped breakfast was almost catastrophic. Hunger was grinding him not so much in his stomach but in his brain, unleashing a chain of queries and a sensation of total discontent. Kosef J was overcome with profound sadness, especially because there was no one to tell him what to do. It was obvious that something *new* was happening, something concerning him and his future, but he didn't know what that was.

'Mr Hoss!' Kosef J shouted, standing in the doorway of his cell, hoping that the old prison guard would hear him from wherever he was, such as the lift tower, for instance.

No one answered, so Kosef J placed his palms around his mouth to form a trumpet, and shouted again: 'Mr Prison Guard! Mr Prison Guard, this is me, Kosef J!'

He would have liked to continue: Mister Prison Guard, what the hell, this is me, surely you know who I am.

'Mr Hoss, can I go to the kitchen garden?' Kosef J asked again, delighted that it occurred to him to ask for permission.

No response this time either. But Kosef J was suddenly feeling more confident. The fact that he *did ask for permission* gave him the conviction that he didn't do anything wrong. Basically, he wasn't formally forbidden to go to the kitchen garden on a Sunday. He had been *carrying out*

Sunday gardening duties for a few good years now and always proved to be a conscientious and diligent fellow.

Sure of himself, he headed towards the lift. He had never used the lift unescorted. He checked out the six or seven buttons corresponding to the various floors. He pushed the button with the arrow pointing upward and the lift rose to him. He entered the liftcage, which reminded him of his own cell, closed the safety railing, and pressed the button marked zero. The lift jerked into motion. Kosef J felt sick. He squeezed his stomach with his fists and huddled in a corner. He was disgusted with the thought of throwing up in the lift and tried to suppress the urge. He held his breath and tightened his jaws. The lift came to a halt but Kosef J didn't dare stand up. His stomach suddenly felt very heavy. Something was poking him from within, filling him up with a gluey and poisonous liquid. Kosef J closed his eyes, clenched his teeth even stronger and huddled up even more. He was shaking all over and his muscles tightened.

The lift door was suddenly propped open and Deputy Fabius's head appeared in the doorway.

'Do you need to puke?' Fabius asked, unperturbed, as if the lift's sole purpose had been to transport people about to get sick to the ground floor.

'Yes,' groaned Kosef J.

'Come with me to the lavatory,' Fabius said, helping Kosef J to his feet.

The two men dragged themselves along the corridor, hanging on to one another. Fabius, limping and gasping from the effort, and Kosef J in pain and just about to explode. This was the first time Kosef J set foot on this corridor, yet he was able to figure out that Fabius was taking him to the lavatory reserved for prison guards. He felt overwhelmed by a strange pride, which spread all over his body despite the fact that he was shivering in pain and feeling quite nauseous.

Fabius helped him to throw up, holding him by the back of his neck. Kosef J had the impression that he was pouring all his guts out, one by one. Sweat was streaming down his neck and face, while tears borne by the effort mingled with sweat. Fabius tried to calm him down:

'Almost there, Mr Kosef, almost there.'

But Kosef J continued to throw up over and over again, and kept on groaning until his groan began to echo, absolutely convinced that he would be vomiting like this until the end of his days. This was the moment when Fabius, holding him by the nape and shoulders, advised him that, as of that morning, he was a free man.

3

Kosef J announced that he was feeling much better and asked Fabius to allow him to be on his own *a little*. Fabius got out a handkerchief, wiped Kosef's face and mouth, and, gently forcing him to keep the handkerchief, responded: 'Yes, of course.'

Left alone, Kosef J calmed down little by little. The prison guards' lavatory was spotless; he could almost see his reflection in the tiles. It smelt of quality disinfectant and Kosef J breathed in the air with delight. Then he tried for minutes on end to remember the exact phrase Fabius had told him. He was not sure of its *wording*. He was trying to remember it, rummaging through his head. His brain echoed something along the lines of 'Be brave, Mr Kosef, you were freed this morning.' But no, this was too long, Fabius used other words. 'Take it easy, take it easy. From now on you are a free man.' Not this either. Fabius used an official term, something like 'your period of detention has come to an end.' Still not there. What Fabius told him felt like a piece of information conveyed with great concern: 'Beware, as of today you are free as a bird.' No.

Kosef J would have liked to feel something really special, to be blissfully happy or moved to tears. But he didn't experience anything like this. He was given the news, his brain made a record of it, and that was that. All he could feel was stomach ache, and a terrible hunger. What Fabius told him would certainly explain all the strange behaviour that morning. He was allowed an additional three hours of sleep because he, Kosef J, was entitled to it. In his capacity as a free man. Yet he was not informed of this fact, of being a free man, straightaway. He slept his first sleep as a free man without being aware of this freedom. The two prison guards were rather strange, and, to be fair, they behaved nicely but strangely. Perhaps it wasn't their job to tell Kosef J that he was suddenly free, and this would explain everything. But if it wasn't their job to tell him he was free, whose job should it have been? Kosef J gave up thinking about all this and made a real effort to feel pleased. He tried to be pleased with his stolidity, and concentrated on this with all his might.

'This is the most beautiful day of my life,' Kosef J whispered to himself, hoping to get a little emotional.

He waited for a few moments to savour the impact of this sentence, and then, disgruntled, he repeated it much louder: 'This is the most beautiful day of my life.'

'Did you say something?' Fabius asked, and Kosef J had to make use of all his strength to prevent the guard from opening the door.

'Do you need anything?' Fabius asked again, checking whether there was a need for him to pull the door open.

'No, nothing at all,' Kosef J answered in a soft voice from within the lavatory.

Except for hunger, nothing bothered him any more. He glanced at his reflection on the tiles and smiled. The tiles were white and his skin gained a pearl-like glow. He noticed, mounted on the wall and in a marble frame, a ring-shaped toilet-paper holder. He instinctively felt the urge to roll down as much paper as possible and stash away a few sheets for later. His sense of superiority held him back from this urge though. He pulled his trousers up, pulled on the golden chain of the water tank and stepped out of the lavatory.

In the meantime, Fabius had disappeared. Kosef J no longer felt awkward. He took his time washing his hands and face in a sink he spotted on the corridor, right under a window. After savouring the cool water on his face, Kosef J looked out of the window.

The window overlooked a side of the prison Kosef J had never seen before. He realized that he was facing the administrative building, comprising offices, storerooms and the guards' own bedrooms. An alleyway covered in gravel led to one of the side entrances to the prison. The alley was flanked by a few old poplars that Kosef J liked immensely. The gate at the end of the alley was less commanding than entrance Number One, which he had known for so long. Two lanterns placed on either side gave this entrance a discreet, intimate and inviting feel.

The thought that he was now finally free sprouted again in his mind. A tremendous urge to run towards that gate flanked by lanterns had suddenly awakened in him. Good God, what on earth could *freedom* actually entail? Would freedom mean that he was allowed to walk on that alley flanked by poplars? Would he be allowed to return to the window after nightfall and check out the light of the lanterns for himself?

Feeling helpless, Kosef J bit his lip. He practically knew nothing of what his life would be like *from now on*. Someone should have certainly told him a thing or two, but that someone hadn't yet come forward. The two guards appeared a little uncomfortable, too. Perhaps it was up to him to ask a few questions, to ask for more precise information. After all it was *he* who got freed. Yet he found it quite difficult to imagine that old Hoss had never granted anyone else their freedom before. 'I'm an idiot,' Kosef J said to himself, and headed to the kitchen garden with determination.

He could spot the two guards from afar, sprawled on a bench, enjoying the few sunrays that had managed to miraculously break through the clouds. The two were eating sunflower seeds and Franz Hoss had his eyes closed.

The detainees were busying themselves happily among the cabbage and tomato patches. They stopped work when they caught sight of Kosef J, and, with astonished yet respectful expressions, started whispering to one another. For a moment Kosef J felt guilty that he'd slept all morning instead of coming out to work alongside everyone else, as usual. He got over this quickly, though, saying to himself that he was now a *free* man after all and had other *responsibilities*. As he was heading towards the bench where the two guards were slumbering, Kosef J decided to ask for no less than to be escorted as soon as possible to the main prison gate.

'How's it going?' Franz Hoss probed, opening his eyes just before Kosef J could get close enough to engage them in conversation.

Fabius rose to his feet for no apparent reason. Kosef J's breathing stopped and all his plans to ask a few questions suddenly evaporated. The detainees resumed work.

'Fine,' Kosef J said, realizing that the old guard was clearly awaiting a response to his question.

'Would you like to sit with us?' Fabius asked and Kosef J said yes.

'It's a miracle that the sun still breaks through,' Franz Hoss muttered.

Fabius handed a bag of sunflower seeds to Kosef J.

'Here, have some.'

Kosef J accepted gladly. He was extremely hungry and would have been able to eat just about anything. He would have liked to dash to the garden and pick a few peapods, but for some reason he was embarrassed to do this.

'Look at these sluggards,' the old guard croaked again, 'they haven't made any progress since morning. They've filled their bellies, that's what they've done. They filled their breadbaskets. That's all.'

Kosef J blushed suddenly, fingers frozen in the air. He managed to spit out a few shells and, with his mouth open, was waiting for air to somehow penetrate his lungs. Was this a veiled reproach from Franz Hoss?

'What a shame that today's Sunday,' Fabius said, resting his gaze on Kosef J, but the latter failed to grasp the actual meaning of this sentence.

For a while all three kept quiet. The break in the clouds was about to come to an end, to the regret of Franz Hoss. When the last ray was abruptly severed by an avalanche of clouds, the old guard jumped up and issued a command. The detainees lined up immediately. It was mealtime and everybody was awaiting their return to their cells.

'So that's that,' Fabius said to Kosef J, wrapping up a conversation that had never really taken place.

The prisoners fell into formation. Franz Hoss was shouting down the line, issuing all sorts of commands and insulting someone or other. Fabius shook out the shells from his beard and followed Franz Hoss.

All of a sudden, Kosef J felt incredibly lonely. A hard and oppressive loneliness, veiled in an almost unbearable sadness. He had never felt so abandoned, had never experienced a greater state of confusion. Of all the contradictory impulses that had tried him, Kosef J chose the most natural one. He decided to re-enter his cell and wait there for lunch.

So he ran to catch up with the inmates.

4

This time Kosef J was really angry. For the second time
that day the guards had passed by his cell without handing
him the regulation tray of food. The customary *mealtime*
racket was echoing all over the prison floor. He could
make out sudden bursts of laughter and the odd belch,
though the cutlery itself didn't add much to the noise as it
was made of plastic. The already muttered sounds ended
up entirely stifled, as if coming from a beehive shrouded
in steam.

Kosef J hated being hungry. In fact, he was willing
to endure anything except hunger. He was prepared to
understand a great deal, but he couldn't possibly compre-
hend why he wasn't *given* anything to eat any longer. He
had a feeling though that *the imprecision* of his release
was connected to the special Sunday atmosphere, after all
this was a day when routine was somewhat neglected.
Contemplating what happened in the garden, Kosef J was
telling himself that Fabius's words 'what a shame today's
Sunday' couldn't have had any other significance but this.
Had it been any other day of the week, things would have
probably turned out *differently* and he, Kosef J, would
have found himself already on the other side of the
lantern-flanked gates. Yes, one could contemplate such a

situation, one could understand and accept any number of other things. But not the business with breakfast and especially lunch, not these.

Kosef J set out to look for Franz Hoss without calling his name from the door of this cell and asking for his permission to make a move, like he'd done only a short while ago. It wasn't without a sense of pride that he passed by the heavily locked doors of the other cells, though hunger was driving him crazy and made him rather resentful.

Franz Hoss and Fabius were having lunch at the end of the corridor, just by the lift. The two guards were so immersed in what they were doing that they didn't hear Kosef J get closer. Franz Hoss had already finished his soup and moved on to a piece of meat. Fabius, who was eating more slowly, savouring every second of that moment, had still another five or six spoonfuls left. It seemed to Kosef J, for reasons unknown to him, that the guards' meal was somewhat *richer* than it should have ordinarily been. A bowl, the purpose of which was hard to figure out, seemed to be concealed under Fabius's chair. This helmet-shaped bowl was swaying gently, as if it had just been tucked in there and as a result, it didn't yet manage to find a state of total stillness.

Kosef J slowed down, but held on to his determination and the stubborn look on his face.

'Oh, Mr Kosef,' mumbled Franz Hoss with his mouth full.

'Mr Hoss, please, I have no idea what's happening,' Kosef J babbled.

'What?' the guard stopped chewing, deeply alarmed and with a fixed gaze.

'*Food,* sir,' Kosef J whispered, grunting and on the verge of bursting into tears. His Adam's apple, set in motion by an overstrung nerve, was jumping up and down and made him dry swallow every now and then.

'Food?' the guard echoed him.

'Yes, food, food indeed,' Kosef J spelt out.

The two guards looked at one another. Franz Hoss winked, presumably scanning his brain for secret connections between the word 'food' and Kosef J's presence.

'Well, Mr Kosef,' Franz Hoss mumbled, 'I thought you were told.'

'Told what?' Kosef J asked.

Franz Hoss looked reproachfully at Fabius.

'Was he or wasn't he told?'

'He was, he was indeed,' Fabius insisted.

'There you are,' Franz Hoss shrugged.

'What? What do you mean?' Kosef J struggled to voice a response.

The situation was as awkward as possible, or at least it so appeared to Kosef J. Looking at Fabius's plate he realized that the last spoonfuls of soup have gone cold by now, and this would have normally chafed the old guard no end.

'You're free, Mr Kosef, you're free,' Franz Hoss howled, though his aim was to make Kosef J understand *the idea* rather than convey hate or impatience.

'They are at it again,' Kosef J said to himself.

'Do understand,' Franz Hoss continued. 'This is it. You are *off the list.*'

Fabius burst out laughing, which somewhat encouraged Kosef J, despite feeling a gradual urge to run back to his cell and bury his head under the pillow.

'You're no longer entitled to meals,' Fabius explained very calmly. 'Your portion was *taken off* the list. Do you get it? You are off the budget. At this point, since you are free, you know, the prison isn't obliged to provide you with anything. Do you understand?'

Kosef J did understand. The other two carried on with their meals.

'But if you wanted to buy something . . . ' Kosef J heard as if in a dream, without being able to tell which of the two guards was talking.

'Something good,' the first voice resumed.

'Sausages OK with you?'

'What shall I do, what shall I do, what shall I do?' Kosef J mulled over this dilemma in his head. Freedom hit upon him in the shape of something very distant and surreal. And he, former detainee in cell number 50, just released, had no point of reference whatsoever, none of his actions were consistent and no thought was powerful enough to trigger deeds. Fabius quaffed his last spoonfuls of cold soup with the same pleasure he experienced when slurping the hot ones. Franz Hoss finished his meat and was now gathering the leftover breadcrumbs and swallowing them with the pleasure he had swallowed the meat with. Fabius was eating his portion of meat with the same pleasure with which Franz Hoss had eaten his. 'For them,' Kosef J mused, 'everything is really simple—they know what they are supposed to do in each and every moment—for them everything makes sense . . . '

'This man is hungry,' Fabius stated.

Kosef J tried to look Fabius straight in the eye to thus show his gratitude.

'Shall I take him to the kitchen?' Fabius asked, without addressing the question to anyone in particular.

'Yes, take him,' Franz Hoss echoed, and Kosef J quickly directed his gaze to the old guard, spurred by the same childish desire to show his gratitude.

'Come,' Fabius sighed heavily, like a man who knows full well that his afternoon break has gone to the dogs.

'They are wonderful people after all,' Kosef J concluded, and followed Fabius into the lift.

Despite being famished and rather dizzy after such an exceptional day, Kosef J was pleased that he could finally tread the alleys leading to the kitchen. This was a different zone of the prison altogether, and he had never set foot here before, although he had always spied at it from a distance with a sort of perverse longing. He was eager to see new things and, behold, new images were rolling out in front of his eyes. He could make out the gravel under his feet, as if it were something he had already seen in his mind's eye, something capable of reinvigorating him. As he was nearing the kitchen he rejoiced at the sight of the large chimneys above the large roofs, and the giant windows of the staff dining room.

The sky was overcast with tattered clouds. A rather cold wind made the poplar leaves shake. The black smoke coming from the kitchen chimneys left an unpleasant imprint in the sky.

'We are going to have a long winter,' Fabius remarked disheartened.

Kosef J would have liked to answer as warmly and amiably as possible, but could only muster the following words: 'Perhaps.'

'There will be seven long winters in a row, you'll see,' Fabius continued. 'There have already been seven short winters and now it's time for seven long winters.'

Kosef J tried to recall whether the last seven winters were indeed short ones. But all winters seemed rather exasperating to him, or, to be precise, identical and equal, strikingly equal in their exasperation.

'There will be, of course there will be,' he responded, scolding himself for resorting to such idiotic statements.

They entered the building that housed the kitchen. The hallway was already much warmer than any other room Kosef J had ever set foot in. It also smelt extremely good.

'Rozette!' Fabius shouted. Then, turning towards Kosef J, he added: 'she must be having lunch.'

Kosef J didn't find it unusual that a person named Rozette, being in a kitchen, should *not* eat.

'Rozette!' Fabius shouted once more, so loudly that he nearly choked and started coughing.

Kosef J felt obliged to say something, especially since all this journey was undertaken for his sake. So he also decided to have a go at shouting, as politely as he could possibly manage: 'Rozette!'

'Bloody hell!' Fabius suppressed a scowl of iritation. 'When she's eating she doesn't hear a thing.'

They entered a fairly large hall with several electric ovens. Kosef J slowed down, intimidated yet eager to see these fantastic appliances from as close up as possible. But Fabius pulled him by the sleeve; they walked past two or three dishwashers and were heading towards one of the most concealed nooks of the hall, beyond the cutlery cupboards. At a table a woman was feeding a child.

'She's Rozette,' Fabius said and, exhausted, flung himself onto a chair.

The child looked amusedly at Fabius as Fabius smirked.

'This is Kosef J. I spoke to you about him,' Fabius continued. 'He'll eat here.'

Kosef J drew his breath to say something but absolutely nothing came to his mind. The child was sizing him up, so he decided to smile at him.

'Fine,' one could hear Rozette's voice.

The woman had such a pleasing voice that Kosef J pulled back and waited for her to say something else. But Rozette had nothing to add. She put some lumpy yet warm and steaming substance onto a plate and placed it in front of Kosef J.

'Eat as much bread as you like,' Fabius added.

Kosef J began to eat, feeling incredibly content. The child carried on staring at him so he wondered whether he had actually satiated his hunger. But no, the child had eaten *all* up, and now was simply curious. 'I'm a stranger to him, am I not?' Kosef J said to himself. Chewing carefully, he looked at the child again. The child smiled at him. Kosef J registered this smile with boundless delight. 'He's a good kid,' he said to himself. 'And the food is good, too,' he added. Everything was extremely warm and welcoming in this part of the prison.

'Is the food OK?' Fabius asked, laughing.

Kosef J nodded and laughed with his mouth full. The woman joined in the laughter, too. All three were watching him with an expression of profound sympathy on their faces. Kosef J felt happy for the first time in his life.

'You can have some more if you like,' Rozette said in that pleasing voice of hers.

'Thanks, I'd rather not,' Kosef J responded.

'Don't be shy,' the woman encouraged him.

'Do talk to me, please talk to me as much as you can,' Kosef J thought. He would have listened to Rozette forever, even if she were to talk about operating dishwashers. 'I'll give her a hand once I'm done,' he decided. Yes, it was high time he did something in return for these people. 'I'll also give Fabius a hand,' he continued, although he didn't yet know in what way he could possibly give a hand to Fabius.

Without asking, the woman handed him a second helping. All three smiled again and he resumed eating. 'They are kind, they are good, they are genuine people,' Kosef J kept saying to himself. This was life, this was freedom; lo and behold, it was freedom itself that had eventually appeared in front of him.

'I'm off,' Fabius announced.

'Thank you, thank you very much indeed,' Kosef J called out after the guard.

'Would you like some water?' the woman asked.

'Yes please,' an eager Kosef J responded, hoping to engage in a dialogue, however brief, with her.

'Bring Mr Kosef a glass of water,' Rozette said to the child.

The child jumped off his chair and fetched him a glass of water. 'What a good boy,' Kosef thought to himself.

'What a good boy,' he went on to observe, this time in a loud voice, because he wanted to say something and couldn't find anything other than repeat his earlier thought.

'Yes, he's very obedient,' the woman concurred.

'He's very well brought up,' Kosef J added, proud that he could come up with this sentence, yet astonished that such a thought could linger in his mind for so long without him being aware of it.

'I brought him up,' the woman said. Then she gave the child a kiss, as if prompting him: 'Didn't I?'

'Can I give you a hand with anything?' Kosef J asked when he finally got up from the table.

'No,' Rozette answered.

Kosef J insisted: 'I'll do any job.'

The woman shook her head firmly and Kosef J experienced an alarming wave of regret. He headed towards the exit. The child followed him.

Once they made it to the alley, Kosef J came to a halt. So the child stopped a few steps behind him, too. The weather carried on being unpredictable, though every now and then sunrays would strike the walls and the bluish gravel. Again, Kosef J felt extremely confused. On the one hand, he was very pleased that he managed to satiate his hunger, but on the other, he didn't know what he was supposed to do with himself from then on. He turned around and looked at the child. Taking this as an encouragement, the child twitched and came up to Kosef J.

'I have some pebbles,' the child said.

'Say it again!' Kosef J replied.

The child giggled. Holding Kosef J by the hand, he dragged him past a few buildings Kosef J hadn't been aware of until now, and came to a halt in a kind of blind alley, near a damp and blackened wall.

'Here,' the child said.

At the base of the wall, someone had dug a small pit and filled it with gravel.

'These are mine,' the child added.

Kosef J couldn't make sense of any of this. Instinctively, he adopted an astonished look.

'All of these,' the child continued. 'You can come here whenever you like.'

'I shall come,' Kosef J said, 'I'll come for sure.'

5

Kosef J rested in a deep and dreamless sleep. When he woke up, on Monday morning, he was really surprised to find that he hadn't heard anything from the usual breakfast racket. He stepped out to the corridor and found all cell doors wide open. Everyone had left for work. Suddenly it dawned on him that he was *free*. He went downstairs, to the ground-floor basin reserved for prison guards, and washed his face.

He looked out of the window. The small gate, the two lanterns, the poplar-flanked alley and the sky covered in tattered clouds and fleeting sunrays were all in place. The words of Fabius, 'he'll eat here', still echoed in his mind, so he headed off to the kitchen.

Franz Hoss and Fabius were playing dice at the wooden table. Rozette has switched on the dishwashers and she seemed to be hard at work. The child was nowhere to be seen. The air was unbreathable. The steam coming from the dishwashers reeked of detergent and fat.

'Look who's here!' Franz Hoss commented when he saw Kosef J. Fabius said nothing. Franz Hoss shook the dice in a tin cup, looking totally immersed, with cheeks red from excitement. He fixed his gaze somewhere beyond his immediate surroundings, and for a few seconds it

28

looked as if he was praying. Then he rolled the dice. The two old prison guards leant forward, both at the same time, nearly bumping their foreheads. Fabius broke out in a merciless laughter.

'Your way of rolling the dice is rubbish, and that's that,' he said. 'This is no way to roll. You don't roll the dice as if they were grains.'

Franz Hoss didn't react. Glum-faced, he was trying to look Kosef J in the eye, as if he wanted to seek his help.

'This isn't the proper way to roll,' Fabius carried on mercilessly. 'You roll by way of your mind, not by hand.'

Rozette brought over a tray with two large slices of bread and two cups filled with some yellow liquid. She placed the tray on the corner of the table and left without a single word. Kosef J looked around hoping to spot a chair somewhere. He couldn't see any so he began to eat while standing.

'This isn't the way to shake, either,' Fabius carried on with his theory. 'When you shake, you don't look at any-one at all.'

Kosef J decided to eat as fast as possible and then get away. This time he didn't find the kitchen to his liking. The steam was making him choke and tiny drops of fat were landing on his hair.

'Have you been to the clothing-supply room yet?' Franz Hoss suddenly tackled Kosef J.

'No,' he responded swiftly.

'Well, you should go,' the old guard said begrudgingly.

It was Fabius's turn to roll the dice and Kosef J stopped chewing. One could only hear the muffled sound of the dishwashers. Fabius rolled the dice and then immediately picked up his running commentary where he left it: 'See, I told you! Did I or didn't I?'

Franz Hoss produced a large handkerchief and blew his nose. He behaved like a sulking child.

'Get it now?' Fabius pressed on. 'You need to go easy, really easy. That's all. As easy as possible.'

Kosef J gave his all to figure out why Franz Hoss asked whether he *had been* to the clothing-supply room. What business would he, Kosef J, have at the clothing-supply room? No one had told him that he should go to the clothing-supply room. He didn't even know that there was such a thing as a clothing-supply room in the first place.

'Why?' he asked in an indifferent tone, as if this was about something totally unimportant.

'For clothes,' the reply came.

Again, Kosef J felt taken over by an inexplicable emotion that localized, like a claw, at the root of his neck. For clothes then, of course, for clothes! How could he not realize before? This was so obvious. Freedom had to be marked in some way, and the clearest *sign* was changing clothes. It was his own fault that he had become so accustomed to his prison clothes that he couldn't imagine wearing anything else.

'You should go tomorrow,' one could hear the voice of Franz Hoss, followed by the sound of the rolling dice on the wooden table.

'Sure, I'll go,' Kosef J replied, trying to avail himself of the same indifferent tone as before. 'But why tomorrow and not today?' he could not help but wonder. The clothes, being so important, should have been dispensed to him in

30

the morning. If not yesterday even. But yesterday was Sunday, and it goes without saying that the clothing-supply room couldn't have been open on a Sunday. It had to be closed for sure. But today? Why not today? It was his own fault, and only his, that he didn't enquire about his rights. Franz Hoss was no doubt a kind and helpful man, but he had no obligation to drag Kosef J to the clothing-supply room, and then to the other side of the prison gate and say, 'Mr Kosef J, this is where your freedom begins.'

'Still, why tomorrow and not today?' Kosef J continued to fret. He didn't have the courage to actually ask Franz Hoss. This would have appeared outright rude. As if you regretted something you didn't even know about, and then suddenly found out you can't get. Tomorrow was near enough, a delay of just *one day* didn't really make any difference. Not to mention that perhaps there was no delay whatsoever, because the clothing-supply room wasn't open on Sundays and Mondays. This was possible. Anything was possible.

'Would you like to have a go?' Fabius asked, handing him the dice.

'Yes, I would,' Kosef J said happily.

He threw the dice into the tin cup, shook the cup twice and placed it on the table, mouth facing down. Then he lifted the cup and all three leant forward, eager to see the outcome of the dice.

'There!' Fabius blurted out. 'Mr Kosef rolls *correctly*.'

Kosef J had no idea whether his score was very good, good or merely acceptable from the point of view of the two prison guards. He wasn't particularly keen to clarify either. The fact that he rolled 'correctly' was more than enough for him.

Rozette came to collect the breakfast tray. Seeing her, Kosef J felt a sudden urge to hear her speak and eagerly offered to lend her a hand with washing the dishes.

'OK,' Rozette said, and a delighted Kosef J followed her on her way back.

He put in a hard graft until nearly midnight.

6

The hall with the dishwashers was much larger than anything Kosef J could have imagined. It looked like a factory floor due to the large number of appliances lined up in three rows and connected by what looked like conveyor belts. At the moment, only two dishwashers were in operation, the ones used by Rosette and him respectively, yet the noise of the engines, pistons and conveyor belts was already near-deafening.

Rozette had shown him by way of mere gestures, without making use of words, how to start and stop such an appliance and what he needed to do with the individual dishes. Basically, the plates, trays, spoons and knives arrived on a conveyor belt from an entirely different part of the kitchen, a mysterious place where thousands of dishes and items of cutlery had been gathered together. 'What kind of feast could have possibly taken place in order to leave such a stack of unwashed objects in its wake?' Kosef J wondered. There was no way so many plates could have been used by the detainees alone. Unless the prison was adjacent to another, much larger prison that he didn't yet know about.

The pace of work was downright hellish. Each and every item had to be checked for size and placed accordingly into an appropriate drawer. Every so often he'd drop the odd item, but this wasn't really a problem since absolutely all the dishes were made of plastic.

Every half an hour or so Rozette would leave her workstation and come over to bring Kosef J fresh supplies of detergent.

She wouldn't smile or be delayed beyond saying 'well done Mr Kosef' or 'you've got no idea how much help this is to me.' Anyway, this was enough for him. What bothered him the most was the hot steam squirting from all the joints of the two mechanical monsters. The steam was so dense at times that Kosef J could barely see a few inches ahead of him. This was just about enough for him to decide whether the next dish should be placed in the drawer for large or for small items.

All of a sudden the child turned up in the midst of this hot, oily and stinking steam, holding a glass in his hand. Kosef J was so astonished that he dropped a few dishes and then stopped altogether. Surprisingly, the conveyor belt slowed down. The child went up to Kosef J and handed him the glass. There was some white liquid in it. 'Milk perhaps,' Kosef J thought.

'Here,' the child said.

'Thank you,' Kosef responded. He knocked the drink back and added: 'It was good.'

'Would you like some more?' the child asked.

'Later,' Kosef J said.

Suddenly a terrible rattle could be heard from the direction of the dryer, as if some cogwheels were about to rip these fragile plastic objects apart.

The child started to laugh. So did Kosef J. The child handed him one of those pebbles he had shown him earlier in that pit behind the kitchen.

'It smells nice,' the child said.

Kosef J took the pebble, sniffed it and discovered that it did indeed smell incredibly nice. But he didn't get the chance to ask how a pebble could smell so nice. The child vanished, leaving Kosef J with the pebble in his hand.

Kosef J put the pebble in his pocket and carried on stacking the machine with dirty dishes.

When everything was all done and dusted, Rozette flung the kitchen windows wide open. Outside, there was a soft breeze, milder than the one on Sunday. The sun was about to set. Half the sky had cleared up, but the other half was still overcast by dark and ragged clouds. Kosef J took to heavily breathing in the poplar-scented air.

Rozette brought over some bread, meat and wine. Kosef J couldn't resist coming to the conclusion while he took a seat at the table that the food finally produced by Rozette was in lieu of both lunch and dinner. The only thing that had started to bother him since he had been freed was this unpredictability of meal times.

He couldn't recall when he had last seen or, better still, drunk wine. The woman probably wanted to surprise him.

'So what's next?' Rozette inquired after seating herself at the table in order to take a better look at him.

'What do you mean, what's next?' Kosef J shuddered, perplexed.

'Where will you go?' she made it clearer.

'Oh, to town!' he said.

'When?' she asked.

'Tomorrow,' he said. Then added: 'Tomorrow I'll get my clothes back.'

'I see,' she nodded and then fell silent again for a while.

He took great pleasure in eating while being watched by her. He took a few sips of wine and said, 'It's good.'

'It's red,' she replied.

He was finished with his meat and bread, and now wanted to drink his wine as slowly as possible. The thought that 'she is fat but pretty' suddenly crossed Kosef J's mind, though he immediately felt ashamed for harbouring such thoughts. He cast his eyes down, hoping that Rozette won't be able to read his mind. But the woman continued as if she had just picked up on his thoughts.

'This awful steam makes me bloated,' she said.

Kosef J felt so ashamed that he nearly boiled over. He had the impression that he had been caught in the act, and was seen committing an appalling deed he could never clear his name of.

'Oh, no, *this* isn't what I meant,' he just about managed to mumble.

'Excuse me?!' she reacted, dumbfounded.

'I didn't mean *this*. Please . . . forgive me!' he lifted his gaze to see whether there were any chances for the woman to forgive him. But Rozette was so flabbergasted that Kosef J no longer knew what to make of all this. They looked at each other in silence, one as baffled as the other.

'I'm off to lock up,' she said and Kosef J sighed with relief, without the slightest desire to find out what exactly she wanted to lock up.

7

He walked over to the side entrance, hoping that the lanterns would be lit. He couldn't hear any footsteps behind him. The evening seemed utterly calm and quiet. Suddenly the wind ceased to blow. The clouds stopped in their tracks on the sky, while the sun found itself pinned just under the horizon to scatter a soft and delicate light. In their peculiar stillness, the poplar leaves appeared as if they were momentarily frozen.

One couldn't even make out the sound of heavy boots treading the gravel alley. Perhaps one couldn't have even heard if someone snapped their fingers or clapped.

Kosef J was in a state of bliss. There was nothing to make him hurry up or worry. Silence has permeated the very depths of his brain. He was able to spot from afar the two pale dot-like sources of light, and his body started to tremble with excitement. The two lanterns were lit. Perhaps it was someone's job to light them night after night. 'But for whom?' he couldn't help wondering. 'It doesn't matter,' he hastened to answer his own question. What mattered was that there were *two* live flames, acting as beacons on either side of a gate one couldn't quite figure out the use of. at least he, Kosef J, couldn't yet work out the role of this so-called *side* entrance.

As he was getting closer, the sight started to dominate his imagination more and more. The rays of light stemming from the two spheres lent the sunset an additionally warm and inviting hue, and made this sensation travel far and wide, as if the entire sky had been kitted out in the colours of the prison lanterns. Kosef J slowed his pace down, entirely focusing his gaze on this wondruous experience.

He only noticed with some delay that the gate was wide open.

When this fact dawned on him, Kosef J experienced a staggering reaction. He simply felt like running away. But whereto? He had no idea. Somewhere back, of course. To his own cell perhaps. Or at least to the prison guards' room, *to let them know*. Franz Hoss would need to be notified immediately, of course. A gate opened wide in a prison wasn't something that could be considered normal. Kosef J sensed this and, though unsure why, he felt *responsible*.

An array of thoughts cropped up in his mind, but he was unable to make a move. After the first few moments of stupefaction he remembered that he was, in fact, a free man. There was no reason for him to be so scared, after all he was free. To prove this: he could even afford to stroll into the relatively *out-of-bounds* wings of the prison. It was no business of his to wonder whether that gate was meant to be open or not at that particular time. Since the lanterns were lit, someone must have already passed by there. Someone had been tasked with a mission they had accomplished, and that someone had probably also seen the open gate and had chosen not to react, which is why the gate was still open. In conclusion, there was nothing strange and against regulations in the gate being *open*.

'To hell with them!' Kosef J decided, angrily.

He went up to the gate to look *beyond* it. Again, he realized he should feel something, like he did when he had been told he was free. But he felt nothing. He realized that under normal circumstances he should have felt tremenduous curiosity or suffocating emotion. But he hadn't looked *beyond* for such a long time, and he felt absolutely nothing.

He stopped right in the gateway and took a good look *on the other side*. The light had faded in the meantime, so Kosef J focused his attention the best he could in the circumstances. He had to admit that not much could be seen beyond the gate. Yet he wasn't disappointed. He could make out a country road leading to an orchard. Left and right there were bare fields, dotted about with shortgrass.

Kosef J sat down on the grass. He loved it when his palms would get wet just by touching the grass. He lay on his back and stared at the sky. A puny star had already appeared above the kitchen.

'It's OK,' Kosef J's brain mused.

'It's nice,' Kosef J said to himself.

'It's exactly the way it should be,' Kosef J's brain mused again. Then he got startled because he had the impression that he heard some barking.

'A dog, it must be a dog,' Kosef J's brain chuckled.

He quickly got to his feet and tried to scan the horizon. It seemed to him that there must be something beyond the orchard, something lumped together along the horizon itself. 'The town,' Kosef J said to himself, this time a little uneasy. So this is where the town was. Odd. For years he had imagined that the town was situated somewhere behind the courtyard where they had their daily walks. In other words, in an entirely different direction, some ninety degrees to the right, if he could put it this way.

Trying to get a glimpse of what was beyond the trees, he realized that the trees were laden with fruit. He couldn't quite distinguish the exact kind, but he was overwhelmed by a sudden craving, not so much for eating but for picking some fruit. He headed towards what turned out to be an apple orchard. There he found mature trees, with tired branches hanging through and almost touching the ground *also* because of their abundance of fruit. Kosef J strolled up and down among the hollow trunks like a sleepwalker, careful not to step on the hundreds of fallen fruit or the branches that had reached down to the grass. It took him ages to muster the courage to stretch his hand out and pick an apple he'd so wanted. On the distant horizon, a few lights got switched on in what must have been the town. The dog barked again.

'Quite some apples!' Kosef J indulged himself.

The sun had set below the horizon but the sky was still quite bright, partly aided by the sparkling reflection of the stars and of the city.

Kosef J finally brought himself near an apple, and without picking it from its branch, he took a bite. He slowly chewed that sweet and scented matter that sneakily spread out from his palate into his bloodstream and into his entire being. He kept looking at the bitten apple, still hanging from its branch, and laughed.

'Good God, why am I laughing?' Kosef J wondered, also anxious of the fact that he had instinctively appealed to God. He, Kosef J that is, was an atheist. Could he possibly turn into such a fool? To allow himself to be bothered by such simple things as the night, the grass, the dog, the apples. 'It must be late,' *someone* surmised in his inner self, 'Franz Hoss must have gone to bed.' A sense of deep concern had immediately lodged in his heart that made him turn around and cast his glance towards the walls from behind which he had come. His concern increased further when he realized how far he'd ventured from the prison. He couldn't believe that he had moved away quite so much.

'This is no good,' Kosef J inferred.

Sure enough, he was now a free man. But strictly speaking his *release* hadn't been completed. 'This is my fault, and my fault alone,' he blamed himself. Take, for instance, that he had moved away in a completely irresponsible manner from the prison building while still wearing a prison uniform. The fact of the matter was that anyone could have believed just about *anything* in such a situation. Whoever would meet him could believe *anything*. They could even shoot him because whoever would meet him could easily believe that they were dealing with a prisoner on the run.

'This is bad. Really, really bad.' Kosef J reasoned and started to run.

He had no other wish but to re-enter the prison courtyard, his *shelter*. Perhaps Fabius and Franz Hoss were playing dice. What a relaxing treat a game of dice with Fabius and Franz Hoss would have been!

He kept running as fast as he could but the prison walls were still quite far away. Behind him he could hear the barking of dogs. This could only come from the town nearby.

'Now there's several of them,' his brain registered.

'And so many stars,' Kosef J said to himself, casting a glance at the sky while running.

Right ahead, one could make out the dark and still distant outline of the prison building.

'There it is,' his brain rejoiced, as if it had finally found relief in the idea that the walls, the office wing, the clothing-supply room, the kitchen and the various floors housing the narrow and perfectly aligned cells were all firmly there where they belonged. This represented a certainty in the universe, a point where one could always depart from and return to.

When he arrived at the gate and saw that in the meantime someone had closed it, Kosef J could barely stifle a howl of anger.

He was angry with himself, above all, for having allowed to be *lured* into such a bad plight. The term *lured* was actually too vague a description, since he had allowed himself to be dragged by a primal instinct, a childish illusion, a chimera, in fact. He had staked his entire *situation,* everything that had just started to bud in his new capacity as a free man. How will he justify himself in front of the the two elderly guards? How will they regard him from now on? Will he be able to make use of their basin and eat at the kitchen? Will Rozette allow him to help out with the dishes?

Overwhelmed by a profound sense of despair he decided to cling on to the gate and try to open it. This side entrance though, and the gate that he had become so fond of because of the two lanterns and the privileged place it occupied at the top of the poplar alley, the gate he had longed to *at least* set his eyes on, well, this gate was now well and truly bolted.

'This isn't right,' Kosef J muttered.

He charged with all his might into the cold metal of the gate, but no matter how often his flesh hit the metal plates, the gate produced no sound.

'Mr Franz Hoss,' Kosef J shouted in depair, having given up hope but nevertheless hanging on by virtue of the fact that he had done this very same thing over the last forty-eight hours.

He tried to gauge the height of the gate and wall. As one would expect, when viewed from the outside, both the gate and the wall appeared higher, more solid and less accessible.

'It's me, Kosef J!' he screamed, ravaged and sweaty, and with bloodshot eyes due to the considerable effort of trying to see in the dark.

He stepped back a few paces to gain impetus. He smashed against the metal side entrance, but the impact of his haggard body on the gate produced no sound, not even an extremely feeble noise, which made him come to terms with the fact that his attempt was an utter flop. He turned around and ran along the wall for a few yards, searching for an opening, an inlet, a window of some sort. He then changed direction and explored about ten yards the other way. After a further flop, he stopped right in front of the gate.

He picked up a stone and smashed it against the gate a few times, hoping that this would lead to an echo, a signal, *something or other*.

'Mr Franz, Mr Franz,' he shouted a few more times, feeling strangled and exhausted.

He tried to climb on the metal gate but only managed to hurt his palms and knees. Then he remembered that the next day he was meant to receive his new clothes, as a mark of his release. Yes, it was absolutely necessary for him to return, to be there within, and make it *beyond* the walls by sunrise at the very latest. He had already lost all sense of time. He stood still for a few minutes hoping that some sound from within the walls would give him an indication as to what the prisoners were doing at that time, and what aspect of their daily routine they were carrying out. But there was nothing except complete silence.

'The main entrance, of course. The main entrance!' The revelation of something as common sense as this reassured him a little. All he had to do was go to the main entrance where there was *surely* someone. There is no way not to have anyone there. He, Kosef J, being now released had no reason to be concerned about showing up at the main entrance and explaining the whole situation, since he hadn't done anything wrong. Such things do happen and that's that, they won't happen again from now on, but what happened, happened. He'll be very frank and give all the details. And the person who'll be there will have the opportunity to verify the truthfulness of his words. So many people used to know him. He had been a model prisoner. He'd done such a great job in the vegetable garden. His cell, cell number 50, was open. Anyone could verify *this*.

'This is what I deserve,' he said to himself as he set off along the wall to find the main entrance.

Unfortunately, he was no longer able to rely on his sense of direction. He had never had a very clear mental map of the prison anyway. He had a very vague idea of key locations, and he knew roughly in what direction this or that particular wing was. Nothing more though. Right now, for example, he wouldn't have been able to ascertain whether it was best to turn left or right in order to find the main entrance. More than that, there were parts of the prison that were entirely unknown to him, as he'd had the sudden surprise to discover over the last couple of days. He took off in a random direction, and, as usual, soon received confirmation that he had chosen the longest and most troublesome road.

The walls were supported by buttresses and he had to go around them. Often enough he had to descend and then climb again because what had initially looked like a vast plain had gradually turned into a rugged terrain, with ravines, mounds, deep ditches and dangerous rocky protrusions. Kosef J couldn't help being amazed at how large a surface the prison, in which he had stayed for so long, occupied. He couldn't spot any paths along the walls so he had no choice but to carve his own way among the weed, rocks and shrubs. The ground was marshy in places, and the recent rainfalls have left a number of puddles behind that he had to jump over or go round. Every so often he'd stop, step back from the wall and look up hoping that he'd catch a glimpse of a lit-up window or a watchman. But he could see nothing and hence became increasingly agitated and hurried. He not only didn't spot any lit-up windows but he didn't see any windows *whatsoever*, not even a crenel or an opening. The wall stretched on ruthlessly without any interruptions, giving the impression that it surrounded an immense but lifeless space.

After a few hours' walk (at least Kosef J's impression was that he had been walking for hours) he took a break to catch his breath. Judging by the number of bends Kosef J arrived at the conclusion that the prison had a most irregular shape, and this was probably the outcome of successive extensions. As a rule of thumb, turning four times at a ninety-degree angle takes you back to your starting point. He had the impression though that he'd taken countless bends and there was no sign of returning to the side entrance.

The landscape around the walls had also changed. The ill-lit and near-illusory outline of the town, occasionaly punctuated by barking, had disappeared for some time. The horizon didn't have the same luminosity, and the stars didn't have the same *impact*. Only the walls gave off some light, and, though increasingly feeble, this was just about enough for Kosef J to keep track of their presence.

Hardened, he set off again. He really regretted that he hadn't picked more apples, because if he had, he could replenish his energies now. The night got more and more humid and cold. His boots repeatedly got soaked in mud and he felt the cold reaching the tip of his toes. It was already too dark to figure out how to get around puddles and water-filled ditches. Not to waste time, he decided to just charge straight through them and, at times, he found himself treading knee-high in water or mud. Yet there were also sections where the tall grass made it easier for him to move forward, offering him respite and cleansing him of the mud at the same time.

When he finally heard a banging sound, as if someone had knocked together a couple of stones, he was overjoyed and would have liked to actually give a hug to these sounds. 'I'm saved,' he said to himself. In his mind, he experienced an even more powerful emotion, amounting to nothing less than a sheer sense of *salvation*.

8

The child was playing, on the grass, with a hedgehog.
Oddly enough, that section of the wall reflected a lot more
light than the others. The grass at the base of the wall was
dry and the air had a sort of nocturnal sheen, typical for
nights with a full moon. Kosef J wanted to say something
to the child but he signalled that he shouldn't speak.

'Can you see?' the child whispered a little later.

'What?' Kosef J asked, whispering, too.

'It's dancing,' the child replied.

Indeed, every time the hedgehog could hear the two
pebbles knock together, it got seized by anger and broke
out into a nervous twitch.

'It's happy,' the child said.

'On the contrary,' Kosef J, 'you're tormenting it.'

'No way,' the child protested.

'Yes, you are,' Kosef J insisted.

The child stood up, looking sad.

'Had no idea,' he said.

'No problem,' Kosef J pacified him.

The child bashed the pebbles together again to make
them sparkle.

'See?' he said proudly. 'They burn.'

The child bashed them a few more times, and then handed them generously over to Kosef J. The hedgehog was still there, as if it was carefully following what these two were up to. Not wanting to disappoint the child, Kosef J had a go at bashing the pebbles together. Sparks broke forth really quickly, as if the pebbles had been charged with a secret energy. Also, just by virtue of being borderline hot, the pebbles made Kosef J feel a pleasent warmth in his palms, and then gradually, in his entire body.

'What kind of pebbles are these?' he asked.

'Didn't I show them to you?' the child wondered. 'They are from that pit.'

'I see,' Kosef J nodded.

All the panic and madness of groping along the wall was now a distant memory. All of a sudden, everything had become *simple* again and returned to *normal*. The presence of the child was clear proof that the prison entrance was somewhere very near. Kosef J didn't even see the urgency of talking about *this*.

'I wonder what the time is?' Kosef J asked, mainly from himself.

The child shrugged.

'It's still early,' he said. Then he produced an apple from his pocket and handed it to Kosef J: 'Want it?'

'Where did you get it from?' Kosef J asked, startled, having the impression that the apple was already *bitten*.

'The garden,' the child replied.

Kosef J devoured the apple with gusto. He could have sworn that the apple was picked from the ground, from under the tired branches of a mature apple tree, from the very garden that had fascinated him so much. The apple tasted of earth and grass.

'It's really good,' Kosef J observed.

'It's from my garden,' the child said.

'Is it far?' Kosef J asked.

'No,' the child replied.

All of a sudden they became aware of a commotion coming from the direction of the buildings right *beyond* the wall. Kosef J couldn't quite figure out what was taking place there, but he was able to sense some kind of human presence that did him good. He then got the impression of hearing Franz Hoss swear, which pleased him no end.

'So what were you up to?' Kosef J asked, mainly to break the silence.

'I'm keeping watch,' the child replied.

'He's keeping watch!' Kosef J reasoned, feeling calm and sated yet somewhat intrigued by the child's words.

'Over what?' he asked.

'Didn't I tell you? the child asked. 'The garden.'

'You mean the apple orchard?' Kosef J probed incredulously.

'Yes,' the child confirmed.

'How weird he is,' Kosef J mused. 'How young, yet how weird. He's so young, so serious and can talk such strange things,' Kosef J continued his line of thought.

'But why?' Kosef J asked. 'Is anyone coming here to steal?'

'No,' the child replied. 'They're coming to take a bite.'

Kosef J had the impression of being overwhelmed by a sort of uncertainty, an uncertainty that had stubbornly been following him for the last two days, and whenever he'd briefly catch his breath he'd be soon caught up in its sharp claws.

'To take a bite of what?' Kosef J inisted.

'The apples,' the child explained. 'They don't steal them, only take a bite of them and leave them hanging on the trees. They come every night.'

'How long has this been going on for?' Kosef J asked, astounded.

'Since summer,' the child replied.

Indeed, the child had a grumpy face. He threw himself into the grass and rested his palms above the leaves of grass as if they were some slender flames capable to warm his hands.

'Get it?' the child carried on. 'They don't steal, only take a bite of their flesh and leave the apples on the trees just like that, in a state of being bitten. *This* makes me awfully angry.'

9

That evening had a few more surprises in store for Kosef J. Finding himself within the prison compound, he headed bone-tired towards the main cell block, yearning for his oakum mattress and iron bed. He took the lift to his floor, walked past a snoring Fabius, who was meant to keep vigil right next to the lift, and headed, as inconspicuously as possible, to cell number 50.

The cell was locked.

Kosef J refrained from wondering why, refrained from thought and in fact refrained from any human reaction. He stayed pinned to *his* door, feeling defeated and paralysed with stupor. Then, after a good few minutes spent in this state of *immersion* and utter prostration, he very gently and without any noise lifted the spyhole shutter to check *who* was inside.

Inside, there was a man.

To be precise, there was a man other than *him*, Kosef J, and this man was in *his* cell.

'Ahem,' Kosef J reacted.

The man was sleeping on his back, with an utterly tranquil expression on his face. The cell had been cleaned, disinfected and the blankets changed.

Kosef J went over to Fabius and woke him up.

'What, you haven't left?' the old guard asked, looking more harassed by sleep than surprised.

Kosef J lost his temper. Where could he possibly go? No one had told him yet *where* he was meant to go. The formalities unfolded very slowly. How could he know what to do, where to go and what to ask for? No one would tell him *anything*. Why would no one tell him anything? What did they hold against him? How long did *they* think that he'd bear this uncertainty? Did *they* know what was meant to happen *to him* that very night? Did anyone show any concern about him? No one. How could this be? What would have happened to him had he not bumped into the child by chance? He was lucky to come across the child and that stone pit of his that he was emptying, which made it possible for him to pass under the wall. Did Fabius know in his capacity as a prison guard that behind the kitchen there was a passage under the wall, a passage filled with nicely scented and sparkling pebbles that could be taken out and put back at will by anyone at any point? Well? What did Fabius as deputy chief guard have to say about this *situation*? Was the existence of an underwall passage a normal occurrence in a penitentiary?

Oh, no! Fabius let out a sigh.

Total havoc, this was the word Kosef J found himself obliged to use.

'Hold on, this is pushing it,' Fabius protested.

So here we are, there is a man in *his* cell, the cell *he* had been sleeping in almost forever. In the cell that had somehow grown part of *him*, had become his shell, the cell that he had gone to carry in his self, in his soul and on his back. And now there is a stranger, an unknown and *random* man in it. What entitles him to this? As long as *he*

52

was still wearing prison clothes wasn't he entitled to make use of his prison cell and the regular meal times and all other amenities? What was he meant to do now? What on earth?

'I don't know,' Fabius said yawning, so all his facial bones made a cracking noise. Then, as if he'd given up, he said it again: 'Don't know.'

All the same, they both wanted to find a solution.

Being so tired, Kosef J would have been inclined to sleep in no matter which cell, had there been any available. But there were none. The guards' own room would have been a little extreme, considering that he, Kosef J, was still wearing *those* clothes. Fabius would have been prepared to stay up all night chatting and playing dice, but Kosef J declared that he was far too tired and had an important appointment at the clothing-supply room the next day.

'The dorm!' Fabius jumped up, delighted with his idea. 'If you like, I can let you sleep in the dormitory.'

Kosef J knew what this meant. It meant bunk beds squeezed in like drawers, imbued in a penetrating smell and crammed with people with an infernal snore who could even tread on you during the night.

'No, thanks,' Kosef J said.

He huddled on the chair that normally Franz Hoss would sit on. He owned up to being *totally* defeated. He was afraid and admitted that to Fabius. He, Kosef J, was finished. He couldn't even track down a single clear thought in his brain, and he couldn't pin down a single desire. Or aim. Or sense.

'Be brave!' Fabius moaned, verging on being emotional. Why now?

Well, everything had come to an end. Kosef J could cope no longer. He didn't even need his clothes from the clothing-supply room.

'Impossible,' Fabius pleaded. 'Your life is just beginning.'

'I'm old,' Kosef J said.

'No, I'm the one that's old,' Fabius stressed.

Kosef J pointed out that he disagreed. Fabius also stated that he wasn't in agreement with what Kosef J had said, but that he, Fabius, was an optimist and believed in the future, in truth and in happiness.

'Bullshit,' Kosef J reacted.

At this point Fabius had a violent reaction. How come that a trifle, something of no importance could so easily bring down the newly released Kosef J, someone who had been a model prisoner, with exemplary endurance?

'Really?' Kosef J asked, keen on the old guard's opinion about himself.

Fabius vouched again that Kosef J had always been a strong and resilient man, without fail. A tenacious, tough and strong man. Nothing had been able to subdue him, nothing whatsoever. He, Fabius that is, was a great admirer of Kosef J, and had always admired him for this. He hadn't come across many detainees with such an inner force and such *gravitas*, if he could put it this way.

'How about when you were beating me up?' Kosef J asked.

'What do you mean?' Fabius seemed puzzled.

'How about then? Were you thinking this even then?' Kosef J probed.

'I was beating you, yes, but I also respected you,' Fabius sighed.

'You'd give me merciless beatings,' Kosef J said, adding: 'What were you thinking while battering me?'

Fabius began to slowly roll himself a cigarette, and this aided his concentration and ability to search for an answer. He wasn't thinking of much, he had to admit that.

'Still, was there anything?' Kosef J insisted.

'I was thinking about where I had to hit,' Fabius blurted out while lighting his cigarette. Then, somewhat ashamed for having forgotten to offer one to Kosef J, too, he asked: 'Would you like one?'

Kosef J swiftly lit the cigarette offered by the guard.

'You were an *expert,*' he mumbled.

'What do you mean?' the guard asked.

Kosef J explained what he meant. Fabius had possibly been the *most callous* of all prison guards. Sure enough, other guards would also beat prisoners up, in fact all would give beatings, but he, Fabius, had a kind of *sophistication.* Franz Hoss, for instance, was more likely to swear rather than batter. Fabius would be silent, and prepared his strikes carefully. His speciality was, as everyone was aware, to strike prisoners without warning. No one would hit harder and choose less unpredictable moments. And no other guard would draw on quite so much imagination to choose a specific part of the prisoner's body onto which to deal a blow.

'Is that so?' Fabius asked fired up, hoping to hear more.

'Everyone was frightened of you,' Kosef J said.

'Everyone, really?' the guard hummed like a wise old man listening to a palpitating story.

'For years and years on end,' Kosef J added.

'This is true,' Fabius agreed. 'Time flies frightfuly quickly.'

'You'd normally hit us on the elbow or the shin,' Kosef J carried on. After taking another drag on the cigarette, he looked the guard in the eye and asked: 'Can you tell me why on earth you'd always hit us in the elbow or in the shins?'

'No idea,' Fabius said, somewhat lost. 'I really wouldn't know.'

'You must have an idea,' Kosef J insisted.

Fabius leant back against the wall with his chair. It looked as if he was thinking of a distant memory that only had importance to him.

'You used to take particular pleasure in hitting us in the *bones*,' Kosef J came to his rescue.

'I may have done that,' the guard nodded. 'But there was a lot of unruliness.'

Kosef J turned the right side of his head towards the guard, brushed his hair aside and showed him a scarred wound behind the ear.

'See? I got this from you.'

'From me?' Fabius asked, sounding apprehensive.

He stood up straightaway and started to carefully inspect the mark. Kosef J could feel the old guard's fingers moving up and down his throat, behind his ears and on his hair. His fingers were soft and warm, pleasant to the touch. One could have said that he had the gift of calming and healing by sheer tactile contact.

'Here?' Fabius asked, his fingers slightly shaking.

'There,' Kosef J nodded.

'Yes,' the guard said, like someone who is searching for an answer in their own thoughts but cannot quite find it.

'Do you know how much blood had poured out of that wound?' Kosef J asked.

'A lot,' the guard replied swiftly.

'It went on for days,' Kosef J clarified.

Fabius sat back and carried on smoking, looking sad and somewhat dreamy.

'One time you kicked me,' Kosef J continued in a calm voice devoid of the slightest reproach.

'I take your word,' Fabius hastened to say, as if he was afraid that the former prisoner might undress to show his scars. He leant with the back of his neck against the wall and cast his glance onto the ceiling. This time he looked rather inspired and involved, waiting for the right time to come forward with a great piece of information.

Kosef J seemed taken down memory lane, too. He had no idea what made him start such a conversation. Yet certain uncalled-for details have simply taken over his memory. He hoped that Fabius didn't feel too burdened or adversely affected by all these *remembrances*.

'No, not at all,' Fabius stated.

'After all, you'd aged right in front of my eyes,' Kosef J pointed out.

Fabius started to blow smoke rings towards the ceiling, as high up as he possibly could.

'As time went by you gradually had enough and gave up,' Kosef J continued.

Fabius asked him whether he could remember the last time he had been beaten up. Kosef J could remember it exactly: ten days ago. Fabius seemed taken by surprise. Ten days ago? Really? Yes, Kosef J replied in a decisive tone. To be fair, this wasn't a proper beating. It was more like a blow. A blow that he, Fabius, had served him in the face while handing him the dinner tray. Fabius looked rather annoyed. He hadn't asked about *this*. He had asked about *the last beating*. The last beating, Kosef J replied after a while in which he collected his thoughts, in the *other* sense of the word, well, he had to admit that the last proper beating had taken place two years ago.

'I remember it well,' the guard said, panting.

'You do?' Kosef J startled, blushing.

'It was a Sunday, wasn't it?' the guard said, turning his emotion-laden rosy cheeks towards Kosef J.

'A Sunday, yes,' Kosef J confirmed.

'After we returned from the garden,' the guard said.

Kosef J couldn't stifle his explosive enthusiasm for the old guard at the sight of such precision regarding their *shared* memories.

'That's right! That's right indeed!' he shouted.

'I hit you real bad then,' Fabius continued.

'In the back of the neck, you hit me in the back of my neck.'

'And teeth, right?'

'Yes, teeth, too.'

'Goodness gracious!' Fabius cried out.

The two men stared at each other for a long while. The guard's wrinkled face revealed nothing except for fulminating old age, layered with minor anxieties. Kosef J would have liked to hug Fabius for remembering so many details.

'You hate me?' Kosef J asked.

'No,' Fabius said. 'I used to be afraid of you. That's all.'

'What?' Kosef J cried out. 'Afraid of me? Me personally?'

Fabius acknowledged without any embarrassment that he, Kosef J, used to make him apprehensive. All the prisoners used to make him terribly apprehensive in fact. This was why he would strike blows at them. Out of fear. Or to banish fear. Franz Hoss, his boss, was more indifferent as a type, he was rougher. For this reason he didn't really hit people, since he wasn't *afraid*. But he, Fabius, was terrorized by the prisoners in their hoards, by their sheer faces and gestures.

'Can you see?' Fabius asked, panting and almost beseeching him, due to the effort needed to explain all this. 'I've lived with this terror day after day for years. I'd aged feeling terrorized. No mean feat, ay?'

Kosef J couldn't believe his ears. So he said:

'I can't believe you, Mr Fabius. Honestly, I can't.'

The guard stood up and started to pace around the room.

'I was afraid, I really was,' he murmured.

After all, what was his life about? Could he actually call what he had lived up till now a *life*? Being there, with all the prisoners, almost *like* them? Living and eating with them, sleeping right next to them, keeping watch over them in exasperation . . . Always afraid of them, every single second feeling a terrible and overwhelming fear. There were nights when fear tormented him to such an extent that he could barely catch a wink of sleep, he groaned, shivered, writhed and had nightmares while being basically half awake. He had the sensation as if all these people in their cells were snakes slithering towards him. Yes, he could feel how *they*, and that includes *him*, Kosef J, too, would dissolve and slip away under the doors and through the tiniest cracks on the prison walls. They would all flow towards *him*, towards Fabius, to snatch him, to devour him, and to make him *be* no longer. He lived with this fear and this agony for years. And he couldn't get over this and restore his energies in any way other than by lashing out. Yet even by beating prisoners up, he didn't achieve a great deal, because all this momentuous outburst and discharge only led to building up an even more intense state of horror. As he carried on beating, his conscience got more and more burdened despite his body managing to relax and those hellish shakes diminishing a little. Because he, Fabius, did have a conscience. Yes, he had.

'You do believe me, Mr Kosef, don't you?' he begged him with tearful eyes and saliva drooling on his lips.

'I do, Mr Fabius, of course I do,' Kosef J replied.

He found some relief *whenever* he administered a beating. Within the spell of half a day, or at times even a whole night, he experienced himself as a new man, in charge of his own self, even touched by a certain sense of kindness . . . He, Kosef J, couldn't forget an essential detail: namely, that in the majority of cases when they had to undertake hard labour it was Fabius who kept watch over them, and then, he, Fabius would never force the prisoners to stretch to superhuman efforts. From *that* point of view, deputy prison guard Fabius was the most tolerant guard possible. He never made a *fuss* about people not working enough or not completing their workload. He never rushed or battered them for not having finished a job. Sometimes he'd even allow them to smoke and thus prolong their breaks, something that no other guard would have been prepared to do.

'Right, Mr Kosef, isn't it?' Fabius pleaded.

'Right, of course it is,' Kosef J confirmed.

After all, the beating he had administered to the prisoners was never fatal! And it wasn't one of those to damage anyone's health or make them unfit for work for who knows how long. He'd agree that it was a very painful beating, perhaps the most painful of all that were given, but only painful for the moment. Kosef J recalled that, didn't he?

'Of course!' Kosef J confirmed.

So no one could claim that they had to lie in bed for very long in order to recover from the blows administered by him, Fabius. Some guards would break skulls and thoraxes, and tear out entire chunks of flesh. Had he, Fabius, ever done such a thing?

'No, never,' Kosef J acknowledged.

Not to mention that he wouldn't beat people very often! Other guards would be up for this this much more frequently. However, he'd give beatings on *particular* days of the week. So he'd give beatings on a regular basis, that was very true, and the prisoners would be familiar with Fabius's beating timetable. They'd know exactly on what days of the week or even at what times of the day, or, more than that, at what minute within the hour would Fabius be seized by *those* furies. Yes, the prisoners would know all this, and perhaps this was *the reason why* they felt so terrorized. To put it differently, they were most terrorized by the idea of having to await those particular moments, and by the fact that one of them had to bear the madness of that moment for sure. Perhaps this was much more unbearable than the beating itself.

'Perhaps,' Kosef J concurred.

Besides, he, Fabius, had never born a grudge towards anyone. Other guards would single out a prisoner for some reason and then carry on beating them over and over again for months and years. But he, Fabius, had never done such a thing. He'd always choose at random. He had never taken exception to anyone. When his moment of *crisis* beckoned and he felt the urge to beat someone at any cost, he'd make his choice on the basis of purely arbitrary criteria. Could this have troubled prisoners more than knowing for sure which one of them was to be on the receiving end of his beatings?

'Yes, awful,' Kosef J replied.

'I'm sorry, really sorry,' Fabius said.

'Well, that's that,' Kosef J summed up.

'And now?' Kosef J asked.

'Now, I don't care,' the guard replied.

Something had happened to him the last couple of years. He wasn't really sure what that was. He had calmed down somewhat. Perhaps he had aged too much. The discomfort he had experienced in relation to the prisoners had transformed into a discomfort towards his own self. The fact that he had aged so quickly was grieving him. He hadn't realized this at the beginning. But, in time, he had become aware of something odd that had turned his entire being upside down. He had noticed that the prisoners would endure the passage of time much better than him. People who should have already been old, or anyway, at least older than him, had been perfectly preserved and they were expecting to get out of prison and still live on. Meanwhile, he had grown old without having something to look forward to, which is why he had actually aged so quickly.

'Don't you find this absolutely awful?' Fabius bemoaned.

'Yeah,' Kosef J nodded.

'Now,' Fabius said, 'I'm at peace. I know that everything's over.'

'Not true,' Kosef J replied in a deeply compassionate tone. 'You have to do something.'

'There's nothing *more* for me to do,' the guard stated.

'This is unfair,' Kosef J retorted.

'Is it?' Fabius glanced at Kosef J, in the hope of a revitalizing spark.

'You have to take pleasure in simple things,' Kosef J pointed out, delighted with his formulation. 'Such as the sky, the grass, water.'

Fabius turned his gaze towards the wall, looking somewhat disappointed. Kosef J was about to catch his breath to dispense some advice but he had suddenly got stuck after uttering 'sky', 'grass' and 'water'.

'Goodness, what can I say to him, what else?' Kosef J wondered. He had an utterly forlorn man in front of him and yet he couldn't come up with anything else to say.

'What could I do for him, what *else* could I do for him?' he wondered.

NOTHING, the response came from somewhere far away. ABSOLUTELY NOTHING.

'Did you say anything?' the guard asked, still facing the wall.

'Nothing, absolutely nothing,' Kosef J replied falling asleep with his head on the table.

10

First thing, Kosef J went to the clothing-supply room. He was determined to do everything in his powers to leave *there* as soon as possible. The conversation with the guard had left him with a bad taste in his mouth, a sense of help-lessness, pity and of deep and murky waters.

'I know about you!' the man in charge of the clothing-supply room said as he entered. The man rubbed his palms together and appeared to be utterly thrilled. 'My son told me about you,' he continued.

'His son!' Kosef J mused, taken by surprise. Who could possibly be the son of this ageless stocky man, with bulging fish-eyes.

'*The kid*,' said the ageless stocky man with bulging fish-eyes.

'The kid indeed!' Kosef J cried out, amazed that this ageless stocky man, with bulging fish-eyes could be the father of the child.

'That's right,' the stocky man confirmed.

'Oh, well, I've had enough,' Kosef J's brain concluded.

'Why?' the other asked.

'I don't know, I've simply had enough,' Kosef J responded in his mind.

'But why now, why right now?' asked the very warm and humane ageless stocky man, with bulging fish-eyes. 'My son said wonderful things about you.'

'Oh well, what difference does it make?' Kosef J asked himself.

'It does make a difference!' the man replied.

'It doesn't,' Kosef J said out loud.

'The child has a clean soul!' the man pronounced.

'I can't get anywhere with him either,' Kosef J mused, thinking about *how* the discussion with Fabius had ended the night before.

'OK, but I'm not a prison guard,' the man responded. 'Guards are swines.'

Kosef J found the responses of this ageless stocky man, with bulging fish-eyes, somewhat odd. He kept silent, leaving space for the other to add something.

'*Still*, fish-eyes . . . ' the man babbled, with a hint of reproach.

'I want to leave as soon as possible,' Kosef J said, determined to put an end to this elliptical and pointless conversation that wasn't leading anywhere.

'Certainly,' the man thought to himself, and it seemed to Kosef J as if he had heard the word CERTAINLY in his brain.

'Follow me,' the man said.

They descended a few damp steps and found themselves in the basement. A few tiny windows at the height of the ceiling let through a greyish light.

'I've always been against this,' the man said. 'Always.'

'Against what?' Kosef J asked.

'See this?' The man gestured. 'All damp. Clothes shouldn't be kept in damp conditions. This is not the way to run a proper supply room. Let alone one for clothes.'

They moved from room to room. All along the walls there were shelves stacked with rolls of fabric, shirts folded up on top of each other, and frayed jumpers and coats smelling of mildew.

'I should keep them in *waxed* paper bags,' the man said. 'According to regulations, that is.'

He grabbed a random musty shirt from a shelf and tore it apart in one go.

'There! *The cloth* can't hold out. How could then *paper*? I laid them all out, hoping they might dry a little. You think they can?

The man seemed seriously disheartened by the problems encountered in the clothing-supply room. He rummaged among a few piles of fabric resembling some kind of sticky bodies, looking like the fat and shapeless trunk of a decapitated animal, put out for a slow rot.

'Any thoughts on what I could do? These are clothes from last year. And they can't be worn any longer.'

Meanwhile they moved on to other, more spacious rooms. Kosef J seemed rather impressed with the heaps of clothes laid out on the shelves. Where could so many clothes come from? Did they all belong to prisoners? There seemed to be so many clothes, much too many, an immense number, there couldn't possibly be so many prisoners. Or perhaps the clothes had been amassed over the years . . . but how many years would it had taken for the clothing-supply room to *fill up* to quite such an extent? The smell became harder and harder to bear. The fabrics had started to rot, each at a different pace, emanating their unique smell. Kosef J was able to distinguish between the musty smell of wool, cotton and velvet.

'Awful,' the man grumbled on. 'It's a great loss, a really great one. There!' he said, picking up and squeezing flattened hat. A greenish liquid squirted from the hat and trickled down the man's fingers.

'Yet management doesn't want to do a thing,' fulminated the ageless stocky man with bulging fish-eyes. 'It's *inhuman*, absolutely inhuman.'

They stepped into a room chock-a-block with metal cabinets. The man opened one of the doors and a huge pile of shoes, boots, brogues and even slippers, as well as many other barely identifiable items rolled out onto the floor.

'Leather rots, too,' the man said, rasping. 'Look, please take a look at these! Could you call these boots?'

He lifted them to demonstrate to Kosef J *the tragedy* hidden behind the metal cabinets. He was able to yank off the sole of a boot in one single move. Two rows of rusty nails appeared in the section left behind, reminiscent of the rotten teeth of a carnivorous fish.

'See?' the man whined. 'Some will tell you all sorts, that I didn't do my job properly, and suchlike . . . But how could I possibly do my job in these conditions? How?'

Grudgingly he stuck a foot into the heap of shoes.

Then he carried on pointing out other wardrobes in which the clothes were kept in plastic bags. This plastic, however, had stuck to the fabrics stored in the bags, and none of the clothes could be salvaged.

'These are clothes from *five years ago*,' the man clarified.

He ripped one of the greenish plastic bags up. An unbearable stench dispersed in the air at once, as if it were the poisonous squirt of a monster's slashed-open stomach.

'What can I do? What can I possibly do?' the man said, wailing. 'I've tried everything I possibly could.'

The situation was even worse in the room accommodating clothes from *ten years ago*. One could claim that it was actually disastrous. Not a single object could be identified. The various items had dissolved and mingled together like hungry mushrooms: coats and shirts, cloaks and jackets, trousers and sleeveless shirts. This hoarding of disparate things was characterized by something organic and fragile at the same time, akin to marine bodies that, once brought to the surface, dehydrate and decompose at the slightest contact with air.

'I've been *fighting* for years,' the man said, looking really sad and serious, without clarifying who he was fighting against.

He had experimented with all sorts of methods and had a go at all sorts of ideas. For a long time he entertained the belief that by heating the rooms, he'd manage to preserve the clothes. The humid and hot air turned out to be even more voracious, and decomposition went on at an even quicker pace. The method of keeping the windows open didn't help either, as the currents of air played the role of catalysts and, instead of drying the clothes out, they ended up multiplying the hotbeds of infection. He had been toiling like a slave for years, tormenting his mind and body. He'd often take stuff into the open air, to the sun, so that they can freshen up. He had noticed, however, that this method weakened the fabrics no end, and once returned to the warehouse, they underwent a sort of *moral* collapse, unable to present any resistance whatsoever to pathogenic factors.

'Here are the clothes from *over ten years ago*,' the man pointed at a seriously bolted metal door, barricaded with a few suitcases, just to be on the safe side. 'You can imagine what's in there,' the stocky man said in a disheartened tone.

He then confessed that he hadn't had the strength to open that door for a while now. At times, especially during summer nights, he had the impression that he could hear something in there, a sort of bustle, something dodgy in any case.

'Your clothes are in there, too,' the man added with a guilty smile.

'Oh, no, that can't be!' Kosef J cried out.

'What can I do?' the man whimpered yet again. 'Would you like to open this door? If you have the courage to open this door then go for it . . . '

And he handed him a bunch of keys.

Kosef J swiftly and almost violently stepped back a few paces. No, he didn't want to open that door. He didn't want anything. He was just seriously disappointed.

'Can you see my point now?' the man asked, coming closer to Kosef J and seeking to meet his glance. 'Can you please see my point?'

'Sure,' Kosef J replied to avoid appearing discourteous.

'I compiled reports, I explained to everyone, I had an experts' report carried out,' he continued to list the various items, emphasizing the term *experts' report* above all.

By now he had basically given up hope. Or, rather, he had one last hope! A single one. It was Kosef J who represented *this* hope, given that he was now a free man. He was in a position to signal the actual state of affairs to those concerned. He was about to be seen by the prison governor to sort out the paperwork around his departure. Could he, Kosef J, please be so kind and talk to the governor at least for a moment about what he had seen in the clothing-supply room? To remind him that this clothing-supply room actually exists. To tell him that in these humid and damp basements an honest man is battling wardrobefuls of clothes, and that he needs help. It was him, Kosef J who could still salvage *something* in this situation. He was the only person the prison governor would perhaps listen to, given the exceptional circumstances of his release.

'You've got no idea how much weight your words carry right *now*,' the man added.

Kosef J reassured him that he won't forget anything. Yet he was utterly restless within. He had no knowledge of the fact that the formal arrangements towards his release would take him as far as the prison governor. Yet another thing he hadn't surmised and no one bothered to tell him. He had found this out by chance, and only because the man in charge of the clothing-supply room thought that he, Kosef J, was already in the know. All his plans to collect his clothes and leave at once crumbled irrecoverably. Up until then no one had ever told him to see the prison governor, and he didn't have the slightest idea when exactly he'd be called in. Similarly, he had no idea of the other procedures he had to follow in order to be able to leave.

'This is all my fault,' Kosef J kept thinking for the umpteenth time. It was his fault not because he didn't know what to do, but because he didn't put in enough of an effort to find out what he should do.

'And yet what shall we do with my clothes?' Kosef J stuttered.

'Come!' the man said with a perfidious smile.

He dragged him along some corridors and then they started to go up. Just like on his way back from the apple orchard, Kosef J was astounded by how long he had to walk until reaching the surface. They climbed a few flights of steps, crossed a few corridors, and went past a sea of doors.

At last, the man in charge of the clothing-supply room led him to a narrow chamber, which at first sight reminded him of a tailor's workshop. At one of the tables, he spotted the *child*, leaning over a cardboard box.

Kosef J made a sudden turn towards the stocky man, as if he wanted to seek his permission to enter, especially since *this* was indeed *the child*.

'Please come in,' the man said in a jovial tone.

The room was hot and bright. Kosef J went up to the child and started a friendly conversation.

'What are you up to?' he asked.

'I'm choosing buttons for you,' the child said pointing at the box. This response cheered Kosef J no end.

'Buttons for me?' he asked.

'For your clothes,' the child replied.

'I made you a new set of clothes,' the man from the warehouse clarified, throwing an embarrassed glance over Kosef J's shoulders. 'You can pay me when you receive your money.'

'Money?' Kosef J hummed.

'What, you've got it already?' the man asked with a hint of greed in his voice.

'No, not yet,' Kosef J replied, wondering what could this business with the money really mean. Where was he supposed to get money from? What for? And how much?

'This will be ready by tomorrow,' the man pointed at a pair of trousers and a jacket hanging off a tabletop. 'All I have to do is sew on the buttons.'

11

The next day a prisoner escaped.

Kosef J had been sleeping in the liftcage, on a mattress produced by Fabius, and was woken up, ahead of all others, by someone banging on the lift's ground-floor door. This meant that they wanted to set the engine into motion. He immediately jumped up, stepped out into the corridor, dragging his mattress behind him. The lift went down at once.

Still dizzy and feeling a terrible pain in his lower back, Kosef J tried to awaken his senses and figure out whether there was any chance of dozing off somewhere else that morning. This was his second night spent in the liftcage, and Kosef J had no reasons whatsoever for being pleased. The lack of space in the box didn't allow him to stretch his full body out, not even when lying across the floor. He couldn't bear sleeping in a crouching position, and yet the last couple of nights he was forced to adopt the most uncomfortable postures imaginable. He couldn't get the thought out of his mind that he had no opportunity to stretch his bones at leisure, so he had the impression, while sleeping, that he was actually thinking all the time rather than sleeping, and the same phrase kept spinning over and over again in his head: 'I can't stretch my bones at leisure.' Every time he twisted or turned in his sleep he'd hit against the metal walls of the lift with his feet, each strike being followed by a prolonged echo, seemingly intended to drill into his brain and remind him yet again that there simply wasn't enough space for a peaceful sleep.

This being Fabius's idea, however, he couldn't fault it. The old guard was really trying to be helpful—he had actually done *something*, had come up with this improvised solution with the lift and didn't deserve any complaints, at least not for the time being.

As he slowly calmed down and scratched the back of his neck, Kosef J could hear that on the ground floor the racket of screams and stamping feet was on the rise. It even seemed to him that he could hear a dog bark. He looked out of a window facing the prison courtyard, but it was still too dark to be able to see anything properly. And yet, the hustle and bustle of shadowy figures made him of the opinion that something special had happened down there.

He headed towards the cubicle where Fabius was still lying asleep, but he didn't have the courage to wake him up. Fabius was in deep sleep, snoring gently, saliva drooling down the corner of his mouth. His hands were placed over his chest, as if he'd been dead. Seeing him, Kosef J had this same thought: 'The old man would make a nice corpse.'

There was no need for him to wake Fabius because Franz Hoss had already done so. Kosef J saw the lift stop on their floor and then caught a glimpse of Franz Hoss dashing out like a raging bull. And yet, for the duration of the moment they locked eyes, Franz Hoss held his outbursts in check.

'Good morning, Mr Kosef,' he said.

'Good morning,' Kosef J responded. He would have liked to ask him what was happening down there, but he felt that it was wiser to keep silent.

Franz Hoss hurried over to Fabius and shook him without mercy.

'Up! Up!' he shouted. 'Up, you idiot!' Then he turned towards Kosef J, as if he wanted to rely on his witness statement: 'Goodness gracious!'

Kosef J kept silent, content with being a mere observer of what was to happen.

'What?' Fabius groaned while sitting up.

Now that his deputy had woken up, Franz Hoss was in no rush to tell him what it was all about. He sat down on a chair and began to pour last night's leftover tea from one mug into another. He drank the tea, clicked his tongue and got his cigarettes out.

'This is going to get nasty,' he said after a few drags.

Fabius rubbed his eyes, yawned and stretched until he could hear his bones crack before he took notice of Kosef J standing there, mattress in hand.

'Good morning, Mr Kosef,' he said smiling.

'Good morning,' Kosef J replied.

Once done with this ritual, the old guard decided to get up.

'*A prisoner escaped*,' Franz Hoss uttered in a grave voice.

'Where from?' deputy Fabius hastened to ask.

'The first floor,' Franz Hoss said.

As if by miracle, Fabius eased off straightaway, having looked anxious beyond measure just before. At least this didn't happen on their watch.

Franz Hoss didn't appreciate the way Fabius handled this news. It didn't matter which floor the prisoner escaped from, the first, the second or so on. What mattered was that it had been possible in the first place, and this was *a major disaster*.

'Why?' Kosef J asked in his mind.

'Because it was *possible*, that's why,' Franz Hoss yelled, at no one in particular.

Because no one was doing anything in this place, and all employees were basically dummies. *This* was no longer a prison. It was anything but a prison. Because there was no more respect. The prisoners held nothing holy. Everything had degraded and mellowed. Nothing was like in the old days. Those were the days, when everything was thought through and *weighed up*. The prison was a well-oiled machine, prisoners were prisoners, guards were guards, soldiers were soldiers, bosses were bosses, and so on. Everyone had great respect for others, and everyone knew exactly what their particular role was and how far they could go. The place was ruled by rigour, seriosity and competence back then. The inner courtyard looked spotless, and the food at the kitchen was outstanding. The walls were white and shiny, and cracks were filled in weekly. Rats were basically nonexistent because the prison had a regular allowance of rat poison for carrying out *ongoing* pest control, and even if there was a glitch in the delivery, someone would be able to concoct the poison on site. The cells were exemplary in their cleanliness, the prisoners cleaned their cells themselves, including the walls, the floor and the ceiling. Prisoners' clothes would be changed frequently, and all detainees had to shave daily and wash hands before meals.

'Yes, this is how it used to be!' Franz Hoss noted bitterly, taking a long look at Fabius who had instinctively hidden his hands behind his back.

'And the soup!' Fabius cried out. 'The cook's cabbage soup was out of this world!'

'Quite,' Franz Hoss reacted with a spark in his eyes, as if this memory had lit up his entire being.

'And on Sundays there was wine!' Fabius continued.

'There was a chapel. One could go to the chapel,' Franz Hoss added.

'There was no such thing as a *dorm*,' Fabius recalled.

'No, because *there were* enough cells,' Franz Hoss felt obliged to explain, mainly to Kosef J, whom he had been fixing his eyes on for a while.

The two guards carried on reminiscing about the good old days, with a sort of nostalgia entwined with bitterness. The prisoners used to work hard and long. The food was plentiful and tasty. The rules were harsh but precise. Those who escaped were caught immediately. The prison governor could be found at any moment in time in his office. The infirmary had an orderly, and the laundry had a laundress. Dogs were well nourished. The main entrance gate did not screech in *such* a bad way. Bread was delivered three times a week from the nearby town. There was a headcount in the morning, at noon and in the evening. The cutlery was made of tin, not plastic. Fireplaces were well built and the chimney flues were in perfect working order. The guards were allowed to wear clothes made of felt in winter time. The prisoners would line up and sing on their way to work. Their songs were beautiful and sad. When it was someone's turn to get released, well, they were released within the timeframe of a *single* morning.

Following this last relic of memory, the two guards took their time resting their eyes on Kosef J.

'Take Mr Kosef J,' Franz Hoss said, 'how he suffers . . . '

Kosef J gazed down to the floor, so he could get away from responding to this.

'Have you been to see the governor? Franz Hoss asked.

'Not yet,' Kosef J said in a low voice.

'And the cashier?'

'No, not yet,' Kosef J said it again.

'There you have it,' Franz Hoss concluded with disappointment, perhaps meaning that *all* that is happening to Kosef J is the utmost confirmation of their earlier observations.

Meanwhile the hustle and bustle had peaked outside. It was already light, so Franz Hoss decided to switch the lightbulbs off in the hallway and on the corridors. People kept running up and down in the courtyard, crossing each others' paths and barely avoiding a crash. The dogs' bark had become deafening. There was even a gunshot. The plodding of boots on the concrete floor sounded like hail. Someone was giving orders in a guttural tone, yet every now and then they also yelled and swore terribly. A few soldiers had also appeared who at times lined up and then broke out of line.

'They'll catch him,' Fabius mused looking out of the window.

'They won't,' Franz Hoss responded in a calm tone.

'They will,' Fabius said it again, still and sad, looking out of the window with his forehead against the dirty pane.

'They won't catch him,' Franz Hoss stated again, calmly. 'They still haven't caught the one from last year.'

'They didn't because they were stupid,' Fabius opined.

'They'll never catch anyone,' Franz Hoss continued in the same pessimistic tone. 'They still haven't caught the one from two years ago.'

'But they will manage to catch this one,' Fabius said stubbornly.

Franz Hoss got angry. Not a single escapee had been caught for at least ten years. And every year there were at least two or three cases. Soldiers, dogs and guards had searched everywhere, they had turned the plain, the town, the woods and the marshes upside down. Absolutely everything. Yet there was nothing. No one had found anything, as if the escapees had disappeared into thin air. The dogs had wandered about helplessly, chasing imaginary scents. No one had a valid inkling, or a serious suspicion. It was a total failure. Yet another proof that things were in a bad state.

Kosef J listened very carefully and very strenuously. He would have liked Franz Hoss to volunteer a few more things about how the escapees managed *not* to get caught, but the old guard said no more.

'Come,' Franz Hoss suddenly said to Fabius, and both swiftly headed towards the lift.

It would seem that the old guard had realized that down there people needed him. Once they made it past the lift's doorway, Franz Hoss said to Kosef J in a part-authoritarian, part-beseeching tone: 'Mr Kosef, you'll look after this floor, won't you?'

Then they disappeared into the lift and started to make their way down, but after a few seconds one could hear the sound of a door opening and then clacking back again. Kosef J found himself in a state of *responsible* stupefaction.

12

He would have never imagined in his whole life as a prisoner that one day he'd be left all alone on an entire prison floor, with the mission to keep watch over the other prisoners in their cells.

'I shouldn't have accepted,' Kosef J said to himself severely.

But he was taken by surprise. He hadn't had time to think, hence he hadn't had the time to say *no*. He was trying to recall the tone used by Franz Hoss. Was that a request or an order? He was unable to figure it out. He was suddenly overwhelmed by panic and shame. He, a former prisoner, had ended up keeping watch over his fomer comrades in suffering! Utterly monstrous.

'I'm a weak man,' Kosef J said to himself and could suddenly see black spots appear in front of his eye.

'I'm a weak man,' Kosef J reminded himself, 'and they know that.'

He pressed his forehead against the window, like Fabius did earlier, and could feel the cold glass freshen up his skin. He was under the impression that this coolness might help him think more clearly. He followed with his eyes as the two guards blended into the crowd in the courtyard. The noise, stamping of feet and commanding shouts kept streaming in waves. The hustle and bustle had reached utterly erratic and improbable proportions. Kosef J was unable to detect the scope of anything in this commotion. The dogs were barking at the prison guards as if they were the ones needing to get caught.

At first, Kosef J was hoping that Franz Hoss and Fabius would only be gone for a few minutes. All of a sudden, though, he could tell that the people in the courtyard were being divided into smaller groups, and each group was allocated a dog. Then, the groups started to take their leave, one by one. For a while, he could hear the footsteps of those on their way out, and the feeble barking of their dogs. In no time, the prison courtyard was deserted. The noises and shouts had died out. A heavy silence descended upon the inner courtyard and the prison as a whole.

It was a rather chilly morning. Any minute, the overcast sky was threatening with the prospect of an annoying drizzle, and the threat in the air moved into Kosef J's heart, too.

'What shall I do now?' he wondered disheartened.

It was obvious that the usual prison routine had been messed up. The prisoners hadn't been taken to work, but hadn't been given their breakfasts either. One could feel a certain tension coming from the cells. The people in their cells had most certainly heard the commotion in the courtyard. In fact, Kosef J remembered that every time the prisoners were not taken to work, or were not given food or drink and were given no explanation, made them surmise that the prison was turned upside down by some important event.

He moved away from the window and took a few steps on the corridor. He would have liked to sit on Fabius's narrow sofa, but he felt burdened by a sense of responsibility and gave up on the idea. He would have also liked to take a nap for another hour or two, but he couldn't, and what he had to do kept him awake.

As he immersed himself deeper into the situation, he realized that he didn't know what *exactly* he was supposed to do. The two guards hadn't specified anything. Franz Hoss had suggested something, but that was far too vague. He had asked him to look after the floor for a little while. What does looking after a floor mean? That he looks after it *the way they did* when they were there? Kosef J's head started to spin. He'd been woken up very early, he'd slept very badly the last couple of nights, he hadn't eaten anything that morning and, to top it all, he had even received a task he had no idea how to carry out.

'It's my fault,' Kosef J said to himself, somewhat ashamed that he had to go over this short and sharp sentence so often. As a free man, he should have been in an entirely different place. He should have been at home in town. He, Kosef J, had a mother. He hadn't even found the time to write to her and let her know the good news of his release.

'I'm so careless,' Kosef J scolded himself.

With slightly watery eyes, he ventured to check the corridor out. Life was so ironic, so unpredictable and so odd! He, Kosef J, former prisoner was now in a position to keep watch over the others. He found himself on the other side of the barricades, in a position he'd never dreamed of or coveted. He found the boundary between these two worlds, that of *the guarded* and that of *the guards*, frail beyond belief. Long years had passed while he was locked into a cell, and all this time he'd yearned to be on the other side of the cell door. And all these years, the sheer fact of being beyond the cell door seemed like a fantastic and almost intangible goal. He had coveted, yearned and dreamed of one day making it beyond the cell door, of being in another world, on the other side of that awful wall that separated *them* from *the others*. And now, he suddenly found himself *on the other side*, but the difference struck him as negligible. He wouldn't have been too fazed had Franz Hoss unexpectedly returned and locked him, Kosef J, into any available cell on the floor and entasked another random prisoner 'to look after the floor for a little while'.

'This is a mad world,' he concluded in his mind.

Such a fragile line of demarcation between the two worlds was more than enough to drive anyone mad, let alone a former prisoner.

So he decided eventually to take a walk between the two rows of cells. He watched his steps with great care, fearful that the sound of his footsteps could perhaps betray his presence and even incite the prisoners. He slowly walked past the doors and, driven by an irresistible urge, headed towards his former cell at number 50. He came to a halt in front of the door that had, for so long, been his door. He fixed it with his gaze, yet couldn't recognize it. He stared at it but couldn't feel anything within, no emotional impulse or shudder of excitement. The fact of the matter was that he didn't recognize the door because this wasn't *the side* from which he had been used to contemplate it.

'What could *he* be doing in there?' Kosef J wondered, without realizing that he had just referred to the new prisoner in the cell or had named himself. In a way, he had the impression, if not the conviction, that no one else could *live* in that cell except for the above-mentioned Kosef J, the only *legitimate* lodger of the cell. Hence the man inside could be none other than a susbstitute for him, another *Kosef J,* someone who merely acted as his double.

'I could lift the spyhole,' Kosef J said to himself.

But he didn't. The sheer fact that he had the power to lift the spyhole was so overwhelming that the actual act of lifting it paled into insignificance. Had he wanted to, he could have lifted the spyholes of all the cells. Had he wanted to, he could have opened the doors of all the cells. He could have even released the prisoners! Dear me, all this sudden power! What could possibly be the reason behind the two guards having invested him with so much power? Why wouldn't they be fearful of him? How could they possibly have so much trust in him, a prisoner released only three days earlier?

Kosef J felt somewhat humiliated by the fact that Franz Hoss and Fabius had tacitly considered him *one of them.*

'What am I actually doing now?' Kosef J wondered, feeling extremely disheartened.

He had been walking up and down the corridor for a good ten minutes. Gradually, he'd given up on caring whether his footsteps could be heard or not. He regained his usual pace, placing his entire footsole of the floor, and started listening to the sound of his paces on the concrete tiles.

'Could *they* possibly be aware that these are my footsteps?' Kosef J wondered.

Could the prisoners have any inkling that instead of the two guards there was someone else *on the watch*, a man who had been a prisoner himself until recently? Kosef J started to count his paces. From one end to the other, the corridor was exactly 123 paces long. Cell number 50 was at pace 97. Every time Kosef J walked past it he couldn't refrain from coming to a brief halt.

'I wonder whether *he* can hear me?'

'I wonder if he's afraid of me when I come to a halt just outside his cell?' Kosef J continued.

He developed a liking for this game of the paces, and after a while he ventured to make his boots give out a louder and rougher sound.

'They're so quiet,' Kosef J said to himself.

At one point, he stopped in front of cell number 50 and stood there still for almost five minutes.

'I wonder if he knows that I'm here?' Kosef J asked himself.

It was impossible for the man not to realize that there was someone standing still in front of his door for a good few minutes. Kosef J imagined the prisoner waiting in fear, bent over the edge of the bed, agonizing over *why* the footsteps had come to a halt outside his cell. Right outside his cell, of all places! Could this man in there be really scared? Most certainly. He was scared of him, Kosef J, as of something mysterious and unknown. He probably had his heart in his mouth. He was probably holding his head in his palms, prepared for the worst. Probably having a tremor in the back of his head also, due to the strain.

Suddenly, Kosef J disengaged the shutter on the spyhole to check whether this was indeed the case.

Kosef J had been correct. The man inside was crouched up on the edge of the bed, slightly leaning forward.

'As if he was throwing up,' Kosef J observed.

The man was well and truly frightened. He was holding his head in his palms and was trembling all over. Then he turned his head for a second, and the two locked eyes. The man's face was contorted with fear, his skin had a purplish tone and all his wrinkles had deepened.

'I did this,' Kosef J mused. He was unsure whether he should be proud or utterly ashamed of having produced such fear on the face of this man by way of a simple game of paces.

'I could do this to all of them,' Kosef J carried on with his train of thought.

Yes, he could have stopped in front of each and every cell for a minute or two, only to generate a sense of devouring panic in the soul of those *inside*. He could have done *this*, and those inside would have never found out that this was nothing but a game.

'This was what they'd done to me, too,' Kosef J thought to himself.

'This was the game they played, too,' Kosef J added.

'Swine,' he concluded and closed the shutter, withdrawing to the lift end of the corridor to look out of the window.

The courtyard continued to be deserted. Silence was still reigning over the prison building. Franz Hoss and Fabius didn't seem to be in a rush. From the direction of the cells a sort of din started to build up, as if every individual had been talking to himself and all these voices had ebbed into a single flow of sound.

'They are hungry,' Kosef J observed.

But he couldn't do a thing. He was practically as powerless as they. Moreover, being there, on the corridor in between the cells and keeping watch over *them*, he was just as locked up as they were. And, sure thing, he was just as hungry as they were.

'They are hungry and don't do anything!' Kosef J snapped.

'What could they possibly do?' he wondered.

'Make noise, pound and scream!' someone responded from the innermost corners of his mind, so appalled that Kosef J quickly started to look around himself.

That's the last thing he'd needed, a scandal and being involved in something like this. What would Franz Hoss say, what would Fabius say, what would the whole world say? After they'd placed so much trust in him . . .

In there the commotion was mounting by the minute. Kosef J got the impression that he was hearing the thoughts of people locked up in there, that all their brains were generating a sort of electric whirl. For a while he had been feeling terrorized by this near bestial growl. Tension was building up within the cells. The state of disquiet and unrest spilled out onto the corridor and flooded the entire building. Kosef J didn't feel safe any longer *there*. He had the impression that doors could burst out of their hinges any minute, simply exploding, and seriously famished people would rush out into the open.

'Awful,' Kosef J mused.

This savage mob would have most certainly trampled all over him, without showing a shadow of mercy.

So again, he found himself walking along the row of cells, checking locks and latches. He calmed down a little and fell into a sort of lethargic anticipation, no longer having the strength to think about what was actually happening to him.

13

It was already lunchtime when the phone on Fabius's table started to buzz like a bee.

'Hello! Hello!' a delighted Kosef J yelled into the receiver, thinking that it was either Franz Hoss or Fabius.

Someone rang from the kitchen to alert him to collect the lunches of the inmates on the second floor.

Kosef J could suddenly feel his hand holding the receiver tremble. He struggled to put the receiver back on its rest. Anxiety took over his soul again, yet he didn't dare to linger on. The voice on the phone was rather commanding, after all lunch could only be a very serious business.

Kosef J pressed the lift button and, to his surprise, the lift arrived without delay. He went down and got hold of the old trolley used to transport the inmates' food from the kitchen. Then, he collected the portions for the inmates, stacked them onto the trolley and lugged them up to the second floor. As he walked past the cells, he opened all the shutters on the spyholes. He handed everyone their share. He didn't look anyone in the eye. When he reached the end of the corridor, he ate his own meal, which was the same as everyone else's, then waited for the inmates to finish their meals and collected everyone's tray.

He loaded them onto the trolley. He closed the shutters and took the trays back to the kitchen. No one had addressed a single word to him, and no one seemed surprised that he, Kosef J, was dishing out the food in lieu of the guards.

To continue waiting, he settled for the same spot, the corner between the lift and the window. The hours kept trickling away, and reminded him of bored and indifferent fat worms that would leave a wide trail of see-through foam in their wake. Not a single soul was to be seen in the inner courtyard, and not a single sound was to be heard in the entire prison that could disturb its somnolent peace.

Kosef J turned his attention again to those *inside*.

'They stuffed their faces, what do they care?' he said to himself.

Most of them were probably dozing on their hard and narrow beds. Some were probably walking up and down, counting the paces to the barred window and back.

'They are in need of a walk,' Kosef J mused.

At this very moment, the phone rang again and Kosef J was given the command to open all doors and take the inmates to the inner courtyard for a fifteen minutes' walk.

'How can I open the doors?' Kosef J asked, really scared.

'What will *they* say when they see *me* open their doors?' he wondered again.

'What will they think of me?' he asked himself for the third time, profoundly unhappy.

Yet he hastened to carry out the order. The prisoners were indeed in great need of a walk. He did exactly what he knew needed doing. The lift could take six people at a time. He opened the first six doors. The first six inmates stepped out and, without a single word, headed towards the lift. The lift went down and returned empty in a minute. Kosef J opened the next six cell doors. The inmates came out, without looking at him or saying a word to Kosef J, and headed towards the lift. In a few minutes, everyone was down in the courtyard. Kosef J was the last person to join them. The inmates were walking around in the inner courtyard in circles.

'How meek they are,' Kosef J observed.

The inmates were moving along in Indian file, one after the other. Everyone looked straight ahead and no one talked to their neighbour, neither in front, nor behind. Every now and then someone would look up to the sky. Some would take a deep breath of afternoon air.

'Why are they so meek?' Kosef J wondered.

There wasn't a single guard or soldier in sight. The inmates could have easily chattered a bit among them. They could have come to a halt here and there, to take a good look at one another. What was wrong with them? Why were they not *doing* anything? Were they afraid of being beaten up?

At this thought, Kosef J swiftly placed his hand in front of his stomach because he felt as if he had been receiving a blow right there.

Were those people really afraid of *him*? Were they afraid of being beaten by *him*? And could he have really beaten them? And they wouldn't have reacted in any way to his beating?

The sequence of events seemed truly incredible. He tried to look at the inmates' faces, to recognize them. Only three days earlier Kosef J was alone in a cell, thinking, waiting and suffering like any one of these people. Only a week earlier he was taking a walk, with them, in this very courtyard. But neither a week earlier nor at any other point, would he have had the courage to lift his head slightly and look a guard in the eye. It was a well-known fact that it was best not to look guards in the eye.

'I must administer a blow to someone, to see what he does,' Kosef J decided. A sort of morbid curiosity took over him. He didn't hate or bear a grudge to anyone. All such feelings were alien to him, but curiosity had started to devour him and circumstances were *ripe*.

'I won't hit hard,' Kosef J said to himself.

'But if I hit him and *he* doesn't say a word, well then, it's bad,' Kosef J continued.

He didn't clarify what would have been so bad. He carried on staring at the inmates moving around in circles, and continued to believe that nothing from what was happening there was actually true. In conclusion, he had to hit someone, because this was the only way to find out whether this was true or not.

'If no one says anything,' Kosef J concluded, 'then this means that nothing is true.'

'If I hit him and he responds,' Kosef J continued, 'then this means that some of this is true.'

He was looking at them knowing that he'd hit one of them, and his entire being was overwhelmed by a vague yet disturbing sensation. He felt powerful yet humiliated at the same time, because his power over the others had no real foundation. He realized that for those people walking around in circles, he, Kosef J, no longer existed as a person. He was no longer Kosef J, he was a menace, a threat, something best to avoid.

This thought made him somewhat angry.

'Which one should I punch?' he asked, taking a closer look around. He adopted a position from where he could basically get a glimpse of everyone filing past him.

Whom to hit indeed? The inmates walked past him one by one, looking down at the ground. Kosef J scrutinized them in succession. The first looked too old. The second had a little limp. The third seemed so weak and pale that Kosef J felt sorry for him. The fourth had an awfully scared face. The fifth was the man recently moved to cell number 50, and for whom Kosef J had harboured a fellow feeling of sorts. The sixth was a very strong and sturdy man, which didn't suit Kosef J. The seventh looked like a proper thief, and Kosef J said to himself that such a man could only be a coward and a creep. The eighth was wearing glasses. The ninth was shivering with cold . . .

In such circumstances, there was no way he could make any reasoned choices. He simply had to choose at random.

He decided to close his eyes for a little while and count silently to 100. And when he'd get to 100, he should open his eyes and bash into the first man standing right in front of him.

'This way it's fair,' Kosef J said to himself.

He closed his eyes and counted to 100. Around number 10 he said 'Good God, have I gone completely mad?' Around number 23 he said, 'We are all animals,' and around 45, 'I should be ashamed, I should sink into the ground of shame and just stay there, and drown in the mud.' Around 70 he said ,'They turned us into beasts, no less.' Around 82 he noted, 'I should leave here as soon as possible, I should go to town and try to hide there.' Around 87 he said, 'I haven't yet written to my mother, I wonder what she'd have to say?' Around 91 he observed, 'This is no good, this is absurd, this is a really dirty and cowardly business.' Around number 94 he said to himself, 'They will throw themselves at me and rip me into pieces, rightly so.' Around 96 he stated briefly, 'I want to die.' Around number 97 he said to himself, trembling, 'Perhaps *he*'d also hit me.' Around number 99 he simply stated, 'It's pointless.'

He opened his eyes and bashed into someone, hitting a man just under his left ear. The man from cell number 50 wobbled under the impact but carried on walking. As soon as he had hit the man, Kosef J could himself feel the vibrating impact of his strike. One could only hear the footsteps of the people circling the inner courtyard. Kosef J had the impression that he had actually hit *himself*. He was dumbfounded, livid and with leaden feet. He kept following the man from cell number 50 with his gaze. The man would stick to an even pace, and keep the same distance of two footsteps from the inmate in front. He stopped wobbling but continued to look lower and lower at the ground.

Kosef J suddenly heard a kind of sinister laughter in his mind. As if reacting to an unseen signal, the first six prisoners headed towards the lift and went up to their cells. The lift came back, empty. Then the next six prisoners headed towards the lift and went up to their cells. The lift returned, empty again. After exactly fifteen minutes, all prisoners went up to their cells, one group after the other.

Kosef J was the last one to go up, so he proceeded to lock all the cells.

Next, he huddled up in the liftcage, without even putting his mattress down, and tried to fall asleep. His body was shaking, and when he swallowed his saliva, he found it rather sweetly tasting for some reason.

14

They had been on the lookout for the fugitive for three days. When Franz Hoss and Fabius hinted to Kosef J that he could also join them, the latter appeared pleased to do so, because in this way he was hoping to avoid being put in charge of the inmates' quarters all by himself.

Anyway, the formalities surrounding his release were suspended for the duration of the search. There was no way he could be seen by the prison governor in these exceptional circumstances. Even the man in charge of the clothing-supply room was unavailable. Kosef J imagined that he must have also been a member of the search team.

'It's hard when it's just the two of us,' Franz Hoss pointed out to Kosef J. 'Transporting food is the hardest.'

Fabius giggled like a child when he was told that Kosef J seemed interested in joining them.

'Perhaps we'll hit upon the odd clear day, too,' Fabius cried out.

They left first thing in the morning, like everyone else. Tens of search teams had been spread out in all directons.

Franz Hoss wasn't keen on the dog they were allocated to help them with the search.

'It's sick,' the old guard said after a careful look. Since it wasn't yet daylight, he lit a match, then his cigarette, and in the light of the remainder of the flame checked out the dog one more time.

'It surely has something,' he said it again.

Kosef J found the dog perfectly normal. It was that special breed of wolfhound trained to hunt people. Big, with a black muzzle, it was fairly economical with his movements, extremely careful and deploying the reactions of an intelligent being.

They started off in a direction that to Kosef J seemed like the opposite of where the town was. He regretted this somewhat but hastened to say to himself that he wouldn't have made a great impression in town being dressed as he was. In his mind, he reprimanded the man in charge of the clothing-supply room for being so slow with sewing his buttons.

For a while, they were surrounded left and right by other search teams, men and dogs, all heading more or less in the same direction. The dogs could sense each other's presence, so they were fretting nervously and every now and then they'd start barking with frenzy. Gradually, the search teams got to move away from one another. It was almost daybreak, but the sky didn't seem to clear up.

'At least it won't rain,' Fabius said. 'These aren't rain clouds.'

Each and every one of them carried a field rucksack on their back. They weren't too heavy or large. Kosef J had no idea what he was carrying on his back but didn't bother to figure this out.

Franz Hoss and Fabius seemed in a good mood. They were treading along with a kind of vigour that was somewhat unusual for men of their age. Franz Hoss had volunteered to hold the dog by the leash and, as a result, had to put up with all its jerkiness.

After all the other search teams had disappeared from sight, Franz Hoss decided that they were ready for a break. Kosef J found this rather untimely but had no reason to object to something that could turn out to be an opportunity for respite.

'It's good that it's hard,' Fabius mused.

Kosef J needed a good few seconds to realize that the old guard was referring to the ground. It was indeed parched. Next, a tiny forest appeared on the horizon, flanked by a meandering river. Kosef J had never been there before. Nor had he spotted the tiny forest or the river from his cell window, or indeed from any other part of the prison building, and now the sheer throught of getting to the water gave him enormous pleasure.

Then it was Fabius's turn to smoke a cigarette. He handed the packet to Kosef J, too, but the latter refused. Meanwhile Franz Hoss had seated himself on what looked like a giant anthill, though fossilized and abandoned by insects.

'Look at this bummer,' Franz Hoss pointed at the dog that had also lain down.

'Indeed,' Fabius agreed, puffing about with great satisfaction.

'We won't get much done with this one,' Franz Hoss added.

'It's their fault,' Fabius muttered.

'You can't get very far with such a stupid dog,' Franz Hoss continued.

'Dogs aren't what they used to be either,' Fabius stated.

Kosef J got the impression that Franz Hoss and Fabius had only taken this break so they could gossip about the dog at will. Amused, he kept looking at the two guards but couldn't find the right moment to get a word in.

They could hear a bird squawking and the dog perked its ears, rearing up on its front legs. He fixed its gaze on a cluster of trees in the distance, and indeed, soon a bird took its flight.

All four of them, including the three men and the dog, watched it disappear over the horizon with an odd and regretful look, or at least this was Kosef J's impression. Franz Hoss stood up, shook the dust off his trousers and continued to look in the direction where the bird had vanished.

'Partridges, at this time?' he mused.

No one replied. Fabius finished his cigarette. The dog got on all fours, and they all started off again.

They dipped into the tiny forest. They couldn't immediately spot a path so they let themselves be led forward by the dog's instincts. The shrubs were rather spiky, their leaves as sharp as knife blades.

'Is this your first time doing this?' Franz Hoss turned to Kosef J.

Kosef found this a completely ludicrous question but still replied: 'Yes, it is.'

'You'll get used to it,' Franz Hoss said encouragingly.

Kosef J had no idea what to make of this. What exactly should he get used to? From afar, one could hear thunder.

'Bloody hell!' Franz Hoss cursed, hissing.

'Nothing to worry about,' Fabius observed. 'When it thunders, it doesn't rain.'

The dog was unable to find any reliable trails. It would run for ten yards or so in one direction, then give up and spot something else. It would run around in circles, waiting for long seconds, ears perked. So they left the forest behind and decided to follow the meandering river. After about an hour's walk, Kosef J realized that their efforts made no sense whatsoever, and they wouldn't actually discover anything at all.

It started to drizzle. The drops were so fine and rare that they could barely intimate that something a lot worse might also happen.

'This is no proper rain,' Fabius decided, being in a good mood.

Franz Hoss came to a sudden halt and informed Fabius that he was unable to make another step forward. Fabius took the dog from his boss and, most bizarrely, urged the others to carry on. After another hour's walk, it was Kosef J's turn to hold the dog on the leash and endure its whims.

'Enough!' Franz Hoss said at one point.

Kosef J thought this meant that they'd take another break, but Franz Hoss only wanted to feed the dog. He produced a piece of dried meat from his bag and threw it to the dog. He wolfed it down straightaway. Then they carried on searching. Neither Fabius nor his boss complained about the difficulties of this self-imposed march. Kosef J was all wet. Sweat was trickling down his forehead, his cheeks and his throat. He could feel the wet shirt sticking to his skin. He would have liked to tell the others that all this effort was in vain, but he didn't dare. Besides, the two guards didn't seem tired.

'They're like devils,' Kosef J said to himself.

The previously infrequent rain drops had by then turned into a fine yet leaden mist.

'At least it doesn't hail,' Fabius noted.

Kosef J was just about to suggest to the guards that finding some shelter would be most fitting in the circumstances, especially since the dog's vision was likely to be extremely limited by the rain. But at that same moment the dog seemed to have discovered what it had been looking for all these hours. The animal's entire behaviour suddenly changed, turning extremely agitated and impatient. It dashed forward with a force that almost knocked Fabius down, him being in charge of the leash at that time. The dog was barking aggressively, struggling to free itself from the strap that stifled its flight.

'He found it! He found it!' Franz Hoss yelled.

Kosef J found himself overwhelmed by the excitement of the hunter on the game trail. THE TRAIL! Had they really found the trail? He had instantly forgotten that THIS TRAIL was that of a man, of an escapee. He had a single thought in his mind: behold, the effort invested in this day was about to pay off.

'Don't let it go! Just don't!' Franz Hoss yelled to Fabius, who could barely hold on to the dog by the leash.

By now all three were running after the dog, panting and soaking wet.

'We'll catch him!' Franz Hoss whistled into Kosef J's ear, stepping up the pace.

Fabius also let out a victorious howl, as if this had helped him regain his energies. Franz Hoss took the leash over from Fabius. The dog looked ever more self-assured. Kosef J watched, perplexed, how the dog would pick a particular route with an innate precision. Soon they moved on to a hillside and started climbing up a narrow path.

'This can't be true' Kosef J said to himself.

The slope was hellish. The soil had become all sticky because of the rain. Their boots had soaked up a lot of water and so, at every step, they also lifted a decent slice of soil stuck to their soles. Fabius suddenly slipped and besmeared his knees and back with mud. Kosef J bent down to help him. To his surprise, the old guard laughed and stammered:

'We'll catch him! We'll catch him, you'll see!'

Kosef J took over the supervision of the wild beast. He also slid several times into the mud on his knees. The old guards were so transfigured that Kosef J realized there was no point in talking to them. He was fascinated by this *manhunt*. He could no longer feel the tiredness or the rain. He allowed himself to be propelled by this strong animal and had the impression that just a few yards ahead of them there was another human being, surrounded, and about to lose their powers.

'Now! Now!' Franz Hoss yelled.

Just past them, there was a torrent running all the way to the valley. The water was furiously rolling about various bits of rocks and wood.

'This is madness,' the thought flashed through Kosef J's mind.

The air got cooler and cooler as they climbed uphill. Rain turned into hail.

'At least it's not dark,' Fabius noted.

Kosef J no longer knew what to think. He had entered this vortex, wanted to be the first to get to the *prey*, and was almost convinced that they were doing something very important. As they got closer to the highest peak, all three of them were complicit in the sensation that the hunted one was up there, on the summit. They covered the last hundred yards basically crawling along, holding on to herbage and roots to propel themselves forward. The dog had turned into a total savage, howling as if driven mad by some demonic presence.

A few yards before reaching the summit Franz Hoss shouted to Kosef J: 'Let it go!'

Kosef J let the dog go. In just in a couple of jumps it vanished into the unknown. 'There'll be blood,' Kosef J thought. It was strange how relieved he felt just by not being pulled along by the dog. His palms were itchy though, and he had deep cuts caused by the leash.

The three of them reached the summit at the same time. The rain had slowed down a little, but the air was cold enough to cut their breath off. Kosef J was expecting to find a crashed and bleeding man, with the animal's fangs stuck into his throat. Judged by the feverishness with which they were looking around, Franz Hoss and Fabius were probably hoping to find the same, too. The dog had disappeared though. They were all struggling to guess the direction in which it might have headed off, while being faced with a plateau devoid of any trace of life. All they could see were shafts of steam, rising from the rain-soaked earth akin to a bunch of menacing figures.

They kept twirling about on the summit, intrigued and looking out in all directions. Then they heard a wailing sound coming from the scutch grass.

'That is no dog's wail,' Kosef J jumped up.

The two guards, red in the face with effort, mouths hungry for air, eyeballs falling out of their orbits, were greedily awaiting their reward for such a day. Slowly but surely, all three came closer to the place where the wailing came from. They were treading slowly, not wanting to rush, and savouring that moment of suspense prior to victory. Kosef J could see himself walking the line with them, eager perhaps to encounter the same sight that the guards also wanted to see. They came up to the swirl of herbage and took a look inside.

Crouched and foaming at the muzzle, the dog was wailing like a human being. Every now and then, it would twitch, turning its belly up. Its eyes were red, sporting an erratic look.

'Didn't I tell you?' Franz Hoss screamed. 'Didn't I tell you that this was no proper dog?'

He spat on the ground, crouched down, then took his backpack off, opened it and started to rummage in it.

Kosef J couldn't take his eyes off the wailing dog. Fabius didn't seem too impressed, though he showed some obvious signs of pity.

'What's wrong with it?' Kosef J asked, troubled.

Franz Hoss finally found what he was looking for: a bottle of rum. He took a few mouthfuls and a couple of very deep breaths.

'It's epileptic,' he said, handing the bottle to Kosef J.

15

As soon as the dust around the prison-break had settled, the clothing-supply room man got back to his duties, and Kosef J resumed his daily visits. This was, by the way, the wish of the short, stocky and cheerful man, who didn't miss a single chance to ask Kosef J not to avoid his little workshop.

'So we can have a word,' he added each time.

Apart from that, the short, stocky and cheerful man had some actual business to conduct with Kosef J almost every day. The new clothes had proved to be very difficult to make. The short, stocky and cheerful man wouldn't stop taking measurements. He was always dissatisfied with something or other, and kept asking Kosef J to stand straight and still in front of the mirror one more time, so he could take his measurements yet again. The man had a sadistic glee in his eyes every time he came up to Kosef J, armed with a tiny piece of soap and a tape measure that he unrolled from a round metal box.

He measured the width of Kosef J's shoulders, shook his head, closed his eyes, thought for a little while, seemed to mumble something judging by his impossible-to-read lip movements, and put a bizarre mark on a piece of fabric. He then opened his eyes with the joyful look of a diver who had finally come up for air.

'It will do,' he said, and moved on to measure the sleeves.

The game continued like this day after day. The short, stocky and cheerful man kept concentrating on taking measurements, mumbled something, closed his eyes, seemed tormented by some mysterious calculations and mathematical transformations he carried out in his mind, and then wrote *everything* down.

'There, this is the way to do it,' he added, perhas to put Kosef J at ease.

So he carried on taking measurements. The waistline. The length of the legs, thighbone and spine. He measured the circumference of the neck, waistline and thorax. He took complicated measurements in the area of Kosef J's armpits, forcing him to lift his arms up for several minutes, while he kept giggling as if he had actually tickled himself rather than take someone else's measurements.

'It's OK,' he reassured Kosef J.

Kosef J tried a few times to remind the short, stocky and cheerful man that last time, prior to the prison-break that is, there was only talk of choosing the right buttons. This was what the short man himself had said, namely that he only had to sew the buttons on. Why did they have to start from scratch then, day after day? What was the explanation for this?

The short man either didn't respond to such questions, or chose to be vague on this matter. Could he really not hear or just pretended to be deaf? Whenever Kosef J tried to address the question of *time,* in order to draw his attention to this *aspect,* the short man adapted an impassioned tone and started to complain of the array of jobs he had on his plate.

'Just look at all this,' he said. 'Please take a look! Utter chaos!' he added. 'Chaos, nothing else!'

The child was there most of the time, too, rummaging in the button box. On such occasions, he'd usually lift his head, as if the word *chaos* had been of great interest to him.

'I have to do something about *these*,' the short man said. 'I simply must.'

Kosef J finally figured out what the short man meant by *these*. Every day further piles of clothes would appear on the tables, just brought up from the damp basements into the workshop.

'This is the only way to save them,' the short man said with a cheerful spark in his eye. 'The only way.'

'What do you mean?' Kosef J asked one day, intrigued.

'I transform them,' said the short man, panting.

Indeed, the short, stocky and cheerful man would undo and then recompose tens of outfits. He'd turn coats into jackets, jackets into waistcoats, he'd change the lining, cut off the cuff hems on trousers and add cuff hems to other pairs that didn't initially have this feature. He'd replace shirt collars, jacket pockets and coat buttons. He'd make an overcoat from two to three jackets, and a pair of trousers from an overcoat. He'd move everything that could be moved from one place to another, simplified whatever could be made simpler and, conversely, complicated whatever could be made more complex.

'I force them to live on,' he explained. '*This* is the way I coerce them.'

The clothes he'd just transformed were then returned to the warehouse, only to be taken out again and subjected to further transformations two or three weeks later. No piece of fabric or lining would be wasted in this *upheaval*. Each and every patch awaited its turn in a new operation, and each and every button became indispensable at just the right time.

'This is the only way,' the short, stocky and cheerful man concluded, after having generously permitted to Kosef J to *understand* the significance of his labours.

'OK, but how much longer?' Kosef J asked after about two weeks of daily visits at the workshop.

'Until the end of my days!' the short, stocky and cheerful man replied proudly. He then grabbed Kosef J by his lapel and forced him to look him in the eye: 'This is my battle,' he stressed, 'my battle and only mine, understood?'

'Yes, of course,' Kosef J hastened to reply.

What Kosef J had actually understood was that at this pace the short, stocky and cheerful man wouldn't be able to finish the job he started on his clothes. Yet Kosef J didn't get upset. He liked coming to the workshop, were he felt sheltered. He'd be always met with a pleasant warmth, and the short, stocky and cheerful man would always be up for a chat. He'd almost always find something to flatter Kosef J with, and the latter would be secretly pleased to hear these.

'What a great posture!' the short man exclaimed every time he took Kosef J's measurements.

Or, whenever he got Kosef J to try on a sleeveless jacket or a pair of yet-unlined trousers, the short man couldn't get enough of moving around Kosef J and marvelling at him.

'How classy!' he'd cry out.

He'd also often declare that Kosef J was simply *made* to wear ordinary civilian clothing, since he had that rare thing only few people had, namely, *allure.*

'Without allure,' he elaborated, 'it's pointless to even wear clothes. Allure is everything. Allure and nothing but allure.'

'What a chatterbox,' Kosef J said to himself, although he enjoyed letting the short man handle him.

He gradually became aware that the short, stocky and cheerful man effectively rejoiced whenever he, Kosef J, agreed to try on some of these transformed clothes. Another discovery astonished him even more: *all* these transformed clothes fitted him perfectly; in other words, they were made to measure. Thus he realized that in about a fortnight he had become the virtual owner of an impressive collection of coats, overcoats, jackets, trousers, waitcoats, shirts and other bits and pieces. All these items, however, made their way to the warehouse as soon as they were completed as if *cut out for* Kosef J.

The little man worked feverishly, from morning till late at night. Arguably, Kosef J's presence was an inspiration for him. One day, Kosef J didn't go round the workshop, and this led to a minor tragedy. The man waited and waited, but then went off to look for Kosef J himself. He found him in the kitchen where Kosef J was trying to calm Rozette and fix one of the dishwashers. All the spare parts were lined up on the floor and Kosef J was just wondering whether he'd ever manage to assemble them again.

The little man barely dared to walk up to Kosef J in the lightest of fooststeps, and tap him on his shoulder.

'You've forgotten me,' he whispered, tiny tears in his eyes.

16

Kosef J didn't have much time to wonder why his appointment with the prison governor, *the colonel*, kept being delayed. After the business with the prison-break, he was told that the meeting would take place any day. He then found out that the poor colonel had locked himself into his office. Being extremely saddened by the events, he didn't want to see anyone. Franz Hoss mooted that he perhaps had pneumonia.

'This is what he tends to do when he's ill,' Franz Hoss stated in a regretful voice.

The days passed remarkably fast. Kosef carried on eating in the kitchen and sleeping in the liftcage. In the morning he'd visit the short man at the clothing-supply room, and in the afternoon help Rozette with the dishes. In between, he had a little breather to go for the odd walk. Never again did he happen to find the side entrance open, nor did he have the desire to go *beyond* the prison walls. He was pleased with the poplar alley, and the occasional exploit behind the kitchen where the child had initially taken him to point out the gravel pit. Having said that, he was actually unable to come across that pit ever again.

Then he got into the habit of playing dice with Franz Hoss and Fabius, and, most gratifyingly for him, even started to win at this game.

'See, see,' Fabius alerted Franz Hoss, 'Mr Kosef has got the hang of it.'

Franz Hoss would keep losing, so he just panted nervously.

'See, see,' Fabius would carry on maliciously, addressing Franz Hoss, 'Mr Kosef is rolling the dice *correctly*.'

Despite losing, Franz Hoss was dead set on playing dice even more frequently, panting and puffing like a bloated and peevish animal.

'Mr Kosef is much younger,' he'd say, trying to come up with an explanation.

Kosef J would usually win in a manner that appeared utterly devoid of logic to him. If, for instance, he needed thirty points and set his mind on 'needing thirty points', then the next minute he'd roll the dice to earn himself thirty points.

'Impossible,' he'd think and stare in astonishment at the dots on the dice.

'Impossible,' Franz Hoss would yell, having just scored twenty-nine points right before it was Kosef J's turn.

'See, see,' Fabius would remark, 'this is because Mr Kosef J is disgruntled.'

Whenever Franz Hoss heard the word *disgruntled,* he'd turn all red and his entire double chin would visibly tremble.

'Mr Kosef is just a beginner,' he'd say, but Kosef J didn't quite get the point Franz Hoss was trying to make.

'Thirty-six,' Kosef J said to himself and rolled the dice. All three leant forward to count the result and the dots on the dice did indeed add up to thirty-six points, in other words, to the rarest and highest of scores.

'See, see,' Fabius observed, 'Mr Kosef is a *good hand*.'

'Mr Kosef is the devil incarnate,' Franz Hoss muttered in response.

At times, they'd carry on playing dice until well after midnight. The two guards would go to bed tired and, at times, couldn't manage to get up on time in the morning. Breakfast would be left uncollected at the kitchen. The prisoners would vegetate hungrily in their cells, and they wouldn't be taken out to work either, something that seemed beyond belief to Kosef J.

Calmness reigned over the prison, and it felt like a giant and suffocating dome. Everyone moved very slowly, as if they were swimming in some kind of dough. For days on end, one couldn't hear as much as a single sound, since those being guarded and those doing the guarding would hibernate in their dens alike, unseen by anyone.

It seemed to Kosef J that life used be more active and varied in the past. Even now he couldn't really complain of boredom, only of *sluggishness*.

What really managed to get him out of this slumber was the discovery of the enormous *internal* scale of the prison. When he was trying to find his way around the external prison walls he already had the inkling that the prison must have been massively extended. And now, being in a position to walk around unimpeded, absolutely anywhere he liked, he got full confirmation of this first impression.

One day, he came across an internal courtyard where nothing whatsoever would happen. It was obvious that no one had shown up here for ages. Weed had sprouted from the tiles and started to spread about at will. The walls surrounding the internal courtyard were also in a sorry state. Wound-like cracks emerged in-between the stones, and in places, entire sections of the wall had collapsed. The upper edge of the wall seemed to have been crunched up by a montruous aerial being, and in the wake of this beastly feast the entire masonry was left jagged, mangled and in fringes. All along one side of the courtyard one could catch sight of the remains of a former row of cells—now giant black sockets, overgrown with moss.

Kosef J went a little closer trying to figure out the mystery of this abandonment, the reason for this *negligence*. He climbed up on a stone ladder in tatters. He then carried on towards the deserted corridors, taking in, left and right, the sad spectacle of these premises left without doors, windows, bars or flooring. Everything seemed to have been plucked out, everything that wasn't made of stone. All that was left on the inside were the scratch marks of those who had lived there. Oddly though—and this is the oddest of all the things he saw—the words and drawings scratched by the prisoners over the years had all been covered with mortar, or at least with chalk. Someone, therefore, didn't want these to be seen, and took the trouble to silence them. This effort to keep them silent had been rather meticulous, since in each and every cell, on each and every wall and even ceiling, one could make out the scars of these wiped-out and eradicated messages.

Kosef J came back the next day, the third day and then the following days. After this first abandoned inner courtyard he came across a second and then a third courtyard, and then several others. These would only give a vague hint at their original purpose since they had been turned into rubbish dumps in the meantime. Kosef J found it impossible to tell whether this was a dump only for prison rubbish or also for the rubbish from the nearby town.

He stumbled upon a pool that had once been paved with blue ceramic tiles. A few tiles had managed to survive here and there, punctuating with delightful colour spots the greyness of the concrete frame. At the bottom of the pool there was a thin layer of stale water, by now turned green and foul-smelling.

He then discovered a structure looking like a fire lookout tower, and a row of cavernous cellars, a disused railway line, a few abandoned warehouses still smelling of rotten grains. He climbed up the tower and noticed that the prison had in fact travelled in time and space, leaving in its trail the ruins of another four or five similar settlements. Kosef J couldn't get to the bottom of what terrible circumstances must have forced the authorities to abandon at one point all installations, courtyards, pavilions and walls, and then build others, slightly farther away but following more or less the same principle. And then to abandon these as well, and dislodge the prison yet again and then leave it to ruin and build another, following the same course, even farther away. And so on and so forth, at least five or six times, at time intervals Kosef J was unable to determine.

A month had passed since the prison-break when Kosef J, rummaging among the heaps of rubbish, encountered in one of the abandoned courtyards the fugitive himself.

17

As he caught a glimpse of this human figure bending over a small groove carved out of the rubbish heap, Kosef J didn't immediately make the connection with the fugitive. He wasn't overjoyed by the presence of the other, either. He'd got used to being all by himself in those places. He felt at ease wandering around and marvelling at the abandoned courtyards. He'd even had the sensation that he owned those ruins and had received them as a personal gift upon his release.

As he was approaching the man bent over the rubbish Kosef J got the impression that the former was about to bury something.

'A dead cat,' it crossed Kosef J's mind, and he stepped the pace up, as if he'd wanted to give the other man a hand to complete the task, and then see him leave, job done.

The other man could hear Kosef J approach, so he straightened his back and waited for Kosef J to get closer.

'A prisoner,' Kosef J said to himself, realizing that the man was wearing the same clothes as him. He found himself unwittingly scolding the short, stocky and cheerful man who'd never got round to finishing his civilian clothes, because in this way the latter was forcing him *to mingle* with the other prisoners for all this time. Without realizing why, he would have liked this man on the heap to know that he, Kosef J, was a free man who was only passing by. But the man on the heap was looking at him as if he had caught sight of a fellow being, as if they were both likely to rummage in that pile of petrified rubbish.

'Perhaps Franz Hoss had sent him,' Kosef J mused, trying to come up with an explanation for the man's presence.

'Hey you!' Kosef J shouted, positioning himself at the bottom of the heap, with a kind expression on his face.

The man responded with a friendly wave with his left hand. In his right hand, he held a metal hook.

Kosef J wasn't impressed with this response. He waited for a few seconds. The man didn't say a word, so Kosef J decided to climb the rubbish heap *himself*.

'Franz Hoss must have certainly sent him,' he confirmed his own supposition. 'What could a prisoner otherwise do at such a place and time?'

'Perhaps he'd also been recently released,' Kosef J thought somewhat anxiously. 'No, this couldn't be true. A free man had no business on *that* heap, let alone with a metal hook in their right hand.'

'Has Franz Hoss sent you?' Kosef J asked, once he was close enough.

'Oh, no,' the man hastened to reply.

'Fabius?' Kosef J continued, being almost certain that the man would respond 'yes, it was Fabius.'

'Oh, no,' the man replied again.

Kosef J got out of breath a little as he went up the heap, and this made him feel embarrassed.

'It's quite cold here,' he said, trying not to look curious.

'Yes, it is,' the man replied with the same cheerful look on his face. Kosef J became more and more intrigued by his short replies.

He checked him out, head to toe. The man was unshaven and had dark circles under his eyes, and his clothes were badly worn out. Yet his face and expression was incredibly cheerful.

'What are you doing here?' Kosef J yelled at the man, as if the first item in the conversation had already been dealt with.

'I gather,' the man responded.

'What sort of things?' Kosef J continued.

'Oh, there are plenty of things.'

'Oh, there are plenty of things,' Kosef J mused, humming this to himself. This man definitely had an annoying manner of speech.

Kosef J looked around, all of a sudden captivated by the landscape that offered itself for viewing from the top of the heap. The man didn't immediately pick up the job where he'd left it. He was perhaps expecting Kosef J to say or do something else first.

In that instant, Kosef J had a revelation: this man was a fugitive. In fact, he was the very prison-breaker *he* had also been searching for himself. The unshaven beard, the rags, the happy and famished face betrayed the incredible truth that this man was an escapee.

'Good grief!' Kosef J cried out.

The man smiled, seemingly pleased to see that the air had finally been cleared between them.

'Oh, no, this can't be, this can't be,' Kosef J muttered looking left and right, bending his back to make himself appear smaller. 'They will get you,' he whispered to the man.

'Who will?' the man asked calmly.

Kosef J crouched down, pulling the man to his level.

'You have no idea what you're doing!' he continued, sounding more terrified than ever. 'Everybody is on the lookout for you, they are all searching for you and they will get you!' Kosef J could suddenly feel himself breaking out in a sweat. He shook his body as if he wanted to shake the drops of sweat off his forehead. Then he continued, in an almost panting voice: 'With dogs, you know? With dogs!'

'Still?' the man asked in his usual curt manner.

Kosef J didn't respond straightaway. He started to think this through. The fact of the matter was that there had been no mention of the escapee for the last month or so, and no one had lifted a finger to actually find him. And yet it seemed inconceivable to him that the escapee should be still hanging around the prison after all that had happened, especially after having been hunted by dogs.

'You must flee,' Kosef J told him.

'Whereto?' the man asked.

'He's mad! He's completely off his head!' Kosef J's brain rebelled, in shock.

'To town!' Kosef J shouted, as if he'd been strangled.

'To town!' the man repeated, sounding disappointed. 'They'd find me there in no time.'

'Anywhere, just anywhere!' Kosef J whispered jerkily.

119

'I have nowhere to flee to,' the man declared, somewhat annoyed by Kosef J's insistence.

Kosef J simply couldn't recover from the feverishness that overwhelmed him. He would have liked to do *something* for this stubborn man but the fugitive simply refused to take note. He then remembered that the city had been actually turned upside down by the search patrols. In fact, all the surroundings had been gone through with a fine-toothed comb: all woods, villages, marshes, meadows and gardens. How odd that only the abandoned prison court-yards and the rubbish heaps had been left unsearched.

'For how long have you been here?' Kosef J asked him.

'From the beginning,' the man answered.

'From the beginning of what?' Kosef J asked.

'From the beginning of the beginning,' the man replied.

'Mad as a hatter,' Kosef J said to himself.

'You're mad!' Kosef J whispered.

'I'm not,' the man said.

They paused and stared at one another. Kosef J suddenly noticed a buzzing sensation in his head. He felt so burdened by his discovery that he sensed danger straightaway. What would Franz Hoss say if he found out that the man they'd been chasing for a whole day in the rain had been hiding all that time and was in fact still hiding among the rubbish heaps? Anyway, Kosef J now *knew* one thing: he would have been a thousand times happier had he not been aware of the man's whereabouts.

'What on earth am I doing?' Kosef J wondered.

'Would you have some food on you by any chance?' the man asked.

'No,' Kosef J replied.

'Or a penknife?'

'No, neither,' Kosef J replied with some embarrassment, as if to suggest that he didn't bring these items because he didn't know they'd be needed.

'Perhaps a belt you no longer need?' the man continued.

'No, I have nothing on me,' Kosef J responded, sounding desperate.

'Maybe tomorrow, in case you pass by here.'

Kosef J would have liked to flee and forget about coming across this man. He would have also liked to forget that, for a moment, he had shown concern about the man's fate.

'Don't know!' he struggled to respond, sounding almost suffocated.

'Are you OK?' the man asked in a calm voice.

'I don't know,' Kosef J shouted back. After a brief pause, he added: 'I was in fact released, you know.'

'I see,' the man replied.

Kosef J pinned his gaze on the hole the man had carved out with the help of his metal hook. The rubbish had been disposed in successive layers, which had gradually cemented under its own weight and the impact of the cold weather. The man had to struggle to stir these layers and couldn't really find much of interest. He managed, however, to pull out a boot without laces or sole. He was probably aiming to search for its pair, too.

'It can't be far,' Kosef J noted, taking a good look at the boot and imagining its matching pair.

'This is more like it,' the man replied.

For a while, they carried on stirring the layers together. Kosef J also found a metal hook and eagerly got started with the job. He dug out a few empty and rusty cans. The man put these to one side and Kosef J didn't enquire about his designs on them. He managed to save a biggish plastic foil without tearing it too much. He found dozens of nails and a few rolls of wire.

As he got immersed into this work, Kosef J calmed down. His mind cleared up and he suddenly found himself in a good mood.

'I'll come tomorrow, too,' he said.

He carried on rummaging for a little longer, not finding anything. The man put aside a shred of tyre and a rusty metal pot used for boiling water, with a broken handle.

'I'll see what I can do,' Kosef J said again.

The man found a thimble and a tin plate. Kosef J, the backrest of a chair, and two boot pegs. Then the man pulled out a candle holder with all three arms broken. They both stared at it, in silence.

'How lovely,' Kosef J observed.

'Yes, it is,' the man agreed.

Kosef J went on to find half of the bellows originally belonging to an accordion, a blackened but intact glass jar and a fork.

The man found a fingerless glove and the tip of a candle.

Kosef J then stumbled upon a ribbed cardboard box and an iron horseshoe.

The man found a cork, a handful of blue tile crocks and dozens of bolts, some screwed on to nuts.

Kosef J also found a nickel buckle.

The man found two book covers on which one could only make out the letters A, T and E, an alarm-clock casing, a time-worn rabbit skin and another metal hook, identical to the one he had used earlier to stir the rubbish up.

Kosef J found a rusty but yet-unopened can, a knife handle and a belt.

The man found a single playing card, an ace of clubs.

Then Kosef J found the second half of the bellows that used to belong to the accordion, a pen lid and two bicycle-wheel spokes.

The man also found a few bicycle spokes and some sweet-smelling gravel. These pebbles would spark even when clattered very gently.

They only took a break when they came across the corpse of a dog.

18

After dinner that night, Kosef J played dice with Franz Hoss and Fabius in Rozette's kitchen. They talked a bit about the colonel and Kosef J found out that the former was doing 'a little better'. Then they spoke about Rozette, whose cooking had gone from good to great and excellent lately.

'It's because of the plates,' Franz Hoss went ahead with an explanation.

After each had taken their turn at rolling the dice, Franz Hoss continued to expand his theory.

'The cleaner the plates, the stronger the flavour.'

Then they rolled another round of dice. Fabius, who had started to lose lately, would comment with noticeably less enthusiasm on everyone's score. Franz Hoss concluded his theory with the finding that *everything* was down to Kosef J, since it was him who'd help Rozette with doing the dishes. Kosef J was so skilled at dishwashing and he'd get the plates so impeccably clean that the food eaten off these plates would miraculously acquire an exceptionally good taste.

'Simple, isn't it?' Franz Hoss summed up.

Kosef J won two games out of three. Relaxed and somewhat flustered by his victory, he steered the conversation to the topic of the prison-break that had taken place a month earlier.

Had the prisoner been caught?

No, he hadn't.

But had the search continued at least? In Kosef J's view it was the duty of *those in charge* to continue the search day and night.

No, the search had been suspended.

Why had the search been suspended? How come such an important matter was abandoned so abruptly? He, Kosef J, was of the opinion that *all* those who had embarked on searching for the prisoner hadn't been following a well-designed plan.

Oh yes, they had been following a plan, in place for very many years, and which plan had been very well designed.

But hadn't Franz Hoss himself mentioned that about ten years earlier a fugitive hadn't been found?

Yes, Franz Hoss had indeed said that.

From this, it follows that the plan wasn't good. He, Kosef J felt that the plan hadn't been good enough. That all searches had been conducted in the wrong places. Those whose job was to search for the fugitive should have put themselves in his shoes.

'Well, this is exactly what they were thinking, Mr Kosef,' Franz Hoss burst out laughing. 'To catch him and to put themselves in his shoes.'

Oh, no, this wasn't a joke. He, Kosef J, meant something else. He meant that the fugitive should have been looked for in places where it would have been normal for him to hide, and, therefore, easy to find.

'What?' Franz Hoss snapped, staring at Kosef J.

The reasoning was very simple. There was no point searching for the fugitive everywhere. He only needed to be looked for in places that were naturally likely to offer him a perfect hideaway. In places that were *plausible*. Would Franz Hoss agree with this claim?

'I would!' Fabius gushed.

'What?' Franz Hoss yelled.

They had been searching for the fugitive all along the river and among the briars, for example. How long could a fugitive possibly survive while hiding by the river and among briars? Especially in winter? How long indeed?

'Next to no time,' Franz Hoss replied.

Or on the fields, how long could the fugitive survive while hiding in the open fields?

Not very long indeed.

Or in town! Would a remotely intelligent fugitive have hidden in town, where he could have been exposed by just about any resident?

No, not in town either. This was obvious.

In the woods perhaps? Would the fugitive have been able to survive in the woods? Or in any of the surrounding villages, or in just about any place frequented by people?

No.

Well, then?

Then what?

Well, then, which was the place, the only place where the fugitive would have been able to live and survive without being found?

'I swear to you, I've got no idea,' Franz Hoss yelled.

'Think a little longer,' Kosef J insisted with a sense of elation.

'I don't know, Mr Kosef, I really don't. Perhaps you do, Mr Fabius?'

Fabius jumped up, frightened and somewhat embarrassed by this parade of ideas taking place just as he was losing at dice.

'I don't know, Mr Hoss, I really don't.'

Well, he, Kosef J, *knew*, he had a *firm* opinion in this regard: the only place where the fugitive would have had a chance for safe hiding without being found was the prison itself.

The two guards froze for a few minutes, arms up in the air.

'Had anyone looked for him properly in the prison?' Kosef J asked in an inquisitive voice.

'I hadn't,' Franz Hoss admitted. 'Perhaps you had, Mr Fabius?' he asked, turning to Fabius.

Fabius shook his head as a sign of negation, eyes fixed on the last roll of dice. Kosef J was ahead of him again, by just a single point.

'The man could be among us,' Kosef J uttered solemnly.

Franz Hoss looked at the clock and immediately got up from the table. He was already half an hour late. He quickly grabbed the prisoners' dinners, loaded them on the trolley and headed off towards the pavilion.

'You're thinking along the right lines, Mr Kosef,' he said on his way out.

Fabius kept on fretting for quite some time, staring at the dice. He couldn't come to terms with the fact that after he had rolled a maximum of five times six, Kosef J also rolled five times six and now they were about to go for another round.

19

Kosef J managed to snatch a pair of boots from the short, stocky and cheerful man. He had to work on the man for a whole morning to convince him to get this pair of boots out of the clothing-supply room. The short, stocky and cheerful man suffered terribly when he found himself in a situation where he had to give in.

'Mr Kosef, Mr Kosef,' he kept saying, 'your boots are in a perfectly good condition. Your boots can last for another five winters.'

This was the very first time in Kosef J's life that he acted in a way that could be called shifty. He made use of veiled threats. He insinuated that he wouldn't have enough time in the future to help the man with trying on the clothes. After all, he was a free man. He should have left the prison compound a long time ago. He should have been wearing *plain* clothes for ages. What would the prison governor have had to say if he found out that Kosef J hadn't yet received his plain clothes all this time after his release? Who was responsible for this delay?

The short, stocky and cheerful man turned all red in the face.

'Are you threatening me, Mr Kosef?'

'Yes, I am,' Kosef J admitted with some regret.

The short man looked disheartened.

'This is what everyone does. They're all threatening me. Everyone is punching me right where it hurts.'

Kosef J felt disheartened, too. He had no intention to upset the short, stocky and cheerful man. The short, stocky and cheerful man asked Kosef J for permission to share a few stories from his life. Kosef J agreed. The short, stocky and cheerful man brightened up a little. He told the story of his entire life in no less than two hours and forty-three minutes.

'It's sad, isn't it?' the short, stocky and cheerful man sighed at the end.

'Quite sad,' Kosef J agreed.

'Now you understand, don't you?' The short, stocky and cheerful man asked with a hopeful look on his face.

'I understand perfectly,' Kosef J replied.

Somewhat relieved, the short, stocky and cheerful man brought up a pair of boots from the clothing-supply room.

Kosef J went to the kitchen and asked Rozette for some leftover bread. Rozette gave him some. Laden with a loaf of bread under one arm and a pair of boots under another, a merrily whistling Kosef J headed towards the rubbish heaps.

He couldn't immediately find the fugitive. At first, he only spotted a few tiny holes in the compact mass of the heaps, proof that the man had passed by in the course of the morning. Then, behind an abandoned warehouse, he came across the remains of a fire. Someone had been warming up during the night there. The cinders were still hot, and around the fire, there was a scattering of gravel and bits of wood.

The man had got into the pool with the green water and, with the help of a stick, was trying to skim off the vegetation from the surface of the water.

'Hey, you!' Kosef J shouted.

The man waved at him again, in the same friendly manner as the day before.

'I brought you some bread, and a pair of boots,' Kosef J said when he got down to the man.

The man put the boots on and ate a piece of bread.

'Once there were frogs in this pool,' he said.

Kosef J scratched his temple to give the impression that everything the fugitive had said preoccupied him honestly and profoundly.

'I've seen the fire,' he said.

'Yes,' the man replied.

He then bent down and had another go at removing the vegetation that was throttling the water. Kosef J had no idea what else to do or say. He waited. The man pulled out that gelatinous matter and put it on the dry rocks. A soft and moist heap had already been gathered there, a most horrible sight to behold. Kosef J couldn't make sense of what this man must have had in mind.

'There will be a cold snap, tomorrow or the day after,' the man said, still skimming the surface of the water.

Kosef J nodded, although he didn't make head or tail of this explanation either. The days had indeed become colder, there would be a hint of ice in the mornings and a freeze-up could arrive any minute.

Looking around, Kosef J discovered several gelatinous heaps, noting to himself that the man *had already made serious progress*. He found a stick and proceeded to help the fugitive. For a while, they worked in silence. The surface of the water smelt of stale vinegar, and the stirred-up algae produced a toxic whiff.

'Enough,' the man said and stopped. He set the stick aside very carefully, so he could use it again.

This time the man seemed a little lost in thought but his cheerful expression hadn't left his face.

'I might catch a rabbit one of these days,' he said.

He even giggled, as if he wanted to pull off a farce, and dragged Kosef J after him. They walked around the empty shell of an enormous building. Its roof had retained some of its metal arches, so it now looked like the meatless carcass of a prehistoric animal.

'There used to be a *manège* here,' the man said.

They squeezed past the semiderelict manège walls, onto a path peppered with rocks and gravel. The path meandered between the manège walls and the external wall. From place to place, the wall was hollowed out by narrow tunnels that led to *the other* side.

'Here they are,' the man said.

As they walked, he'd come to a halt in front of each and every hollow and analyse it carefully. Kosef J noticed that each hole could house a wire curtain, together with tin boxes strung on the wires and a soft blanket of dried algae.

'And at the first frost, *snap*!' the man clapped his palms as if he'd caught some tiny flying creature mid-air.

'*Snap*, what?' Kosef J asked.

'The traps,' the man explained.

'These are traps?' Kosef J gushed, finally in the know.

'Yes indeed,' the man said, looking very pleased with himself. 'For rabbits and perhaps for foxes, too. Though that may not work out, but for rabbits, it's a sure thing.'

Kosef J bent down to take a closer look, but he couldn't figure out how such basic traps could possibly function. Perhaps the animals would come to look for food there?'

'Do they like algae?' Kosef J asked.

'No,' the man said. 'They come here to sleep. They come at night to find shelter,' the fugitive giggled. 'And then, *snap*!'

'I don't get it,' Kosef J burst out, about to blow his top.

'They come to the warmth. And then, *snap* . . . '

The man led Kosef J to another area, where only the wall was hollowed out but the traps hadn't yet been installed.

'I'm going to set traps all over,' the man said with a wicked smile.

They continued to carve holes into the wall. The man had already made marks here and there, to flag the places to be hollowed out. Hollowing out the wall was much harder work than strirring the rubbish or gathering algae. The stones would easily break off the wall but they were lumpy and would hurt the skin. As the hole got deeper the work turned into drudgery, and to move forward they had to wriggle themselves like worms carving tunnels in fruit. As for tools, all they had were blunt blades and broken kitchen knives, most probably found among the rubbish.

Kosef J managed to make only three holes, during which time the fugitive made five.

'Not to worry,' the man reassured Kosef J, seeing him look so dispirited.

They shook the sand and traces of mortar off their clothes. Kosef J had got really tired, but the man retained his sprightliness and good mood.

'What would you say to a drop of wine?' he asked.

'Bring it on,' Kosef J replied.

He would have liked to ask where the man could have possibly laid hands on any drink, and what this drink actually consisted of. But he was feeling worn out following all this effort, and a decent sip of any liquor would have done him good.

He followed the man and found that this abandoned world had many more hiding places than one could have possibly foreseen, say if viewed from the watchtower. They had descended into a fairly deep basement, and started to make their way forward through various damp and narrow corridors. A few random airing vents allowed some light in, just enough to ensure that they don't smash into the walls. Then they made it to a welcoming vaulted cavity that sheltered several rows of barrels.

'Are they full?' a thrilled Kosef J asked.

'They are still good,' the man replied, beckoning him to sit on a crate.

Kosef J was waiting for the man to show him how to extract the wine. He had a burning sensation in his throat and his nose started to rustle because of the slightly sour scent in the air, heralding the presence of wine.

'It's great that we have bread,' he man said and started to fondle the first barrel with expert hands. Having examined it for a while he managed to break a sort of lid off and sticked his hand into the barrel. After a few seconds, he pulled his hand out, smelt his fingers and clicked his tongue as a note of satisfaction. He took the bread and broke a small corner off. He introduced the piece of bread into the barrel through the hole, moved it around the alcohol-sodden wood, and then took it out.

He handed the piece to Kosef J, who ate it. Indeed the bread had a strong taste of wine.

'How do you find it?' the man asked.

'It's good,' Kosef J said.

This time the man broke off a piece of bread for himself, rubbed it around the inside of the barrel and ate it.

'Excellent,' he said.

He handed the bread to Kosef J, who also broke a corner off and repeated the required movements in order to obtain a taste of wine. His entire palate quivered with delight while chewing.

'It's quite strong,' he said.

'It's strong because it's aged,' the man said.

'A good barrel,' Kosef J added.

'There's cognac, too,' the man said.

They moved on to the cognac barrel. Kosef J felt a slight sense of elation as he gulped down two or three crusts of bread rubbed into the cognac barrel.

'You have to chew it a little longer,' the man whispered, slightly staggering. He then started to giggle: 'There's champagne, too.'

'Let's not mix things,' Kosef J opined.

'There's also vermouth, calvados and apple brandy,' the man continued.

Kosef J got the giggles, too. By now he was also light-headed, as if he were a glider about to fly off a mountaintop.

His eyes had got used to the dark, and he could already tell the difference between objects, outlines and green spots . . . This vast space with a vaulted ceiling was to his liking. It was heart-warming, and he felt protected. He found a mattress of dried algae between two barrels. This lair was just as inviting as the one by the rabbit traps, and Kosef J realized that this was where the fugitive slept.

Kosef J pointed at the lair between the barrels and laughed. The man nodded and joined in the laughter. He then pointed at the leftover loaf of bread and laughed again. Kosef J nodded, laughing. 'He's a good guy,' Kosef J said to himself, and replied to his own point: 'Yes, he is.' He had to laugh hearing himself respond, and the man laughed, too, as if he had heard the reply.

Each broke off a piece of bread and started to rub it against the inside of the cognac barrel.

'What's terrific,' the man said, 'absolutely terrific and entirely and utterly unbelievable, is that it doesn't taste of barrel in the slightest.'

They both broke out in fits. Kosef J's mind was still gliding above gentle yet endless slopes.

'Does it?' the fugitive wanted to double-check.

'You're right,' Kosef J agreed, and they were both in hysterics again, as if this 'you're right' had been the funniest thing in the world.

'This is so simple. Good God, how simple indeed,' Kosef J thought. 'Isn't it?' the man concurred. 'Right?' the man mused. 'The fact of the matter is that we are both free,' Kosef J thought. 'That's right,' the man agreed. 'More or less free,' Kosef J continued, looking into the void. 'What do you mean?' the man thought, staring at the piece of bread he was holding with two fingers. 'In fact, nothing actually changes,' Kosef J thought. 'So?' the man mused, slowly moving the piece of bread towards his mouth. 'No one is afraid of me any longer,' Kosef J confessed, bringing his head to his chest and placing his palms on his cheeks. 'No one,' the man thought as well. 'I could have been in the city by now. I could have been in any other place,' Kosef J continued. 'Not quite,' the man thought. 'He's not afraid of me,' Kosef J spelt it out again in his thoughts. 'Not at all,' the man confirmed. 'Something isn't right,' Kosef J thought. 'True,' the man thought. 'Neither Franz Hoss nor Fabius are afraid of me,' Kosef J added. 'Because you don't *exist*,' the man concluded.

'What do you mean?' Kosef J yelled.

He made such an effort to utter these last words that he almost got out of breath.

'I didn't say anything,' the man said.

'You did,' Kosef J insisted.

'No, I didn't,' the fugitive whined.

Kosef J tried to stand up but he found his knees too weak. He rolled to the ground, and burst out laughing while rolling. All along, he could hear the man's laughter.

He stopped rolling. He lay there staring at the cellar vaults, just like he used to look at the sky in the apple orchard. White circles kept spinning around above him, right above the places he'd look at. He remembered the piece of bread he was still holding in his left hand. It had been rubbed against the inside of the barrel. He brought the bread to his mouth and took a very slow bite. He could hear himself eat and breathe. He could hear his facial bones rub against one another while chewing.

'There's a rat in that corner,' he said without being aware when exactly he'd seen it.

'Yes, there is,' the other man giggled.

'It's dead though, completely dead,' Kosef J giggled, too.

'It has totally given up its ghost,' the man guffawed.

'It should be thrown out at some point,' Kosef J roared.

The echo of their roars could be heard all along the cellars, getting louder and louder.

'Tomorrow I'll bring a penknife and a belt,' Kosef J announced.

'Tomorrow I won't be here,' the man replied.

'Tomorrow he's not here!' Kosef J screamed to himself, and almost passed out from all this laughter.

'Tomorrow I'm gone,' the man explained, pressing his stomach with his hands. Suddenly they became aware of smoke seeping in through the skylights. 'Watch out, smoke!' Kosef J thought, and the man replied in a loud voice: 'Yes.'

'It has gone dark,' Kosef J said to himself.

'There are so many more holes to make,' the man thought.

'This is roughly what death must be like,' Kosef J thought.

'I could use a pickaxe,' the man thought.

'Perhaps I'm dead already,' Kosef J reasoned.

'Someone should dash to town,' the man continued.

'It doesn't matter,' Kosef J mused, 'what matters is that I'm a free man.'

20

He woke up with a terrible headache just before sunrise. He had shed a few tears in his sleep and now these dried-up tears were stinging his skin. He had a stomach ache and, bizarrely, his fists were also hurting, as if he'd been sleeping with a clenched fist and his finger bones had crumbled.

As he got to his feet, he noticed the man lying still on the ground.

'He can't be dead, can he?' he wondered.

He didn't have the strength to respond. He realized that he has been absent from prison all night, and he'd never done such a thing before. The sheer thought gave him the shivers. He listened carefully for a few seconds, as if convinced that there should be dogs barking and boots plodding outside. He couldn't hear a thing. So he hurried up to get out, to get some air, to get away, to run straight back. If he managed to smuggle himself back to his lift shelter perhaps his night-time absence would go unnoticed.

He breathed in the cold and clean morning air with all his might. He calmed down a little, and remembered snippets of what had happened the day before. He smelt his fingers and had an immediate urge to throw up. His entire being stank of rotten wood and vinegar. He looked around trying to figure out in which part of the prison he would possibly find himself. He started off striding towards what he thought to be the abandoned *manège*, and took the path seemingly peppered with rocks and gravel. He tapped his fingers in front of his face and had almost got pricked by his own beard.

'I'm really unshaven,' he said to himself.

He went past the holes he had carved the day before.

'How insane!' he observed.

Next, he made it to the pool, and all of a sudden felt a tremendous urge to see himself reflected in its murky waters. He decided to sit on the edge of the pool and wait for the sun to rise a little higher. His anxious mind had also calmed down. He now knew that he had nothing to fear since he was a free man. Yet he was experiencing a terrible unrest. He was afraid. He was a free man overwhelmed by fear, and that was that.

He looked at his reflection in the murky pool water. The first sunrays of the day had also plunged in there.

'I look so ugly!' he noted with sadness.

He would have liked to wash himelf but he was too cold. All he wanted was to slip back unnoticed into his prison pavilion, huddle up somewhere and forget about everything. He would have wanted to make sure that Franz Hoss wouldn't scold him.

On his way, he kicked one of those algal mounds over, in anger. By now they had dried out and were soft and silky, and floated in the air like flakes. Then he kicked again and yet again, turning all mounds put up by the fugitive the day before upside down. For some unknown reason he was convinced that Fabius and Franz Hoss would have patted him on the back had they known what he was up to.

'I'm an absconder!' it suddenly occurred to him and he couldn't stop saying this word over and over again: 'A wretched runaway!'

He carried on, following his usual route towards the rows of interior courtyards. The day looked just as overcast by tattered clouds as the one before, and like the one about to follow next. As he got nearer to his pavilion, he was able to make out the hubbub of the usual morning routine. It seemed to him that he could hear Franz Hoss, or, rather, hear him scream. He had the impression of hearing the sound of slammed spyholes, together with clinking and the smashing of plates and mugs.

On his way, he bumped into a guard pushing a food trolley. The guard paid no attention to him and Kosef J didn't say a word either.

'Why doesn't he say anything?' he wondered, feeling a little resentful.

But then he replied to himself that no one had the right to say anything to him any longer.

'This isn't quite so,' he replied again, somewhat later.

Right in front of the pavilion there was a kind of military cart. Two horses were harnessed to it. Fabius was slumbering on the box, looking cold. Kosef J had never seen this fairly spectacular vehicle before. He came to a halt and looked around, particularly pleased with the sight of the horses. He had never seen Fabius hold on to a harness before, so this made him smile. He was almost convinced that the cart's actual driver had just taken a short break for a few minutes, and therefore asked Fabius to keep his place for a while.

'Hey!' Fabius shouted when he spotted Kosef J.

Kosef J was really pleased to hear this rather friendly yell.

'Good morning,' he replied.

He had instinctively opened his mouth to explain his lateness, the wasted night and other things but Fabius cut him short: 'Would you care to join me?'

'Sure,' he said with a sense of relief, and climbed up to the box next to Fabius.

Fabius cracked the whip and the horses set off. Everything was so unforeseeable and happened so quickly that he no longer knew what to make of it. In a way it seemed as if Fabius had actually been expecting him, and now that he had come, they could finally leave.

'This is stupid, really stupid,' he scolded himself in his mind.

This sudden departure made him feel dizzy again. It was obvious that they were heading to town. To town! While he was still dressed in his old clothes . . . and was looking worse for wear than ever.

'What if Mum sees me?' it crossed his mind.

He tried to look Fabius in the eye. He wanted to make sure that all this wasn't just a joke. But Fabius didn't look like someone who was joking. He was grumpy and mumbled into his beard, as ususal. Every now and then, he'd lift the whip and whack the horses on the rump. He'd whack them for no reason since the cart carried on moving at the same pace as before.

'He enjoys flogging horses,' Kosef J mused.

They left through the main gate. Then they made their way onto a gravel road winding towards the horizon defined by the outlines of roofs, trees and spires.

'Would you like some?' Fabius asked offering him a piece of bread.

Kosef J's entire stomach turned.

'No, thanks,' he said placing his hand on his mouth.

'It's hard,' Fabius explained, taking the bread back and biting into it.

'Whose horses are these?' Kosef J asked, mawkishly.

'They are old,' Fabius pointed out.

Kosef J had a slight inkling that the old guard hadn't answered his question but let it drop.

Fabius decided to whip the horses again. He'd swear and mumble between his teeth, then begin to tell a very confusing story. Something about horses that *grind* their teeth.

'Get it?' the guard said, 'they'd live longer but they have nothing to chew with.'

He didn't get it, so Fabius explained again. Greedy as they were, the horses would keep on grinding their teeth. They'd wear their teeth down ahead of time, because they'd mindlessly gnaw and chew on everything. They'd continuously gnaw on pretty much anything, from wood to their harness, so their teeth would wear down in a few short years and then they'd die of hunger because they simply would have nothing left to chew with.

'Get it now?' Fabius asked again. 'The heart works, the legs work, everything works, except that they have no teeth left.'

'Is he talking to me?' Kosef J wondered. Something in the guard's manner, he was unsure what exactly, made him feel suspicious.

'This is bad,' Kosef J responded.

'It is,' Fabius agreed and Kosef J felt a pang in the chest.

These curt answers reminded him of the fugitive, but also of the fact that just recently he also thought of himself as a *runaway*. Could it be that Fabius's short answers were intended to make him, Kosef J, understand something special? He was almost certain that the old guard was *in the know*.

In the know of what?

He knew everything. He knew of the abandoned courtyards, the rubbish heaps and the fact that the fugitive would find shelter there. He also knew that he, Kosef J, would regularly wander about those parts. And even that he'd chat to the fugitive, and help him to make holes and remove the pool algae and rummage in the rubbish. Yes, Fabius knew. He knew that Kosef J had given that man a pair of boots and a loaf of bread.

'If he knows, why is he so quiet?' he wondered.

With his hand holding the whip, Fabius pointed at the horizon: 'A house had burnt down over there.'

'When?' Kosef J asked.

'Last night,' Fabius replied serenely.

Kosef J regarded this news as a bad omen. He was now even more awestruck and the thought that Fabius would put him to the test came back to haunt him. The fact that a house had burnt down in town, the very night he had been absent from prison for the first time, sounded like a reproach. He felt somewhat guilty for this fire, seeing this as an unfortunate coincidence, and in his mind he rebuked the fugitive. Only this fugitive with his rabbit traps could have been behind this.

As they got nearer the town Kosef J noted with horror that he had started to recognize places. He recognized each and every bend in the road and each and every tree. They got to the barrier at the edge of town and he recognized it, too. He recognized the man that was in charge of lifting the town barrier and he recognized the booth where he'd take shelter. Nothing seemed to have changed in all the years that he hadn't set foot there. The road was the same as before, paved with small cubes of granite. The pavements were the same too, narrow and paved with pebbles from the river. The houses on the edge of town all had the same green fences and the same red roofs. Everything seemed to have frozen in time, even the dried leaves of grass seemed identical to the ones from the day when Kosef J had left town through the very barrier that the watchman had now just lowered behind them.

How close this town had actually been to him all this time! Kosef J found it really incredible that the town should stay the same, just as dusty as before, and just as close yet inaccessible as always.

He'd take a good look beyond the fences, into the deserted courtyards and would come across the same old objects. He'd soon catch sight of faces that should have aged in time, but oddly enough, they looked exactly the way they used to look like all these years ago.

'Where are we going, in fact?' Kosef J finally mustered the courage to ask, after he realized that he didn't even have the slightest inkling as to their destination.

'To the bread factory,' Fabius replied.

This response scared Kosef J beyond belief, to an extent he hadn't imagined to be actually possible. The road to the factory led past his house! He could already see the bend beyond which his house would appear on the horizon. He suddenly turned around and looked back. Had he been able to jump out of the cart and run back, he would have chanced that. He looked at Fabius again, trying to figure out whether he knew all this. Fabius was in the middle of whistling some stupid tune, and he obsessively kept repeating it over and over again. Every now and then the old man would cough and spit, trying to get rid of a hair strand stuck to the tip of his tongue.

'That's my house,' Kosef J pointed out.

'Really?' Fabius replied.

Kosef J started to feel as if a claw was being thrust deeper and deeper into his throat. He turned around, looked towards the bend in the road, then looked back again. Next, he almost stood up in the cart, then sat back. He huddled up so tight on the seat as if he was trying to go unnoticed. He kept peeking left and right, fearful of the thought that people could spot him from their windows or courtyards.

Yet no one took any notice of him. Only a dog barked as the cart went past, so Fabius had another excuse to start swearing.

'What would my mum make of this?' the thought crossed Kosef J's mind.

They reached that fatal bend and the road revealed itself exactly as Kosef J recalled it. It was the same old narrow street, flanked on either side by ditches, and he found the houses he had known since childhood emerge one by one in front of him.

'What could she possibly say?' he wondered, looking around feeling ever so tense and terrified. What if his mother would happen to be standing by the window or working in the courtyard, doing the laundry, as she'd normally do? What should he say to her then? Would it perhaps be better to ask Fabius to stop for a moment? Should he perhaps call out from the street? What should he say to her though? He swore between his teeth, for letting himself be *dragged into something* he disliked so profoundly. He gazed at Fabius with a look bordering on hate.

'This is where my mother lives,' he said as they passed his house.

'Really?' Fabius replied.

'He's mad,' Kosef J concluded upon this response, but then specified that it was actually him, Kosef J who was in fact the mad one. He had been released precisely because he had gone mad, and, as a result, from the others' point of view he had ceased to exist.

'Still, this is my house,' he mused.

'It looks as if there was no one there,' he noted, looking back and swiftly checking out the empty courtyard and the windows dressed with white curtains.

'I must get off, I must,' he screamed within himself.

But he didn't budge. He looked back one last time, somewhat ashamed. Fabius didn't say a word. He didn't even appear curious about the house they had just passed, and which belonged to Kosef J.

'Swine,' the latter ventured to conclude. 'Had it been his house, I would have taken a look.'

He felt overwhelmed by an excruciating hate. He no longer tried to cover up. He'd sit on the cart seat holding his head high, with a determined look on his face, wanting to be seen, and awaiting to be seen. He started to deliberately look out for people, aiming to shout out and attract someone's attention.

'I'm here, you losers,' he said to himself.

'Shall we go for a beer?' Fabius asked, disrupting this silent dispute.

'A beer?' he jumped up. 'Sure.'

They made it to the bread factory and were about to enter the forecourt when a tired worker stepped out, trying to shake the flour out of his hair. Without uttering a word he opened the cart doors and pulled the empty crates out. A rather light-footed Fabius jumped up and produced an armful of hay from under his seat. He put it in front of the horses, and despite swearing at them he patted them on the muzzle, and said to Kosef J.

'Let's go, Mr Kosef.'

They crossed the street and headed to the beerhouse. Kosef J walked like a sailor on dry land, staggering and wobbling along. He could feel the ground of his home town under his feet, and this was an incredible sensation for him. He entered the beerhouse, yet he couldn't quite believe he was actually doing this.

'This is too simple,' he said to himself. 'It can't be this simple.'

There weren't many patrons in the beerhouse—mainly old people gathered around a few tables in groups of two or three. The newcomers took a seat at another table and found themselves being studied with a curious look. This didn't last long, only for half a minute, perhaps less. By the time the two pints Fabius had ordered made it at their table the patrons' curiosity had long been appeased. They knocked back the beer, and Kosef J wiped himself on the mouth with his sleeve.

'Goodness, I'm a new man,' he said to himself.

'This beer is excellent,' Fabius observed. 'Next door, at Bruno's, it's less good.'

'Indeed,' Kosef J replied, pleased that he was also able to pull off talking in sound bites.

'On our way back we'll gulp down some bread,' Fabius added and guffawed, being probably very excited at the prospect of sampling some bread.

The publican brought two more pints over. A darkish fellow entered the pub while two of the elderly men left. A child was screaming somewhere in a nearby house, and an enticingly soft female voice was calling the hens in a courtyard. Kosef J felt beyond pleased.

'One of the horses died,' a sad Fabius said after taking a sip from his second pint.

Kosef J startled again, unprepared for such news and yet again taken by surprise at Fabius's seeming willingness for chit-chat. A horse? Which horse? Where?

'Last night,' Fabius clarified with the same sad face, as if horses had been his great passion in life. 'They didn't manage to drag it.'

'From where, a well?' Kosef J wondered.

They left the pub, followed by the publican. Fabius got in the cart and checked whether all the crates had been filled up and in their proper place. He handed the publican four loaves of bread, and invited Kosef J to reclaim his seat. Then they started off on their way back, following the same route.

When they got to his house, Kosef J turned towards Fabius and said: 'Shall we pause a little at my place, too?'

'We shall indeed,' Fabius confirmed.

Kosef J was the first to jump off the cart, and opened the gate. He stepped into the courtyard, followed by the old guard. He could see his mother through the kitchen window, and knocked gently on the pane. His mother looked up and Kosef J took note of the fact that she appeared unchanged.

'It's me,' he said.

His mother opened the door. For a moment, she felt the urge to run towards him, but then spotted Fabius and held back.

'Please, do come in,' she said.

'This is a friend of mine, Mr Fabius,' Kosef J announced.

His mother nodded.

'Take a seat,' Kosef J said and made sure that Fabius was sitting as comfortably as possible. Then he turned to his mother, and in a very calm and soft voice said: 'We've been to get some bread.'

His mother took a long look at him. Then she turned to Fabius.

'Would you like something to eat?' she asked.

'No, because we're in a rush,' Kosef J replied and looked at Fabious, to get an idea of what the latter made of this response.

Fabius looked disappointed.

'OK, something light,' Kosef.

His mother produced some rabbit roast and black currant liquor. The two tucked into the food and drink, and the mother soon gave them another helping without taking her eyes off them. Kosef J snooped left and right and noted that everything was in its place, as before. He would have liked to tell his mother that he was free, but he was too bashful so he kept silent.

Fabius ate with gusto and kept mumbling:

'Thank you, thank you so much.'

At one point the mother laughed, looking rather cheerful, and Kosef J realized that Fabius had winked at her.

Then they were about to leave and the mother accompanied them on their way out, sporting the same cheerful expression on her face. When Fabius handed her a loaf, just as he was to set the cart in motion, she simply burst out in laughter.

They drove away, yet his mother's roars of laughter kept resounding in Kosef J's perplexed mind long after they made it beyond the town barriers.

21

He decided not to tell anyone in town that he had been released.

He had been accompanying Fabius or Franz Hoss to pick up bread for about two or three weeks, and their routine was exactly the same each and every time. They'd stop at the beerhouse, except that Franz Hoss had a preference for Bruno's. The people patronizing both beerhouses were the same, a few elderlies and a bunch of cripples, and each time the two guards paid for their pints with bread pilfered from the prisoners' rations.

Kosef J observed that people were looking at him with *respect*. Every so often, he managed to exchange a few words with the odd elderly man hanging around the beerhouse.

'Well, Mr Kosef,' some elderly man would say, 'it's just fine as it is.'

Kosef J didn't quite understand what the man meant but nodded enthusiastically regardless.

'At least it's not worse than before,' said another man, and he hastened to agree: 'No, it's not what it used to be indeed.'

The elderly men would have obviously preferred to talk longer to Kosef J, but his stints at the beerhouse were always very short and rushed. Franz Hoss and Fabius would only rarely enter into conversation with the other patrons, which is why Kosef J was also reluctant to cross the line. Yet, he couldn't help but acknowledge the sympathetic looks in the locals' eyes.

'How much longer do you have?' one of the men finally slipped in the question with a conspiratorial smile.

'What should I have much longer?' Kosef J asked, perplexed. The elderly man smiled as if he understood the situation, and didn't insist. It was only later that Kosef J realized what the question had meant: the man was asking about the rest of his sentence, the time left for Kosef J to do. Yet he didn't have any further time to do. At the next opportunity he went up to the man to let him know that he had *nothing left to do*.

'I have *nothing* left.'

He elderly man couldn't make head or tail of this, and Kosef J realized that the man had in the meantime forgotten about his question.

'You'd asked me how much longer I *had*,' Kosef J explained.

'Oh, yes!' the man smiled, looking around with a fearful expression and rather briskly making himself scarce.

'What's going on with all these people?' Kosef J kept wondering.

'It's great that you managed,' a man with a short right leg put it to him next.

'I'm glad, really glad,' another man said tapping him on the shoulder.

'Let's hope it lasts,' a third man whispered.

'Clench your teeth and just carry on,' the second man continued.

'It's better for your mother, too,' the first man added.

Unexpected that it may seem, Kosef J's mother was proud of him. Kosef J observed this every time he'd see her walk about in town, holding her head high and smiling. At times she'd meet him already at the barrier or at the factory gates, or in front of her house. Often enough, she'd not say a word. All she wanted was to see him, to know about his presence in town. Increasingly, she'd be accompanied by another elderly woman, or even two or three distant relatives or neighbours willing to listen to her and kill time with her. His mother would never make him say anything—against his will—or insist that he should stay longer. She seemed to perfectly understand how important this work that her son and his guard had to carry out was, and she didn't dare to disrupt them in their activities.

'You've got a wonderful mother,' Fabius would burst out every now and then, usually with a mouth full of bread.

Kosef J would occasionally get upset because his mother was so kind to the two guards. Especially when his mother didn't even pay attention to him, and only took care of the so-called guests, continuously urging them to help themselves to more food, have another drink, opt for the most comfortable chair, wash themselves on the hands and face, sit nearer the fireplace and so on . . . Having said this, the mother's pride was nonetheless visible, even if she were to neglect her son every so often. The fact of the matter was that his mother was proud of him, and he had no idea why.

He discovered the reason later. His mother *didn't actually know*. She didn't know that he had been released. And neither did the others in town. No one in town knew that he'd been released, and the guards were in no rush to tell them.

'What are they up to?' he wondered.

So he realized that this was the reason for everyone's sympathy and also for his mother's pride. They all thought he was still a prisoner, and probably admired him for succeeding to earn this amount of respect and obtain such a rare treat as to be allowed out on the town to accompany the bread cart.

'This can't be true!' he said to himself when he figured this out.

'They are mad!' he concluded.

He experienced a sense of disappointment, because being released was a source of pride for him. As he kept thinking about this though, he realized that in his heart of hearts he felt more pride for being a model prisoner who had done well. In the others' eyes he wasn't just an ordinary prisoner. He was the prisoner tasked with accompanying the bread cart. This was no mean feat. And a prisoner who'd be asked to go to town with the guards two or three times a week wasn't just any old prisoner either.

'Oh my God, what a mess!' he cried out every time he went through all this in his head.

'And Franz Hoss says nothing, nor does Fabius.'

'Goodness, what if they find out?'

Kosef J decided to act just as attentively and obligingly with the two guards as his mother. He didn't want to even chance it that Franz Hoss or Fabius should blurt out something untoward. They hadn't done it so far, and there was no reason for them to do it in the future. And yet, they were the people who knew. Unwittingly Kosef J felt that he had to be grateful for their silence.

The sympathy of the town dwellers has turned into a sort of energizing drink that Kosef J avidly imbibed every time he came to pick up bread. He had started to enjoy these journeys. As soon as he got past the barrier, he took care to adopt a sombre and slightly gloomy posture, dignified yet immersed in thought. He could sense that it wasn't appropriate for him to look too cheerful or happy. Only dignified and calm. Every time he became aware that he was being observed, Kosef J experienced a sense of profound satisfaction. And the number of those watching him kept increasing from one visit to another.

'How nice of them,' he said to himself whenever he spotted them in the courtyards, by the windows or balconies, and could tell for certain that they had come out for his sake.

'How nice of them,' he said to himself, whenever he saw them coming out on the street or in front of their houses, so they could see him better, perched on the bread cart, next to the guard.

Little by little people started to greet him too.

'Good morning, Mr Kosef,' the man in charge of the barrier would say.

'Good morning, Mr Kosef,' the old people would say.

'Good morning, Mr Kosef,' the slim old man loading the bread into the cart would say.

'Good morning, Mr Kosef,' Mr Bruno would say.

'Good morning, Mr Kosef,' the other, nameless publican would say.

'How's it going?' the old man with a short leg would ask, laughing.

Soon Kosef J's arrivals would turn downright triumphal. And his appearances at the beerhouse would have the impact of an extraordinary event that magnetized all patrons. Kosef J was seen as a proper hero and he was given proof of this by way of a myriad of small gestures: a smile here, a greeting there, a certain expression on someone's face, the way the publican would bring his beer.

'For goodness' sake, what should I do now?' he wondered every time he remembered that these people were in fact dealing with a free man.

'Should I tell them the truth?' he agonized.

'The truth? What truth?' a voice replied in his thoughts.

'Truth is what these people actually wish to believe,' he firmed up his decision to let things *carry on as before*.

So he made sure not to visit the short, stocky and cheerful man. The short, stocky and cheerful man kept begging him, driving him up the wall with his theories and luring him to come to try on his clothes. Except that he was now afraid. He was afraid that the short, stocky and cheerful man might indeed finish his clothes after all this time, and Kosef J has started to see this possibility as a catastrophe. So he did his best to avoid the short, stocky and cheerful man as much as he could. He did everything in his powers to be given jobs in the kitchen or in town. The thought that his prison clothes could be taken away just now, at this very moment, had started to truly obsess him.

He also started to fear the meeting with the prison governor. He had been told on several occasions that the poor colonel had fully recovered and that he could be called in any minute to sort out the final procedures.

22

'They are waiting for you,' the child said to him one morning.

Kosef J had just got out of the liftcage. He hadn't seen the child for some time. This is why he had a good look at him, and also because he could sense a change in his way of being. He couldn't tell whether it was only his face that had turned sadder or perhaps the child had become more pensive.

'He's growing,' Kosef J said to himself.

The child had been waiting for him at the corner, this was obvious to Kosef J, and this made him a little apprehensive. Who could have possibly sent the kid? The short, stocky and cheerful man? The prison governor perhaps? Kosef J felt a slight shiver. Could it be that the wretched day had finally come when he was meant to be thrown out of the prison for good?

'Who? Kosef J asked sensing a bad omen.

'Come,' the child said.

Kosef J didn't repeat his question, in fear of the response, so he just followed the kid. They left the main prison compound and joined the gravel path. They crossed the two–three deserted internal courtyards that had become so familiar to him, and headed towards the rubbish heaps. The child led the way, walking a few steps ahead, without turning his head to check what Kosef J might have been up to.

'Should I flee?' the idea suddenly crossed Kosef J's mind, but he immediatey shook his head to brush such a stupid thought aside.

The child led him to the derelict pool, where they came to a halt. Then the child went up to the edge of the pool, knelt down and started to stare at the water. Kosef J stopped right behind him.

'This water is really clear!' the child observed.

Kosef J came closer and looked at the water, too. Someone had skimmed off all the algae and the thin film of water had turned into a mirror in which one could indeed see the reflection of the sky.

'What are you doing with the hedgehog?' Kosef J asked, having suddenly recalled an earlier image by way of a mysterious association.

The child turned towards him, looked at him for a moment or so, and smiled. He didn't reply, and Kosef J was sure that in his heart of hearts the kid didn't find the question worthy of a response.

They continued to walk. They headed towards the cellars with all those barrels and Kosef J started to have an inkling as to what all this was about.

The fugitive was awaiting them at the cellar door. Not without a sense of pride, he was wearing a leather apron and he was armed with a trowel.

'You've come!' he cried out.

Kosef J didn't dislike seeing this man again. After all, the fugitive hadn't done any harm to him, and his cheerful face reminded him of his mother's equally cheerful face.

'Hey!' Kosef J greeted him.

The man untied his apron and put the trowel down.

'I'm really dirty,' he said, pointing at his hands.

'What the hell is he up to now?' Kosef J wondered.

The man had no intention to wash his hands. He had owned up to having dirty hands, as he probably thought that this was the right thing to do. Then he pulled Kosef J inside.

'Let me show you something,' he said.

There wasn't much to see inside. Kosef J looked around for a while and then, intrigued, turned towards the man.

'I covered the holes,' the man explained.

Indeed, Kosef J got the impression that there were signs of preparation for the winter.

'I want to build a fireplace,' the man said. 'I know how to do it, and will do it.'

He then urged Kosef J to look behind the barrels.

'The mattresses,' the man said. 'Here they are!'

And he threw himself on one, to demonstrate just how soft they were. Kosef J gathered momentum and also threw himself on a mattress. The man laughed. The child laughed. Kosef J laughed, too. The mattresses were made of plastic foils filled with dried algae. They were soft and sweet-smelling.

'Now,' the man said, 'we have to get started on the fireplaces.'

'To get started . . . ' Kosef J repeated what he heard. 'What did this man really mean? He had plans to put him to work again?'

'This is why we want to ask you something,' the man continued.

'You, meaning who?' Kosef J asked.

'Us all,' the man replied.

'Us who?' Kosef J wondered.

'You know,' the man said, 'there's a few of us. And we'd like you to buy us a spade.'

Kosef J didn't expect such a turn. How unpredictable people have become. All people. The guards, his mother, the elderly men, the kid, the short, stocky and cheerful man, Rozette and all the unknown people who'd keep greeting him, standing by their front doors and waiting for him to turn up in town. And once again he had the impression that all the others knew something that he wasn't yet privy to.

'But what?' Kosef J wondered.

'We've saved up the money,' the man continued as if this could act as the decisive factor in convincing Kosef J to buy the shovel.

'And the others, where are they?' Kosef J asked, quite ruffled by the thought that they were several.

'At work,' the man replied.

'At work, I see,' Kosef J's brain echoed.

'OK,' he responded to the earlier question regarding the shovel.

'Thank you,' the man blurted out, and started to count the coins he'd been clutching in his fist.

Kosef J didn't only buy a shovel. After a couple of days, he was also asked to buy a pickaxe. Then he was asked to buy a box of nails. In about ten days he also got

161

around to buying a ball of string, an axeblade, a sawblade and a whole lot of other bits and bobs that could only come useful in a carpenters' workshop.

Put in a situation to respond to all these requests, Kosef J felt quite anxious. The coins were rattling in his pocket, and he wasn't sure how to behave in front of Fabius and Franz Hoss. How on earth was he meant to buy a shovel without anyone noticing? How could he possibly slip it on the cart without any of the guards getting wind of it or spotting it?

To make all these strange purchases, he relied on all the enthusiasm he kept stirring up in town. His presence on the streets had become such an important event that Kosef J had the impression that the entire town had suspended their activities only to spot him for a fleeting moment. People's glances did no longer convey mere sympathy but something quite different, something outright *conspiratorial*.

'Mr Kosef,' the elderly men would say, 'in case we could do something . . . ,' and held a long silence after the word *something*, looking him straight in the eye.

'Mr Kosef,' the man with a short leg added, 'I'm here for you. Just so you know. You can always find me here.'

'And I'm always here, too,' Bruno rounded this off.

All these glances carried the same meaning, as if wanting to convey that we trust you, Mr Kosef, give us a sign and you'll see.

The day Kosef J was meant to buy the shovel he had the impression that all eyes were on him, basically saying, 'Yes, Mr Kosef, we are the ones who can do this, just ask us and we'll do it.'

'Could you perhaps buy me a shovel?' he quietly asked the old man with a short leg as they bumped into each other at the beerhouse.

'Yes, of course!' the old man with a short leg replied, looking over the moon.

The day he was meant to buy a pickaxe, all faces in town looked as if they were waiting for nothing else but to fulfil Kosef J's requests. The only thing they all seemed to wish for was to buy him a pickaxe. And in the forthcoming days they all had a desire to purchase string, axeblade, sawblade and all sorts of carpentry sundries.

'You succeeded at something very important,' the nameless publican put it to him.

'This is the way forward!' an elderly man encouraged him.

'We're lucky to have you,' another man whispered.

'This is perfect!' the third man rounded off each brief conversation.

Journeys into town almost always ended in long minutes spent at the beerhouse, minutes which turned into quarters of an hour and, after a while, half an hour. What was strange though, that never would more than one or two elderly men approach him at the same time. In fact, they almost always took their turn, and only very rarely would two of them arrive at the same time. As for the people on the street, even if they were awaiting him as a group, they'd greet him and then immediatey disperse in various directions.

Regarding the guards, Kosef J solved the problem quite easily. He just said to Fabius 'I bought a shovel,' and kept the shovel on his knee for the duration of their journey. Fabius didn't grant any importance to this event.

Same thing for Franz Hoss. 'I bought a pickaxe,' Kosef J announced, and indeed Franz Hoss gave no importance to the pickaxe.

Yet Kosef J was tortured by the fact that he couldn't suss out how far he could actually go in this tacit relationship with the two guards. Most probably the two men wouldn't have objected if he just let them know that he had decided to spend the night at home. He was afraid though that such an event might have made people in town suspicious. He would have certainly lost some of his kudos had people found out that he was even allowed to spend the night in town. Little by little, Kosef J started to wish for a good old scolding from Fabious or Franz Hoss, preferably in front of everyone, so they could all see how much he suffered.

As soon as he'd wake up each morning, he'd run to the guards' sink and check himself out in the mirror. He'd no longer give himself a clean shave but deliberately leave a three-day stubble to make himself look slightly tired and tortured yet, at the same time, dignified. Whenever he'd get wind that he'd need to pick up bread, he'd make sure to sleep less, so he had black circles under his eyes and a somewhat creased face. The world needed to see him as they wanted to see him—dignified, heroic but also tired and tortured. He was after all the victorious prisoner, and a victorious prisoner couldn't show up with a double chin and red cheeks.

He also paid attention to his uniform. He stopped washing it like he used to, aiming to keep it in one piece yet also make it look quite tattered. These worn-out and tattered clothes would add to his image of a dignified warrior who wasn't at all ashamed of his war clothes.

23

Still, Kosef J couldn't figure out what was happening in town. After the elation of his first cart journeys, he started to scrutinize people more carefully.

First of all, he discovered that grown men were absent from this town. He came across old people, ill men loitering about the hospital yard, even a few madmen, but he couldn't spot any grown men whatsoever. Men who could go out at night, to buy bread and then pop to a beerhouse or suchlike for a short while.

He couldn't see dogs either. In the old days there used to be dogs at every household, not to mention the stray ones roaming the streets. Now there were hardly any dogs roaming the streets and there were only a handful of them at people's houses. And anyway, these dogs hardly ever barked.

One could also never hear any music. People rarely went out on the town because there was nothing to do in town. There were very few shops, and even the shops that were still in business would have their shop windows boarded up. All fences had been levelled and all tree trunks had been painted white, up to about the height of an average person. The pavements were very clean, because everyone was obliged to tidy up the pavement in front of their house. Rubbish would be collected once a week, on a Sunday.

There were signs that, years ago, someone had tried to get some work done in town. Sections of a few streets had actually been paved. But then the operation had been abandoned, as if one had run out of asphalt once and for all. In some places pavements had been built, too, in one instance even a very wide one at that.

But even the pavements had met the same fate. There were several streets where the pavements had only been marked out by way of cement edgings, without the actual work ever being completed. And the bits that had nevertheless survived had been damaged beyond repair.

In the town centre a large number of houses had been demolished, and an immense square-shaped area was thus made available to be utilized in some way. It would seem that some foundation had been laid, but the overgrown weeds and scattered about rubbish had suppressed everything. On one side of the square-shaped area a strange building had been erected, sporting several floors and a sophisticated roof. No one lived there and all the windows had been boarded up. The corrugated roof, ornate with several turrets, had rusted, since it had been made of cheap and low-quality metal.

At a crossroads in another area of town, an artesian well had been started. Yet no jet of water would spurt from the rockery laid at the middle of the fountain, however, a considerable amount of rainwater had been gathered which had started to nourish an abundant vegetation.

Kosef J had no understanding of these signs. He sensed though that townlife had been perturbed and that people had been somewhat marked by these building sites. Among the people he discovered hilarious faces, which were somewhat new to him as he hadn't seen anything of this kind before.

Yet it was his own mother who had surprised him the most. He couldn't make sense of the fact why his mother would laugh quite so much and that she'd even answer some questions laughing. Most of the time she'd layer laughter with an expression of suffering, especially if it happened to be a case of him being alone with her. It seemed to him as if his mother had been privy to some information that couldn't be communicated in any other way but through glances further framed by a giggle or a face pull.

The old men at the beerhouse would also pull the most unexpected faces. Some would look at him with a straight face that simply froze one's blood. Others would have one side of the face light up while the other would suddenly darken, all this within the breath of a single banal sentence.

'How nice that you managed,' the man with the short leg would say, his face freezing on a smile imprinted on every single wrinkle. Then his eyelids would slowly start moving up and down, as if he had said YES, YES, YES . . . And soon the rhythm of this moment that tried so hard to make a point had become too painful for the old man to bear, and this pain made its way to the wrinkles at the corner of his eyes and then downwards, to the corner of his mouth. His mouth had opened, as if the man had been in need of extra air, and he remained transfixed in this position, frozen in a large grin of anticipation.

'I'm glad, honestly, I am,' the old man would say, placing a hand on Kosef J's shoulders. Meanwhile his face would turn flushing red, as if these had been his final words. Then this excitement would slowly dissolve into an ironic expression and settle on a wicked smile, about to degenerate into an explosion of hate at any point.

'Let's just hope that it will last,' an elderly man whose name was Adam as Kosef J had found out, kept saying over and over again. Old Adam tended to adopt a most humble stance most of the time, and whenever he uttered the word *just* in his extremely slow manner, he'd cast his eyes down to the ground. Whenever he uttered the word *that*, his chin would start to tremble as if his shyness had struck him down, and when it came to the word *last*, he'd only whisper it, looking rather unsure and seemingly ashamed of himself.

'What a disgusting creature,' Kosef J would say to himself.

'Good afternoon, Mr Kosef,' Mr Bruno would say, clenching his teeth as if he'd been trying to conceal the fact that he was in a great pain. He'd keep staring at Kosef J with such clenched teeth, his entire face ribbed with jaw tension.

After a while, Kosef J was also taken aback by the comments of the two guards.

'What an amazing mother you have!' Fabius cried out and sighed, adopting a melancholy look out of this world. He'd stare at Kosef J, as if expecting some reaction, this delay acting as an indication that Kosef J owed *something* to the world.

'You managed something really important,' the nameless publican would tell him. The man had a pale, gaunt and wilful face, and he looked as if he was only waiting for Kosef J to motion him in order to move to action. He had no idea what the message should contain, and being late didn't seem to matter either. Who cares that Kosef J had no clarity over these things, the others seemed all too keen to follow him regardless.

Even the child had acquired a strange look every time he'd say, 'They are waiting for you.' It would happen more and more often for the child to wait for him at the corner of the pavilion, only to tell him in a very serious and sad voice, 'They are waiting for you.' Kosef J would try to make him smile, he'd ask him about small yet fun things but the kid would be in no mood to come out of his shell.

'Come,' he'd say in the most serious voice in the world.

Meanwhile, the fugitive, the man with a cheerful face who was awaiting him beyond the abandoned courtyards of the prison compound, would cry out in a voice of trust: 'You've come!'

The things the man with a cheerful face would ask for had also become more and more bizarre. After the string of items purchased in town, Kosef J was asked to keep a closer contact with the kitchen.

'Why?' Kosef J asked, somewhat disappointed.

'You know, *we* are making preparations for the winter.'

By now Kosef J had stopped finding the use of the plural intriguing. He had already had the opportunity to see for himself that work was going on among the rubbish heaps, and what was being done out there on a daily basis couldn't possibly be down to a single person. One couldn't actually see a great deal, of course, but there were signs of hard work carried out *underground*. He was able to spot, for instance, that the rocks had been moved from one place to another. He'd discover over the course of two or three days that hundreds of rocks had been piled up, which then would simply disappear overnight. Or that fresh heaps of soil would appear, without any trace of actual holes having been dug nearby. What's more, these would be heaps of fresh, almost warm soil, brought over by someone with the express aim of storing them here.

Kosef J looked at the man with a cheerful face with envy. He envied him because the man with a cheerful face was always busy and focused on some task or other, seemingly optimistic about the job he had to do. His requests were precise and as he put them across he gave the impression that something extremely important was behind it all.

'Anyway, what could I possibly do at the kitchen?' Kosef J asked.

The man replied promptly, as if he had been memorizing the various stages of this schedule for days:

1. Kosef J was urgently asked to observe the way leftovers were collected, such as the number of bins used and where these bins were then taken.

2. Kosef J was beseeched to find out who was in charge of transporting the bins containing food waste, and whether it was always the same people or there would also be changes of shift. If so, at what intervals.

3. It would be extremely important to know whether these bins containing food waste were collected after a number of them had been filled up over several days, or whether collection was taking place on a daily basis.

4. Were those collecting the food waste being watched over by prison guards, by soldiers or just by kitchen staff?

5. Was there anyone interested in food waste, in some way or another, on the stretch between the kitchen and the place where the bins were handed over for collection?

6. What was Kosef J's opinion of Rozette, the cook?

24

As time went by, winter was making its presence more and more felt, and people's faces betrayed a heightened sense of expectation every time they encountered Kosef J. It would have been fair to say that as the days got shorter and shorter, as well as colder and colder, people had become needier and needier. Fabius had long come to terms with repeatedly losing at dice, and every time Kosef J rolled the dice, he'd break out in cries of wonder. It seemed obvious that both guards were quite happy when they lost.

Dice games would take place mainly in Rozette's kitchen after dinner. Almost every time Franz Hoss would produce some greenish liquor, and they'd take turns sipping it from the bottle. Rozette would often make an appearance, too, and watch them while standing behind them for hours.

'Impossible! Impossible!' Franz Hoss would warm up after the first round, taking a sip from the bottle. He'd then turn to Rozette and ask: 'Did you see this? Did you?' In case the short, stocky and cheerful man was present, he'd turn to him, too and ask: 'What do you make of this? Well?' And in case the child was also there, he'd paternally place a hand on his head and tousle his hair: 'Well, what do you think, ey?'

The kid would shake his head disgruntled, since nothing annoyed him more than having his hair tousled.

'Fantastic, fantastic!' Fabius would say, leaning back in his chair in order to take a better look at Kosef J.

Each time the mood would heighten gradually, cigarette smoke gently shrouding them, alcohol taking its effect and making them feel better, Rozette letting out the odd giggle, and the short, stocky and cheerful man embarking on yet another amusing story. And yet, Kosef J would occasionally hear random phrases whispered in his ear that had no connection whatsoever with the chatter taking place around him.

In the most unlikely moments, someone would slip in the odd question, such as 'And tomorrow? As before?' or, in an even more ambivalent tone, 'Have you thought of what's next?'

Only very rarely did he manage to identify *who* exactly had spoken. At times everyone would be leaning over the table to count the dots on the dice, and suddenly someone would say, 'I trust that you won't forget about me.' Or while everyone was roaring with laughter at one of Franz Hoss's stupid jokes, somebody would slip in a comment like 'Still, you should pay heed.' Obviously, there would be no specification as to what exactly he should be paying heed to.

Every so often he'd manage to catch the person who had just spoken in the act, and when finding the right moment he'd hasten to re-open the conversation.

'What did you mean by . . . ,' he'd begin, at which point the person in question would start fidgeting and immediately change topic. Or, akin to the old man in town, they'd simply decamp.

So he soon gave up these attempts to find out who'd address him and to understand what exactly their words would mean. He'd simply stick to memorizing the words, sentences and phrases that bombarded him.

'Don't forget what I said,' he could hear in his right ear as Rozette was collecting the dirty dishes.

'You'll be on your own there, so do pay attention, people can be mean,' he kept hearing in his right ear while the short, stocky and cheerful man was in the middle of explaining how he had managed to save two storeroomful of clothes all thanks to Kosef J.

'It's very important to look him in the eye,' someone whispered in his neck as he was about to roll the dice.

'Now it's time for you to decide,' he heard from somewhere above his left shoulder, as he was taking a sip of the greenish and bitter liquid.

'You are the only truly free person,' a voice whispered through the air.

'You are still very young,' another voice whispered above his right shoulder.

'The very first day is the really important one,' a voice muttered from among the dirty dishes.

'After all, this is something you are entitled to,' he could again hear the voice in the air.

'We are aware,' someone mumbled, from beyond those gathered around him.

'Would you like another sip?' Franz Hoss asked and he could immediately hear a voice saying: 'Make sure to tell us about everything you see.'

'Some more soup?' Rozette asked and straightaway he heard the voice: 'You are the only person who can do *this*.'

'Another beer?' Mr Bruno asked, followed by the voice: 'Remember, secrecy above all.'

'Another round?' the nameless publican asked, whispering in a feverish voice: 'The main thing is to keep your mouth shut.'

'Would you happen to have a lighter?' old Adam asked, the voice following on: 'The day is approaching . . . '

The voices would at times cut across one another and overlap in his ear, tangling and wriggling about as if they were some invisible and highly irritable creatures. At times he was simply assaulted by them, he couldn't keep track as to where they were coming from, not to mention that he couldn't make any sense of it all. The voices had become extremely edgy and would only utter completely random words, mainly odd and disparate ones at that.

'Exactly,' a voice noted.

'Peace and quiet indeed,' a second voice commented.

'Now,' a third voice said.

'Well?' a fourth voice asked.

'Deadly,' a fifth voice added. 'Mortal.'

'Six,' the sixth voice said.

'So?' the seventh voice wondered.

'Oh,' the eighth voice mused.

'Enough!' Kosef J screamed in his thoughts, trying to move away from the others a bit, so he could spend at least an hour on his own.

The voices had suddenly died down the day Franz Hoss asked Kosef J to go to town on his own in order to pick up bread.

'I have an unbearable pain in my loins,' the guard complained with the look of an old and ill man.

Kosef J had no idea how he could turn him down, although the thought of making his appearance in town all alone didn't appeal to him.

'What would my mother say?' he wondered.

He tried to shoo away the thought by speeding his journey up. He didn't go to the beerhouse and didn't even stop in front of his house to say hello to his mother. He helped the man at the bread factory to load the bread into the cart as fast as possible. He was simply afraid to look left or right, and only once back at the prison did he sigh with relief.

'Thank you,' Franz Hoss said upon his return, looking at him as if he were a faithful dog.

Kosef J wanted to respond, in fact he would have wanted to say that he'd rather not do this journey again on his own, but the found himself interrupted by the sound of the kid's voice.

'Come,' the child said, so Kosef J smiled at Franz Hoss and followed the kid out.

The child seemed rather agitated, so Kosef J didn't dare to ask him anything.

The fugitive with the cheerful face also seemed restless.

'The committee would like to see you,' the man with the cheerful face said, but Kosef J didn't respond. He followed the man through the interior courtyards he was so familiar with, and then through the rubbish heaps which had turned into some sort of intimate geography. He arrived at a place he would have never expected, a place that looked like an abandoned railway station. He was able to make out several rail tracks under the anthills and bushes. The carcass of a disused water tower also appeared on the horizon. The very moment they had crossed the first rail track the man with a cheerful face couldn't refrain from pausing for a second and said to Kosef J: 'You have now entered the *free world*.'

25

Kosef J could only see rubble, rusty rail tracks, stacks of switches, disused traffic lights and large spills of petrol. When they reached some old train engines, frozen behind one another for donkeys' years, a darkish man wearing a motorcycle helmet appeared menacingly in front of them.

The man with a cheerful face came to a halt and motioned Kosef J to stay still. The darkish man came so close to Kosef J that he had the impression that their faces would touch. The man looked very mistrustful, and checked him out for a few seconds before motioning him with both arms to turn around. He then started to search him conscientiously.

'What could he be possibly looking for?' Kosef J wondered. He turned his head to ask the darkish man what exactly he was looking for, but the man gave such an evil eye that he lost heart.

'We're going to see the committee,' the man with a cheerful face said.

The darkish man appeared not to have heard this. He finished with Kosef J and moved on to the man with a cheerful face, searching him just as thoroughly. When he was done, he withdrew beyond the row of engines without saying a word.

'This man had escaped four years ago,' the man with a cheerful face pointed out.

They were walking along the row of train engines in silence, and Kosef J couldn't make any sense of what he was experiencing. What was a man who had escaped four years ago doing there? And how did these engines get there, and what was the story behind these railtracks? Had the railway station in town gotten to such a state of abandon and dilapidation? Or he was dealing with one of those buildings that were once quickly started but then suddenly abandoned?

'This way,' the man with a cheerful face said, pulling him towards something that looked like a loading ramp. Once they had made it to the ramp and were already helping one another to climb onto it, the man asked: 'Is it true that you went on your own to town to get bread?'

'Yes,' Kosef J said.

They headed towards some cement domes that looked like astronomical observatories sunken into the ground.

'Is that bad?' Kosef J asked.

'What do you mean?' The man with a cheerful face wondered.

'That I went to town on my own,' Kosef J clarified.

'No idea. We'll see,' the man said.

'We'll see what and where?' Kosef J wondered. And he chuckled to himself. The free world! The words the man with a cheerful face would choose. Then they suddenly came to a halt in front of a dome and waited.

'What are we waiting for?' Kosef J asked.

'They can see us,' the man with a cheerful face replied.

'Who's they?' Kosef J asked.

'The members of the committee,' the man with a cheerful face responded.

'He's driven me crazy with this committee of his,' Kosef J said to himself.

The man with a cheerful face lit a cigarette butt, and Kosef J was dead sure that it came from the rubbish heaps.

'We are just like one big family here,' the man with a cheerful face said.

'Really?' Kosef J reacted.

The man kept silent, and continued to smoke looking cross, as if he had talked too much and now regretted it.

'We'll be soon allowed in and given a seat,' he said in a neutral voice.

Someone shouted from above.

'You'll have to answer some questions. I recommend you don't try to hide anything.'

They climbed up a narrow iron ladder attached to one of those cement domes, and then descended a similarly narrow ladder on the inside of that same cement balloon. Inside there were about a hundred people huddled together on wooden benches. Kosef J looked at them in amazement. He wasn't frightened, only astonished, because those people smelt terrible and were in a deplorable state. The first thing Kosef J caught sight of looked like a bunch of stacked heads. Heads with eyes deep seated in their sockets, gaunt cheeks, and beards unshaven for donkeys' years. Toothless mouths, cracked lips and nostrils enlarged by some kind of a thirst for air.

It was fairly dark inside. Kosef J was led into the midst of this gathering. The people kept roaring as Kosef J went past, and they muttered the odd word to one another or to themselves. Someone spat through their teeth. Most of them were still wearing their old prison uniforms, worn out by time and patched up here and there, now soiled by petrol and soot.

Kosef J was asked to sit on a chair. At his feet, there were displayed all the items he had bought in town at the request of the man with a cheerful face: the shovel, the pickaxe, the nailbox, the ball of string, the sawblade and the other carpentry sundries. The man with a cheerful face patted him on the shoulder and blended into the crowd, so Kosef J lost sight of him.

'Good afternoon,' someone in the front row said and everyone burst out laughing.

'Quiet!' a high-pitched voice shouted through a loud-speaker. Then, addressing Kosef J, he asked: 'Could you tell us your cell number prior to being released?'

Kosef J didn't immediately understand the question. He also didn't expect to be asked any questions.

'Pardon?' he said in an innocent voice.

The crowd laughed again. A few people whistled. Kosef J would have been able to swear that they whistled with two fingers in the mouth, the exact same way he would have done this, too. Someone threw a roll of paper at his feet.

'Your cell, what number was your cell?'

'50,' Kosef J replied.

'50,' the megaphone repeated. 'Who stayed in 50? Did anyone stay in cell number 50?'

For the last two questions, the megaphone turned towards the audience and Kosef J could clearly gather that these didn't concern him.

'Me,' someone shouted and started to elbow their way through the crowd.

Everyone fell silent, expecting that the man who said 'me' should come forward. Kosef J slid forward in his chair a bit, so he could have a better view. A tall old man, with white hair on the back of his head, appeared in the middle of the room. There was utter silence. Kosef J was left standing in front of the old man. He didn't know whether he should sit back or hold his hand out to this *double* of his. So he waited. All of a sudden, the old man hugged him. All started to clap and stamp their feet.

'I am 50,' the old man said, with tearful eyes. 'You are 50A.'

The entire crowd started to shout '50A! 50A!'

Kosef J felt overwhelmed with emotion, and shed a tear.

'Which way was the window facing?' the old man with white hair asked.

'The kitchen garden,' Kosef J replied promptly.

'How many paces was the cell on the diagonal?' the old man asked again.

'Eight,' Kosef J replied.

'A tile had four cracks. Which one?'

'The third one, viewed from the right.'

'Correct!' the old man cried out and hugged Kosef J again.

The crowd started to shout and whistle again, throwing paper balls at the two men. The old man raised his hand to indicate that he wanted silence, and when they were all quiet, he started to speak.

'This man must be killed,' he said.

The entire audience got to their feet as if a storm had broken out in the room. Kosef J couldn't tell whether he was living a dream or finding himself the butt of jokes cracked by someone all too keen to amuse.

'I shall explain what I mean,' the old man continued, at which point the crowd showed signs of settling. Nevertheless, Kosef J found the time to observe that not everyone agreed with the old man. In fact, some had made a very violent point about their disagreement. The old man's explanation was as follows: this man you see here was released so that he could be of use to them, and only *them*!

'Not true!' someone shouted.

'Perfectly true!' someone else shouted back.

'Let him speak first,' a third person yelled.

'Here you go, talk,' the old man said, making Kosef J sit back on his chair.

There was silence again, but Kosef J didn't manage to utter a single word.

'See!' The old man yelled. 'See the kind of people *they* chose to release!'

'This isn't fair,' a toothless man bellowed. 'The man doesn't even know where he is, and besides we didn't bring him here for a trial.'

A storm of phrases broke out again in the air, blasting Kosef J's eardrums. Everyone would talk at once, putting their views across and taking Kosef J by surprise with their energetic commitment. Kosef J had never seen such people and such attitudes . . . A few of them were in agreement with the old man and hence with the fact that he, Kosef J, represented a *potential danger*. A man released *by those on the other side* could only be a man entirely subject *to those on the other side*, or a man who'd sooner or later would play into the hands of those on the others side. And even if he personally, Kosef J that is, wouldn't play into the hands of those on the other side, he'd nevertheless remain a symbol of this dodgy game that those on the other side had actually invented. It was common knowledge that those on the other side aimed to transmit a message through this release, and that he, Kosef J was the bearer of this message by virtue of his status as a released man.

'What message?' someone inquired. A message of hate and menace to those who had freed themselves through their own will. 'Don't forget that this man had purchased a shovel, a pickaxe and a roll of string for us!' another voice added.

'To hell with the roll of string!' a man with a lisp howled, as if completely out of his mind.

'Let's explain to him first what this is all about,' another two or three people opined. 'Sure, let's lay the law down,' others agreed. 'He won't be able to understand any of that,' the man with the shrill voice stressed. 'Do you realize that all of us here are starving?' someone shouted behind Kosef J's back. 'That's another matter, don't get mixed up,' the toothless man pointed out.

'Quiet!' the megaphone yelled.

'Still, he has the right to defend himself,' the man with a cheerful face claimed.

'He should defend himself when he's actually accused!' a man with a baritone voice yelled.

There were rigorous arguments, people standing up and throwing phrases above one another's heads, contorting their bodies while waving their arms as if they wanted to make more room for themselves. In all this time they carried on throwing small paper balls left and right, which astonished Kosef J even more, making him feel as if he was at a gathering of naughty children, or worse still, of madmen.

Opinions of the most varied kinds followed one another. So what if 50A was a man working for *those on the other side*? They could still use him against *those on the other side*. How to make use of a man working for *those on the other side,* to act precisely against *those on the other side*? Perfectly well, everything is possible and justified in the fight against *those on the other side*. But Kosef J hadn't done anything wrong. This wasn't about doing wrong. For God's sake, he, 50A, hadn't done anything wrong because he was no longer able to do good or bad. 'Had he ever tried to escape? If so, he should say so!' the man with white hair shouted. 'Or at least he should have come straight to us,' the man with a lisp howled. 'He didn't come because he didn't know,' the man with a baritone voice proclaimed. 'He's a leper,' someone with a hoarse voice opined.

'This really doesn't work,' the megaphone proclaimed proudly.

'The man has the right to know where he is, and is entitled to have some options,' the man with a hoarse voice insisted.

'To opt for what?' the man with a lisp asked.

All of a sudden, a wave of insane bursts of laughter resounded at one end of this cement dome, and everyone turned that way. Someone seemingly started to make their way down towards Kosef J, rolling over the shoulders and heads of the others in the room, which amused everyone no end.

Someone from Kosef J's immediate vicinity sighed angrily: 'Good grief, is this the sort of impression we want to make on him?!'

'Let's take a vote!' a firm voice urged.

A few others endorsed the idea and shouted: 'Let's vote! Let's vote!'

More and more voices demanding to take a vote were heard, and at the end the entire gathering of hungry and ragged men had started to howl the words *let's vote*! Kosef J was caught up so closely by the course of events that for a second he also opened his mouth to demand the same thing.

The entire room was throbbing to a shared scream as everyone present kept stamping their feet and shaking their fists in the air. Several minutes went past like this and Kosef J became seriously concerned because he was unable to work out who was against this unanimous desire to take a vote and also why they wouldn't move faster to action.

'OK,' one could hear the megaphone, and everyone stopped fidgeting at once.

There followed a highly solemn moment, and Kosef J felt really tiny and humble. He would have liked to do something to win the support of this gathering of men but no suitable idea came to his mind. The only thing he was able to pull off was to stay standing in as respectful a manner as possible.

'Who agrees to take a vote?' the megaphone enquired and everyone raised their right hand above their head.

They remained in this position for a while, in a suffocating silence. Kosef J mused that had there been a fly in the air at this particular time, it would have certainly been felled mid-flight by the tension inherent in this silence.

'OK,' the megaphone concluded.

Everyone lowered their hand, yet this happened so slowly that it made the air vibrate and resound in a sort of prolonged hiss, the rustling of hands in the course of being lowered.

'Who's for?' the megaphone asked again.

This brutal question made Kosef J hold his breath. The question was much more serious than he had expected, and it seemed to concern him most directly. He was overwhelmed by a sense of suffocation also because this time not everyone had raised their hand. Besides, on this occasion the passage of time seemed even slower than at the earlier count, so Kosef J had the chance to look in the eye almost all of those who had raised their hand.

'OK,' the megaphone noted and hands were lowered with a hiss, while someone in the front row whispered in his ear: 'It's OK, you passed.'

Kosef J sighed with relief but then immediately heard the sound of the megaphone.

'Who's against?'

A number of hands were raised this time too, but Kosef J realized at a glance that they were considerably fewer than before, and felt overwhelmed by a terrible sensation of warmth and happiness.

26

For a few days thereafter, Kosef J felt rather anxious. A somewhat new phenomenon was taking shape within his being. Questions would arise, and what's more serious, these questions would persist in his mind, tormenting him and demanding an answer, albeit temporary.

Yet he couldn't find an answer to all these questions. Or he couldn't find the answer fast enough. Or, he'd find several answers to the same question, which only turned the question inside out, into a provocation, leading it to its restless and poisonous slither.

One of the first sinuous questions was 'Do these people really exist?' 'Yes, they do,' he replied and the question disappeared at once from his mind, and he managed to calm down a little.

'And what do they want in this case?' was another trick question, to which he replied with an equally swift and precise answer: 'They want to live.'

'What do they want from me then?' was the next question, one of the most edgy ones in fact. He'd been thinking about this for half a day or so, and every minute he could feel an imaginary snake taking a bite of his brain. 'They want me to help them,' he replied to himself, and for a moment felt relieved. Yet the question continued gnaw away at him. Something wasn't quite right. The answer didn't appear to be convincing enough, so he carried on thinking about it and trying to provide answers:

'They want me to buy them shovels and string.'

'They want me to steal food for them from the kitchen.'

'They want me to leave the prison and stay with them.'

'Bullshit, they don't.'

'They are envious, that's what they are.'

None of these answers managed to respond to the ongoing question, and what's worse, they actually gave a sudden rise to a further onslaught of questions. Shouldn't he, Kosef J, be obliged to inform Franz Hoss about what he'd seen? Was it really wise for him to mingle with that famished and noisy herd? Wasn't he about to do something really stupid? And wasn't it already too late anyway?

His brain had gradually filled up with such unending questions, which had either dilated or split, multiplying suddenly, or swelling up like dough balls, giving the impression that his brain would instantly burst and that throbbing matter would trickle down his face. How had it all started? What mistake had he made? At which point should he have said no? How could he continue on this way when Franz Hoss and Fabius had such a deep trust in him? What were they all expecting from him? What were these voices after, that had terrorized him for so long and would still assault him from time to time? Why would they want to know what he was doing the next day and whether it would be *the same as before*? The same as what, were they completely mad? Why wouldn't they ever clarify anything? And why would he have to think about what was to come, why would he have to think about that? And how about this business with not forgetting them, why would they always repeat that? And whom exactly should he be mindful of? And what about when he'd be on his own? Where exactly should he be on his own? And whom should he look in the eye and what should he take a decision about and how could they tell that he was the only truly free man? And what sort of day were they all going on about, what day was approaching?

All these questions ended up making him nauseous. He was overwhelmed by a sense of emptiness, and it seemed to him that everyone who met him could read all the answers and questions on his face. He felt increasingly guilty towards Fabius and Franz Hoss, and this sensation of guilt had become so suffocating that it started to undermine the simplest acts and delay his reactions. He tried to lose at dice so he could feel relieved towards the two guards, but he failed. Guilt also started to gnaw at him towards the short, stocky and cheerful man who would always expect him, sad and tired, in his workshop. What's more, he also felt less and less comfortable in Rozette's company, to the extent that he'd frequently drop dishes and forget to put detergent in the dishwasher.

'Mr Kosef, we can't do this,' Rozette drew his attention one day. 'We can't wash this many dishes just with water alone . . . '

When one morning Franz Hoss, Fabius, the short man from the clothing-supply room and Rozette were leaning over him to wake him up at least a whole hour before sunrise, he was convinced that they had actually come to kill him.

'Wake up, Mr Kosef,' the short, stocky and cheerful man whispered in a rather faint voice.

'Mr Kosef, Mr Kosef,' Franz Hoss called him, and the air smashed against the mangled walls of his throat in a whistling sound.

'Please, please,' one could hear Rozette's voice.

'Mr Koseeef,' Fabius hummed.

He half-opened his eyes and at first didn't recognize anyone. He could only see four faces leaning over his body, four dark faces at that, because the light of a lantern was seeping in from somewere at the back. He sat up, and only then did he make out the details of each face that conferred it a name of its own.

It was at this same time that the thought occurred to him that 'Good God, they had come to kill me.'

Yet they had only come to let him know that later that day at nine o'clock sharp, he, Kosef J, was about to be seen by the prison governor.

'Understand?' Franz Hoss pressed him after transmitting this information in a single breath.

He was left speechless, and was looking them in the eye one by one.

'The moment had come,' Fabius added.

'What moment?' Kosef J wondered. The news had taken him by surprise, and the way it was communicated only added to this shock. He had of course been aware for a long time that one fine day the prison governor would see him. Lo and behold, this day had just come. But why was it necessary for him to be woken up an hour before sunrise, and, above all, why was it everyone's business to come and wake him up in person?'

'Here you go,' Rozette said in a trembling voice, handing him a cup of coffee.

He took it, warmed his hands on the walls of the cup and started to savour the drink.

'Is it nice?' the short, stocky and cheerful man dared him.

'It is,' Kosef J replied.

Upon hearing this response, everyone smiled, all looking kind and hopeful. The mood had lightened a little. Rozette huddled up in a corner of the lift and giggled when she could feel the tip of Kosef J's toes fight for space under her knees. Franz Hoss laughed out loud and looked up, as if he'd wanted to thank the heavens for the fact that Kosef J had finally woken up.

Fabius shook himself as if he'd wanted to pull himself out from this bustle of bodies. He freed one of his hands and pushed it towards Kosef J, brandishing a packet of cigarettes between his fingers. Kosef J lit a cigarette and smoked in silence, sipping from his coffee every now and then and awaiting the advice his visitors might have been tempted to dish out.

'Mr Kosef,' Fabius started off embarrassed, 'we've been thinking, if I can put it this way . . . '

'In other words we want to . . . ' the short, stocky and cheerful man interrupted.

Rozette giggled again and Franz Hoss panted. Nearly all felt awkward, yet at the same time they looked as if they could barely refrain from bursting out in laughter. Then, one after the other, and in a more or less explicit way, they all uttered basically the same sentence: that *Kosef J shouldn't forget about them.*

In fact, Fabius struggled to explain, they didn't really want much. It was sufficient if at the right time Kosef J simply mentioned their names and gave details of what he knew. Of course, Franz Hoss continued, Mr Kosef J knew an awful lot, and everything that was going on *there* was worth telling. That and nothing more.

'At my place too, at the kitchen,' Rozette added.

'Don't forget the business with the clothes,' the short, stocky and cheerful man hastened to add.

So they all elbowed their way to join in, interrupting one another and building on each other's thoughts. All they asked was that the colonel be told what he needed to be told. And that they *were* there; after all Kosef J knew them so well. This was the moment for him, Kosef J, to say what exactly was going on *there,* and to briefly sum up how things were taking their course.

'Where?' Kosef J mumbled, unable to tell whether he'd asked a question or not.

Seriously, where?! *There.* Things were rather simple yet obvious. He, Kosef J, was now in a position to make a key intervention. Someone burst out in laughter: there was nothing more important to people than knowing that they were the subject of stories told about them. Right? Weren't there countless stories to be told?

They continued to tell him this and that with a drive and liveliness Kosef J had never imagined. They placed their hands on his shoulders, touched him gently on the face, had a good laugh looking at each other, helped him to get up and wash himself, and shake the tobacco leaves off his clothes. They reassured him, whispered all sorts of advice in his ear, asked him to look in the mirror with much more care, and suggested that he held his head high up. They offered him more coffee and cigarettes, made him repeat what they thought to be most important (the word *reality*), and led him out of the pavilion to take some fresh air. They forced him to breathe in several times, to move his arms and legs, and begged him to relax.

27

The colonel was in the middle of helping the child with his maths practice. The room had a high ceiling and was very white and neat, with a glass wall offering a view to the greenhouse. Leaning over his workbook, the kid was busy chewing on his right thumbnail. The tall and pale colonel was unshaven and dressed in a white suit, immaculate apart from being somewhat worn out at the wrists. He was furiously pacing up and down by the table, repeating the task to be solved over and over again. When he caught a glimpse of Kosef J he immediately paused and welcomed him, holding his hand out: 'Please, Mr Kosef, do come in.'

'Thank you,' Kosef J mumbled and held out a limp hand that the colonel shook in a most friendly manner.

'Take a seat,' the colonel said pointing at a chair.

'Thank you,' Kosef J said sitting down.

'I no longer expected to get hold of you,' the colonel said but Kosef J didn't respond since he was unable to make sense of what the colonel had meant.

The child lifted his gaze from the pages of his workbook and stared stupidly at Kosef J. Kosef J raised his hand and waved at him by way of a greeting, but the kid didn't seem to understand this code.

'We're beating our brains here with this nonsense,' the colonel said with a faint laugh. He then turned to the kid and asked impatiently: 'Have you written this down?'

'Yes, I have,' the kid said.

'Listen to this,' the colonel now turned to Kosef J again: 'In a class there are thirty pupils and each of them brings in several jars. How many jars will be collected if half of the class brings in two jars each, a quarter brings in the third of the amount brought in by the first half, and the other quarter twice as many as the amount brought in by the first quarter. Well? Mr Kosef, isn't this utter filth, a lie invented to twist the minds of these innocent children who haven't yet put a foot wrong? Come on, Mr Kosef, isn't this right?'

The colonel almost turned black in anger and started to cough, at which point the child pointed at a glass filled with water. The colonel drank some water and then turned to Kosef J again.

'See? All these things one has to learn as a child. All abominable and false. Only what's really necessary and useful isn't taught by anyone.'

'Indeed,' Kosef J hummed.

'Another example, so you can see how far *they* can go: if two teams are competing at running and the first team's average is 60 km an hour, while the second team's average is 55 km an hour, and each team has three members, how much time do the six participants need to cover 1,000 km? Well? Tell me, Mr Kosef, do tell me! Isn't this utter filth and falsification of the *real*? Can you see the slightest particle of truth in this? And this is what people have to learn from a young age.'

The kid pointed again at the glass of water and the colonel took a few sips. Kosef J swallowed dry.

'Have you written this down?' the colonel asked.

'I have,' the kid replied.

The colonel opened the glass doors facing the greenhouse wide and took a few deep breaths to fill his lungs up.

'This is my way of relaxing,' he explained in a secretive voice to Kosef J. 'We are fortunate to have this garden, right?'

'Indeed,' Kosef J agreed.

Suddenly the colonel started charging towards Kosef J.

'What do you care,' he said. 'You are free and can start a new life . . . '

He sighed and took a seat on a chair next to Kosef J.

'I've heard great things about you,' he continued with a hand on Kosef J's knee. 'I've heard things I liked and I want you to know this. You see, it is so important to hear the odd good thing and to come across the odd genuine person in this sewer and in this horrible process of falsification.'

Kosef J sighed and felt a pang in his chest.

'You know, from the moment I heard that you were released, I've been wondering: what will this man do, how will he look forward to the world, to *reality*, not to these abominable lies that cannot be dispelled. Having said that, these imbeciles, these specimens of human filth have an answer to everything.'

The child listened carefully, shoulders slightly bent, as if he'd been expecting someone to hit him on the head.

Kosef J wasn't feeling at ease either. The colonel grew more and more irate.

'There is no space for us in this world, Mr Kosef. The proof: this child is forced to stay at home and think about things that don't exist. For example, I'm forced to think about all these things and to think about them again and again until my head bursts. Likewise, you are forced to see things that you perhaps would prefer not to see. We are all linked together like insects, like the humps of a giant and disgusting camel. Can you see now, Mr Kosef, why I admire you and why I am in total agreement with you? From the moment I heard that you were released, I kept wondering: what will this exemplary man do, what will he think and how will he move forward in the *real world*? I am convinced, Mr Kosef, that you will move past this filth, without getting soiled, and you will move beyond these abominations that grow in our hearts and fill us with pus and the most shameful disgrace . . . Yes? Yes, Mr Kosef? Promise me, now that the kid is here to witness, that you won't allow to get soiled! Promise me this for God's sake, because only God can get us out of this sewer. Please promise me that you won't allow to get soiled.'

'I promise,' Kosef mumbled.

The child kept staring at the two men, so the colonel barked at him in anger, disgruntled:

'Check out the answers at the back of the book, take a look for God's sake!'

The kid started to leaf through one of the books on the table and the colonel turned his gaze back to Kosef J.

'Thank you,' he said. 'Now we can visit the green-house if you like.'

He stood up and Kosef J followed him into the over-heated greenhouse. The earlier look of hate had instantly disappeared from the colonel's face.

'Are you knowledgeable about flowers, Mr Kosef?' he asked. 'It's really important to know about flowers.'

'I am,' Kosef J said, 'I know a few things.'

'These, for instance, what are these?'

'Petunias,' Kosef J said.

'Not a chance in hell! What makes you think they are petunias?'

'I swear they are petunias!'

The colonel shook his head and moved on. He then pointed at another row of pots and asked again: 'An' those?'

'Rosemaries,' Kosef J hastened to reply.

'No way, rosemaries,' the colonel shook his head with irritation. 'How can you tell this is rosemary?'

'Well, what else could it be?' Kosef J replied, by this point rather irritated himself. 'This is rosemary all right.'

They delved further into the greenhouse and soon large drops of sweat appeared on their foreheads. The colonel was breathing with difficulty and his eyes gleamed as if he had just downed a stiff drink.

'Can you smell the poison in the air? Can you? These flowers are poisoning the air. You can never trust anyone,' the colonel mused. 'You'd think that you are walking in heaven's garden while *they* are poisoning the air.'

'Autumn tulips,' Kosef J burst out.

'Where?' the colonel barked.

'There, in the corner,' Kosef J pointed behind the rows of freesias.

'I've never had freesias in my greenhouse,' the colonel babbled. 'Where can you see freesias in my greenhouse?'

'Here you go, a dwarf cypress. A Japanese walnut. Tibetan sycamore.'

'Enough,' the colonel concluded, 'I've had enough.'

'Red ivy,' Kosef J continued. 'Lilacs, magnolias, mountain fern, sunflowers, immortelles.'

'Let's go back,' he begged him.

'Carnations, crow onion, nettle, sorrel, dry osier, hazelnut.'

The colonel let his side down. He took a seat on a crate of soil, squeezed his cheeks between his plams and looked with great concern at Kosef J.

'Have you collected your money?' he asked.

'No,' Kosef J replied.

'Go to the cashier and collect it,' the colonel said in an extremely faint voice. 'It's a lot of money. You'll need it.' He then swiftly hugged Kosef J and whispered in his ear: 'I've been waiting for this *message* for ages, thank you . . . '

As Kosef J was just about to leave, the child ran up to him carrying a few short tubes, covered in thin foil. The kid placed them into his palm and made him close his fist.

'What are these?' Kosef J asked.

'Megaphone batteries,' the kid whispered.

28

Outside, at some distance from the steps to the entrance, he found Fabius. The old guard looked rather absent-minded, and was leaning against the wall, smoking. Next to him, there was a midget of a man dressed in prison uniform crouched to the ground. For a short while Kosef J was undecided. He couldn't tell whether Fabius was waiting for him or he just happened to have some business there. He didn't move for a few seconds, hoping that Fabius would motion to him. But the guard looked rather blank and seemed to completely ignore him.

Realizing that the old guard wouldn't react, Kosef J decided to head towards him. Fabius was rather reluctant to take his eyes off the invisible spot he had been hooked on. The midget was holding his head in between the palms and his knees under the chin. 'How skinny he is,' Kosef J mused looking at the man.

The old guard was staring at Kosef J without saying a word, so Kosef J pointed at the midget and asked:

'What's wrong with him?'

'I'm taking him to the infirmary,' Fabius said in a bored voice.

Registering a human voice in his presence, the midget lifted his head slightly. The prisoner was indeed extremely weak, with a grey face, and an ugly, livid and treacly swell under the left ear. The man seemed to recognize Kosef J and smiled.

'Is it very bad?' Kosef J asked again.

'No,' Fabius replied. After a few seconds, the guard clarified: 'I mean, I don't know.'

Kosef J couldn't handle the benign gaze of the midget, so he produced a sort of a wave and was about to leave but Fabius suddenly grabbed him by the sleeve.

'Mr Kosef,' he said in a miserable voice and with a gaze that rivalled that of the midget, 'help me to take him.'

They both held on to the weakened prisoner and lifted him up, then grabbed him under his armpits and started to drag him towards the infirmary. The man seemed to be pleased with this outcome and, perhaps wanting to show his gratitude, kept turning his head from one side to the other, smiling.

'He isn't exactly light,' Fabius observed without wanting to start a conversation.

Kosef J coughed. They arrived at the waiting room and planted the weakened man onto a chair.

'There,' Fabius noted and disappeared along the corridor, possibly in search of a doctor.

Kosef J had no idea what to do. The weak and smiling prisoner kept sliding down the chair, as if he'd had a soft spine. So Kosef J decided to stay with him to support him. He'd hold the man tight by the shoulders, who'd keep lifting his head every now and then and gratefully smile at Kosef J.

'What on earth is going on?' Kosef J burst out after about a ten-minute wait. There was a perfect silence in the infirmary. Kosef J looked around hoping to find another chair but he couldn't see any. As he was holding the man by the shoulder he found himself on the side with the swelling, and his eyes couldn't refrain from gazing at the throbbing spot that looked as if it sheltered a small and frightened animal. He could feel his stomach crunch into a ball of hate. Where had Fabius disappeared without a word? What role had he been given, obliged to support everyone and expected to be a jack of all trades? He hadn't even been asked to stay with the midget, he was simply *left* with him. And what about the midget, how come he had suddenly turned so limp to be unable to sit on a chair?

Overwhelmed with anger, Kosef J took his hand off the man's shoulders. As if his body had experienced a shock upon being left without any help, all its muscles had drawn out their last resources and the body stiffened.

'So he can manage!' a voice howled in Kosef J's brain. The irony was that rather than making him feel sorry, the sad state of the midget was actually getting on his nerves. Besides, the man's head had stiffened while leaning to the right, so the swelling found itself displayed in its brutal and somewhat ostentatious fullness. Kosef J tore himself off from the midget glued to the chair, but to his enormous surprise, he didn't head towards the exit but to the end of the corridor in search of Fabius. He furiously opened all doors on his way. Behind most doors there was a dormitory, each dormitory larger than the other, well lit and tidy, with beds placed at the same distance from one another. The beds had been made up by a pedantic hand, the sheets perfectly fitted. Yet there wasn't a single person to be seen anywhere.

Just as he was about to close the door, Kosef J suddenly heard his name being called from the fifth or sixth dorm. This was in fact more of a howl, reminding him of something rather bewildering that took place not long before. He returned to the dorm and looked around. From a bed in corner of the dorm, an arm was waving at him. Kosef J went closer. The man sat up, supporting himself on his elbows.

'How are you doing?' the man asked in a cheerful voice.

Kosef J could see that the man was toothless. He recalled that this same mouth had taken his defence at a time when very many other mouths had barked all sorts of accusations against him. What he couldn't figure out was how come this man had ended up in the infirmary.

'Do you recognize me?' the man giggled, and then made some space on the edge of his bed: 'Please take a seat.'

Kosef J made an effort to smile at the toothless man. He took a seat on his bed. The man laughed with a childish sense of happiness.

'Was it the committee that sent you?' he asked.

Kosef J opened his mouth to respond but the man got in early.

'It's awful, really awful. Did you see what they'd done?'

'What do you mean?' Kosef J asked, just to ask something.

'This is no *democracy*,' the man said grabbing him by the sleeves with both hands. 'This is a gathering of lackeys and toadies. I have been fighting for two years to finally get here.'

'Two years!' Kosef J cried out to endear himself to the man.

'Two years,' the toothless man whistled. 'The things I'd done for this, good God! If you could only imagine, Mr Kosef, but . . . Now that we are here among us, well, I chose to end up without any teeth only to get away.'

'Oh, no,' Kosef J said again, mainly out of complacency.

'Couldn't you tell?' the man jumped up, looking somewhat frightened.

'Of course,' Kosef J confirmed.

'Mr Kosef, Mr Kosef,' the man shouted again, pulling Kosef J again with both hands. 'Genuine democracy, the way I've known it, is gone! You know what I mean? All there's left are some *unfounded principles* that are good for nothing. And that's that. When people are good for nothing, their laws are good for nothing, too. Have you got any idea how much I had to pay to get here?'

'You paid?!' Kosef J cried out.

'Yes, I did pay, and it was absolutely diabolical, but I managed. *There*, if you are no good at scheming, you are completely finished.'

The man was hellbent on chatting to Kosef J, holding on to him with all his might while talking. Did Kosef J realize what danger had he been through back then? There weren't that many votes *for*, just over 50 per cent. A reason for this was also that it had been a cold and sordid day and they were all rather jumpy. Yet it was this very detail that the toothless man was unwilling to accept. In a proper democracy, especially in case the life and death of someone is at stake, you are not allowed to be influenced by a bad day. Irritated people in a democracy? Abhorrent. And yet, in a *democracy of hunger,* like this one, there was no way for people not to be irritated. Was Kosef J aware that it was possible for people to die just because of a rainy day? Such things had happened. It had also happened that a candidate had been rejected because people were jumpy and hence tempted to vote *against*. And one more thing: they are all afraid of yet another mouth to feed. Kosef J had turned into just that after the positive vote, an additional mouth to feed.

'Some want to hate until they drop dead!' the toothless man barked. 'And they'll hate me too until the day they die because I managed to escape.'

Kosef J couldn't make any sense of this. How did the toothless man manage to *escape*? Oh, could it be that Kosef J wasn't up to date with the ways of the committee? No, he wasn't, and in fact he didn't know much about the committee to start with. That's bad, really bad. The committee was the forum that implemented in a democratic fashion the tasks decided in the day-to-day gatherings of the community. The committee was elected twice a year, through a draw. Same thing for the megaphone man. Megaphone? What megaphone? What, he, Kosef J, didn't recall the megaphone? Oh yes, there was something. Someone was always howling into a megaphone. Every day someone else was chosen by a coin toss and tasked with taking on the megaphone. The meetings had to be led by someone, and they were led by the megaphone man. Unfortunately, at the meeting where Kosef J was meant to be received into the fold, the megaphone happened to end up in the hands of a weak and inexperienced man. Yet these were the inherent risks of democracy. It was much better this way, allowing the megaphone to pass from one hand to another by way of a draw. What would have happened if the megaphone had been taken over by a single person? As a rule of thumb, the megaphone man became powerful for the day. The megaphone man was entitled to interrupt meetings or interrupt speakers, and to allow things to develop at their will or to instil a certain sense of direction. In a sense, Kosef J had been lucky that on the day of being received into the fold, the megaphone had been handled by a less than capable and possibly extremely hungry man. For this reason perhaps, the megaphone man had found it acceptable to interrupt discussions, and he had proposed a vote to be taken so he could get away early and carry on rummaging among the rubbish in the hope of finding food.

Kosef J stopped listening. It was clear to him that the man was delirious, yet he couldn't detach himself so easily from the grip of the toothless man. He continued to look at him and nod all along, although the man's words would disperse in his head without making any mark whatsoever.

The toothless man had serious reservations about this lottery principle. Democracy shouldn't have been a lottery, and yet this wretched principle was situated at its foundation since no other more suitable principle could be found. Even those who were ill were *exchanged* following this method.

'What do you by mean those who were ill?' Kosef J jumped up.

Those ill in the community, in the free world that is. Every so often, whenever there was an opportunity, they were exchanged with the patients at the prison infirmary. Obviously they went for people who showed signs of recovery and who had thus the chance of holding out outside the infirmary.

Kosef J laughed mawkishly.

The toothless man didn't appreciate this. Why was Kosef J laughing? Did he object to this particular practice of the committee? In case he did, he was free to make this publicly known at any committee meeting.

No, Kosef J had no objections. But what would happen to these patients from the prison infirmary?

These patients would become free men. The exchange was basically perfectly fair. Those who had fallen ill in the community had the chance of rebuilding their health and hence could save their lives, while the patients from the prison colony were offered an opportunity to rebuild their personality and hence, in a sense, also save their lives. Not a single patient who had been exchanged in this way into the free world had regretted, even for a second, their place left behind at the infirmary. Many of them had of course been initially confused and incredulous. After all they had been *kidnapped* in order to be taken into the free world. After being given the relevant explanation, they'd understand though.

Would some of them die in the process?

At times. There were losses on either side. Even when making it to the infirmary, some of those taken ill in the community wouldn't last long. Life was hard, and the squalor stifling. Hunger and old age wouldn't spare anyone. Yet they were adamant to carry on with their fight. They had developed this method of fighting, and would fight in *this* fashion. Would Kosef J be able to suggest a better option?

No.

Unfortunately, as he had mentioned already, there were very few places at the infirmary. In fact, it wasn't a matter of few places but of few patients. The prison guards, those beasts, wouldn't want to accept that prisoners could become ill. Or, they'd only declare them at the very final stages of their illness. And even then they'd have had to wait for the patient to recover a little before they could engineer the exchange. At times, those finally brought in as patients would die after two or three days at the infirmary, owing to the serious state in which they had arrived. Such deaths represented a massive loss for the community. For this reason they would make sure that the dying were identified early on and exchanged in good time with patients who had a decent chance for recovery. In this way even the dying had an easier end, knowing that their final moments were spent in the free world. The irony was that, from time to time, the so-called dying had miraculously recovered, being spurred on by their new-found status as free men. Such things had indeed happened, perhaps twice or three times in the last twenty years. Thus, these occurences proved that the idea of freedom was rooted in occult forces, able to revive even the dead.

If so, why didn't the idea of freedom manage to heal those already free?

Perhaps because most of those who'd come down with illness in freedom were toadies and profiteers. Also because many of those in the free world pretended to be ill and became willingly ill, only to have an excuse to get to the infirmary. Because the infirmary had turned into an obsession for the free world. The infirmary had become a dream, an illusion, a chimera. Who wouldn't have wanted to enjoy a better meal, to skip work and stay all day in bed, lying between clean sheets? Everyone. They were all obsessed with this *possibility*. And many would go mad because they'd keep thinking about this too much. Half of the community was put on the wait list for the infirmary, catalogued as ill, which was a proper shame on the face of democracy. They'd take advantage of the fact that no one had the authority to establish the existence and seriousness of any illness. In order to put an end to this tendency, the community had abolished the principle of seriousness as far as illnesses were concerned. Future partients were exchanged on the basis of draws, just like all other events in the life of the free world were influenced by lottery principles. Thus, those ill would await their turn for years. He, the toothless man, happened to get lucky. Following this principle, many genuinely ill people were of course sacrificed and they'd give up their ghost. What matters though, is that the *principle* wasn't sacrificed. Moreover, democracy wasn't sacrificed either. For this reason, people were motivated by survival and not by dehumanizing laziness in the infirmary.

How about the guards? Wouldn't they notice anything?

What should they notice? Guards were dealing in numbers, not people. For them what mattered was that a certain number of people should be present in a certain number of beds. According to the guards, there were no individuals, only masses and quantities. No guard would remember for longer than a second the face of a detainee.

This was a horrific aspect of truth, yet one that allowed for the saving of many lives.

By this point the toothless man got really tired. His hands loosened their grip and Kosef J could finally free himself and stand up.

'I have to go,' he said.

'In this case tell the committee the following: at the moment there are twenty-seven people at the infirmary, fifteen of *ours* and the rest *theirs*. Two of their people are in a severe state and could die from one day to another. Five people are an utter waste of resources because they have completely recovered but pretend to be still ill. These five and the dying could be exhanged anytime, including tonight. Another prisoner will be brought in today. Got it? Repeat!'

Kosef J did repeat all this, and the toothless man nodded after each sentence.

'Let's carry on,' he continued. 'The prisoner who's coming in today doesn't have anything serious. Someone had hit him by accident, and this is why he has a swelling of some sort behind the ear. He could also be exchanged fairly soon, in a day or two. Note that cell number 50 in the tile pavilion is empty, so someone could be put in there to recover.'

'What?' Kosef J froze.

'*What*'s what?' the toothless man asked.

Kosef J mumbled and had the impression that he had goosebumps all over. What had happened to the prisoner in cell number 50? He had acquired a swelling behind the ear. How come? Well, these beastly guards tend to hit in the most painful places. But how can one's neck swell so badly after just one blow? Who knows what this man actually had behind his ear. Everyone has a weak spot. Perhaps this man had his weak spot right behind his ear.

Kosef J felt dizzy and sat down at the edge of the bed.

'Repeat,' the toothless man insisted.

He did.

'Now,' the man continued, 'in case they want to exchange anyone tonight they should send the kid to let me know. In today's bins there were soiled bandages and bits of dressing. The cook, who is a bitch, had stolen two portions of food from the infirmary trolley. Repeat.'

Josef K repeated.

'At least two of *our* people are also almost recovered, although I'm not entirely sure of that. Anyway, should there be many people on the wait list, these could be exchanged too. Got it? Bedsheets have been put up to dry right behind the kitchen, so at least one could be easily stolen without any problems. A window in salon number 8 was smashed by the wind and broke into pieces. Half a window is still in good condition though, and could be taken away. Repeat.'

Kosef J repeated all this and the toothless man seemed pleased enough with what he heard.

'Now hurry up,' he said. 'And as far as I'm concerned, tell them that I'm in need of nothing.'

29

The batteries proved to be of use much earlier than Kosef J would have imagined. Indeed the man with a cheerful face asked him as soon as he told him that his name had been drawn: 'Do you happen to have any batteries?'

Kosef J took them out of his pocket and showed them to him.

'Something nasty is going on,' the man with a cheerful face whispered.

There were some laws in place, right? They had to be observed, and observed properly and solemnly, not under duress. There were people who only observed them under duress, and *this* was a serious matter.

The man with a cheerful face handed Kosef J the megaphone used to command order in meetings. He showed Kosef J how to fit the batteries and then urged him to try it out.

'Say something,' the man with a cheerful face insisted.

'Like what?' Kosef J asked, feeling really awkward.

'Say SILENCE,' the man with a cheerful face said.

'SILENCE!' Kosef J yelled into the megaphone, over-whelmed by the thunderous sound of his own voice that made him feel powerful.

'It's fine,' the man with a cheerful face nodded.

He then took to feverishly rattling on with a long tirade. How far could equality go? Until it turned ridiculous? Didn't it suffice that they were sharing the leftovers found in the bins in equal measure? How come that some people would only show their discontent *right now*? Had everyone suddenly taken up smoking? The cigarette butts behind the guards' building had never been declared community property. Wasn't there any hint of common sense whatsoever to be found in these sluggards who have now started to come up with special requirements?

As far as Kosef J could tell, those entering the dome to attend the meeting were all very agitated. An old white-haired man pulled Kosef J aside and shouted something, looking him in the eye. It seemed as if no one was prepared to respect the white hair of the elderly any longer. The white-haired man hadn't caught anything for at least a good few weeks. The reason for this was that programming hadn't been thought through properly. And this was unfair, if not absolutely unjust. The majority of cigarette butts were thrown out between eight and twelve o'clock at night when the soldiers would be chatting away and opening the windows in the dorms to let some fresh air in for the night. Who were those whose turn would always fall exactly between eight and twelve o'clock at night? Who were they and how come it was always the same people?

'What butts?' Kosef J asked bewildered.

The old man didn't get around to answering this because the man with a high-pitched voice squeezed in between them, laughing. He congratulated Kosef J for the way in which he would run the meeting, and advised him to be loud and ruthless. The white-haired man spat and moved away.

Once inside the dome, people headed to their seats babbling and swearing under their breath. The majority were tired, cold, with ashen faces and hands blackened from work.

'Equality will kill us, no other,' the man with a high-pitched voice observed, and briskly got out of sight.

The man with a cheerful face turned up again and dragged Kosef J away, pointing at a chair and saying, 'Here.' Someone pulled him by the sleeve and whispered a few secret words into his ear from behind. 'Pardon?' Kosef J reacted, but the man burst out laughing and didn't repeat his words.

'Take a drag,' another man whispered handing him a cigarette butt.

Kosef J did just that, and felt a commendatory pat on his shoulder. 'Time to get started,' someone said to him from somewhere at the back. So he took the funnel to his mouth and screamed SILENCE. Yet all one could hear for some reason was a sort of long-drawn bellowing. Everyone broke out in laughter. All those men with ashen faces and blackened hands due to hard work were roaring with laughter. Kosef J felt a little ashamed but in no way sad. He had succeeded after all in cheering them up.

'Push the button,' the voice whispered from behind. So he pushed it and shouted SILENCE again. This time it worked out, and a sensation of power took possession of him.

A tall and thin man got to his feet and started to speak in a most agitated manner. He was in no way in agreement with everything that was being shared out, because absolute equality would gradually lead to absolute inactivity. There were some priorities, right? It is agreed that daily food was in some respects a shared problem. Yet everyone had some freedom of movement they could benefit from, right? For years, no one had mentioned those cigarette butts that would be thrown out of the windows in the guards' building. Why would this suddenly constitute a problem *now*?

Because one wouldn't only throw out butts, the white-haired man jumped up. What do you mean one wouldn't only throw butts? How did the white-haired man know that one wouldn't only throw butts? No, one wouldn't really. One would also throw bits of bread and bottles that would at times be still quite full. The tall and thin man let out a long and shrill laugh. Where had the old man seen bottles, that were still quite full, being thrown out by soldiers? Where?

A few voices rose in support of the old man. Yes, bottles were indeed thrown out. And what if these bottles were not quite full? Let's say they weren't full but neither were they empty. Some still had a few drops at the bottom, say three or four drops. Who'd lay hands on all these bottles?

A multitude of voices clashed at this point, ushering in a storm. Who did these bottles belong to? Those who'd be there to catch them at the right time. And who were there to catch them? Just about anyone, according to the law. The rules were unfit for purpose in case some people were able to lay hands on cigarette butts and bottles while others didn't even take their turn. Who didn't take their turn? Was anybody in a position to feel excluded? Everyone was entitled to an hour and everyone took their turn over the span of a few days. Ten days, someone clarified. So what if this happened every ten days?

'Silence,' the voice whispered to Kosef J.

'SILENCE!' Kosef J shouted and everyone fell silent.

A very calm and puny man relaunched the debate. The warm tone of his voice commanded a certain respect straightaway. The puny man produced a few dirty bits of paper from his pocket, and brandished them as if they were some kind of undisputed evidence. He had studied the situation really thoroughly. The fact of the matter was that one would also throw out other stuff, not only cigarette butts and bottles. There would also be leftover canned food thrown away, cardboard boxes, used tape, walnut shells, wet matches and dry bread, in fact an awful lot of dry bread. Moreover, the amount of leftovers thrown out of the windows on these four floors had simply doubled during the last couple of weeks. This is a sign that at least two or three extra companies had been stationed over. Recently a soldier had accidentally dropped his boots out the window. The soldiers would usually get drunk on Saturday nights, so the amount of objects thrown out of the window would be larger, however, the items themselves would be quite unpredictable. Could those who'd had the good fortune of being *there* last Saturday and went away with an old coat, half a bag of bread crumbs and a can of broth stand up?

'The broth was off!' someone shouted.

The puny man carried on cool-headedly. The point wasn't that the broth might have been off. What mattered was the unpredictability of the situation. Some of these thrown-away items could have had a major importance for the community. Let's say that a drunken soldier had thrown out a gun. Shouldn't this object be immediatey declared and made available for common use? No one would have expected people to share their cigarette butts with others, but it would have been wise for everyone to declare what exactly and how much they'd gathered, and also, in some circumstances, to offer a share to the community. In the case of some items, it should be up to the community to decide whether a particular object could belong to those who had found them or whether they had rather a *social* significance.

The storm unleashed again. People shook their fists in the air, talked among themselves, and contorted their bodies as if they had been held down by their feet and dragged towards the bottom of a swamp.

'Silence,' the voice behind Kosef J whispered again.

'SILENCE!' Kosef J bellowed into the megaphone.

And elderly man with a shaven head kept standing up and then sitting back, shouting 'Not true!', 'Not true!' A voice, as if coming from a drink-burnt throat, kept whining somewhere on the floor by Kosef J's feet. No one showed signs of agreement with anyone and anything. Menacing questions rolled out of all mouths and flocked together just underneath the dome, where truth should have probably been residing. Each and every mouth had something to say and shout back at the other mouths. There were people who had made a fortune by selling on their cigarette butts, where were they now? Why wouldn't they make themselves known, for everyone to see them? A few people had grabbed the best time slots as if those time slots had belonged to them and no one else. Why would they pretend that they had no knowledge of what everyone would know anyway? And what about *those* dens at the back of the colonel's house, why would there be no talk of them? The colonel's house tends to generate tens of pounds of food waste on a daily basis. Who would take charge of these so promptly, and why would there be no information on the times when the staff entrance was likely to open and close and when the rubbish crate under the wall would be loaded with new items? And who would keep watch over the short, stocky and cheerful man? How come there was never any talk of the leftovers from the clothes clothing-supply room? Where would the waste and scraps from the tailoring workshop end up? Who had swallowed the myriads of patches and threads? How come the timetable was put together in such a way that some people's turn would come up between two and five in the morning, when there was basically nothing going on, and others could enjoy peak times when an entire swarm of objects would be spurting from the colony's sewers? For how many years had the timetable been *frozen* in this shape?

'SILENCE,' an exasperated Kosef J shouted out loud, overwhelmed by the turmoil in the dome.

For about two seconds silence had indeed been restored.

'What shall I do?' Kosef J asked, turning around and deperately looking for help.

'Shout SILENCE,' the voice whispered again.

Kosef J shouted SILENCE several times, and indeed, there would be silence every time, followed by an even more violent turmoil that would break out straightaway.

It had gradually dawned on Kosef J that the crowd had divided into two camps. One camp wanted that absolutely all objects, irrespective of the location where they had been found, to be stored and shared equally between all members of the community. The other found this proposition laughable. How could seven cigarette butts be shared between two hundred people? Should they all wait until two hundred cigarette butts were found? Every so often those in the second camp would be shaking with laughter. Someone from the first camp had made the point that, at least during the winter when obtaining food was infinitely harder, the fair distribution of all produce was more than necessary. To this intervention, someone retaliated with the elementary truth that cigarettes are not meant to be eaten. Tens of people burst out laughing again.

'We are talking about a principle here, and nothing else,' someone shouted in. 'This principle is rubbish, stupid and void,' someone else retorted. 'It's impossible to survive without a firm principle,' another noted. 'Those who can, survive, the movers and shakers that is,' someone observed. 'It's an abomination to even think in this way,' the response stated, and several people clapped. 'What is abominable is being lazy and expecting society to feed you,' yelled the man whose earlier point led to this remark, and the dome was suddenly invaded by foot-stomping and a second round of applause.

'SILENCE, SILENCE!' Kosef J shouted, and for the umpteenth time people fell silent again.

'We can't carry on like this,' Kosef J shouted again, but there was no reaction. Kosef J turned towards the person who had whispered the word *silence* to him a few times, but he was unable to spot him among the dark and stunned faces.

'Could they possibly fear the word *silence*?' Kosef J wondered, and looked around examining those frozen faces.

'We have to take a vote,' Kosef J said, unaware of how he'd come to this idea.

'Take a vote on what?' the voice from behind whispered inquisitively.

'We have to see who is for,' Kosef J continued in the deadly silence reigning in the space.

All eyes were on him. Clenching their teeth, everyone was awaiting Kosef J's signal. Kosef J couldn't quite understand how such a wretched funnel could possibly trigger such docile behaviour, turning into an almost religious obedience.

'We can only share those things that are suitable for sharing,' Kosef J said.

Some of the audience started stirring, and one could hear splashes and mutterings, cracking joints and a snore.

'We'll do it in such a way so it works,' he continued.

The mood of anticipation persisted.

'Who is FOR?' Kosef J yelled and noted that more than half of these tired people with darkened faces had raised their hands.

30

The man with swollen throat died after a ten-day agony.

On the first day Kosef J visited him, spurred by curiosity and a sort of spite he couldn't quite explain. He did try to say something encouraging and kind, but words simply kept vanishing before he would have had the chance to utter them. Yet the man looked happy and would stare at him with the same expression of gratitude on his face.

'Does it hurt?' Kosef J finally asked, holding out a hand to touch the swelling.

'No,' the man replied letting Kosef J touch his neck. The swelling looked like the belly of a small cat. It was warmish and soft, and slowly throbbing.

The next day Kosef J brought along the soft core of two loaves of bread that he'd nicked from the kitchen. The man with swollen throat pecked at them at leisure. 'It's bread,' Kosef J made it clear, watching the nibbling man with delight. 'Yes,' the man acknowledged. 'It's from the kitchen,' Kosef J felt obliged to point out. 'It's good and soft,' the man replied.

The third day the man looked really tired. His eyes had turned red and his face blue. Yet this didn't prevent him from sporting a permanent smile of goodwill. 'Let me tell you something,' the man said. 'Sure,' Kosef J replied enthusiastically and took a seat on the edge of the bed. The man told him briefly about his life. Kosef J didn't manage to pay enough attention, but he broke out every now and then in exclamations such as 'This can't be true!' or 'Extraordinary!'

The fourth day the man was feverish. His hands were shaking as he was trying to bring a bread ball to his mouth.

'I had a word with the doctor,' Kosef J said to the man.

The man nodded. The doctor thought that things were looking good. The man with swollen throat agreed that things were looking good. Kosef J showed his dissatisfaction with the fact he didn't manage to lay hands on more bread. The man didn't actually need more bread. Kosef J would have liked to say something that was on his mind but he didn't know how to get started. Was the man able to sense what it was that Kosef J had on his mind? Yes, the man understood it perfectly. So? So what? Was he, the man with swollen throat able to help Kosef J in any way? Sure, he, the man with swollen throat was thinking day and night of Kosef J, and yet he didn't manage to come up with a *solution*. Still, he, the man with swollen throat would be on Kosef J's side, listen to him and try to help him. Great, but how? Wouldn't perhaps Kosef J like to talk about his own life, too?

The fifth day the man spoke in a strangely quivering voice. Kosef J had barely slept the night before. The man with swollen throat would have liked to get up and walk up and down in the room for a bit. Why hadn't Kosef J slept during the night? He had no idea. He had helped the man make a few steps in the room. Was he getting dizzy after his walk? No, on the contrary, he had the impression that he was able to breathe in more air. What a horrible day! In the early hours of the morning it started to rain. It was a cold, annoying and endless rain. Nasty, too? Sure. Was another nasty winter on its way? Sure, another nasty winter was on its way. Winters weren't like *this* in his childhood. Obviously. In his childhood winters had never been like *this*. Winters had never been like *this* in anyone's childhood. Would the man like to lean with his forehead against the window? It could be very refreshing. No, he didn't want to lean with his forehead against the window but he did want to have a go at making a few steps by himself. He had been on his own all his life. So, who hadn't? Who hadn't always been on their own? He, the man with swollen throat wanted to say something very important to Kosef J. And he, Kosef J, had a confession to make. What confession? No, first the man with swollen throat. Well, this is it. The man with swollen throat was able to feel something strange, something intense for the first time. This feeling of *guilt* experienced by Kosef J allowed him to die peacefully, saved and almost happy. The guilt that Kosef J couldn't repress was the equivalent of a great happiness, of a devotion able to turn crime into a good deed. What crime? What guilt? What words were these? What was the man with swollen throat babbling on about?

Kosef J stormed out and didn't return on the sixth day.

The seventh day the man was waiting for him, looking pale, with eyes staring at the ceiling. Kosef J brought him some bread balls but the man didn't want to nibble on them any more. The swelling hadn't changed shape or colour, but was throbbing a lot faster. The rain from the day before had turned into sleet and the air had cooled down. Kosef J said something but the man couldn't hear him. Kosef J said it again but the man still didn't catch it. Then Kosef J touched him on the shoulder and the man with swollen throat started to speak all of a sudden. He asked Kosef J not to take this the wrong way. That incredibly cold day and the exhaustion he'd been feeling in his bones had paralysed him and immersed him into a jelly-like aquarium. The patients had been restless all night. Some of them had been chattering till dawn. The majority were frightened. Someone suffering from dysentery was taken away somewhere else, straight after midnight. In his place a white-haired man appeared who just kept sleeping. Many people failed to understand what was going on at the infirmary. But he, the man with swollen throat, knew. What was going on was *a lie*. And Kosef J knew about this lie, too. No, Kosef J didn't know anything about this lie. There was a *feeble* lie, hadn't Kosef J heard about it? No, Kosef J hadn't heard about it. Why wouldn't people call a spade a spade then? After all, things were really straightforward, why was it necessary to convolute everything in this way? Who was twisting things around then? He, the man with swollen throat. No, the man with swollen throat didn't twist things around. To him, everything was somewhat indifferent. Oh, no, Kosef J didn't feel able to put up with this state of affairs any further. How far could ambiguity go? Why wouldn't the man with swollen throat say what he wanted to say? But the man with swollen throat had nothing to say. Lies, lies, nothing but lies. No, there were no lies. If the man with swollen throat thought that he, Kosef J was an *assassin*, why didn't he say so? Who considered whom to be an assassin? He, the man with swollen throat considered Kosef J an assassin. How come, had Kosef J killed anyone? Yes, a thousand times yes. And where was the dead body then? Where was the body? Yes, where was the dead body? The dead body was born there, right in front of them in *that* ambiguity. But the man with swollen throat didn't yet consider himself dead. How come, didn't he claim that he considered himself to be the victim of a benevolent crime? No one had said anything like that, and in case there was any such talk, that was about guilt. Yes, Kosef J felt guilty. Really? Yes, he felt guilty and he owned up to it, right in front of the man with swollen throat, he admitted on his knees that he was guilty and that his soul had dissolved into a burdensome void of impossibility, stupidity and uselessness. What could he, Kosef J possibly do when he didn't understand anything, anything at all from all this burdensome void? Did the man with swollen throat have an answer, was there any *light* at the end of the tunnel? No, there was no light to be seen anywhere. So things were meant to carry on like this, without any meaning, any truth, any ray of hope? Survival had become the only ray. And no one will ever manage to untangle what was so tangled? No, no one will manage to untangle everything, at most to pull at a thread and hold it tight by the teeth. Every time someone would pull at a thread, the confusion would get greater and become even more entangled, so tangled in fact that later it would be even harder to get closer to it. Good God, what were these two going on about? Who were they afraid of, so they talked like *this*? He, the man with swollen throat was no longer afraid of anything.

During the night of the seventh to the eighth day, Kosef J and the man with a cheerful face exchanged the man with swollen throat. This was the first time Kosef J witnessed such an operation. Everything had been meticulously planned. Right after midnight the toothless man opened a window in the ward. He flashed two light signals, at which point the man with a cheerful face and Kosef J left the hiding place where they had been waiting for over two hours. They made their way in, helping one another jump over the windowsill. In the dark, the toothless man led them to the bed where the man with swollen throat was lying. They wrapped the man into a piece of sackcloth, and fastened it around his body with two belts. Then they removed the man through the open window. As they were making their way out of the infirmary, they bumped into two other men coming from the direction of the abandoned courtyards, carrying an old man with shaven head.

They left the man with swollen throat in the former wine cellar. When he woke up the next morning, almost frozen to death and with his feet still tied together, the man with swollen throat found himself surrounded by ragged men who notified him that, from then on, he was a free man.

31

On the ninth and tenth day, Kosef J stayed glued to the dying man, who experienced long spurts of delirium. He wasn't even able to sit up any longer. Oddly enough, as he was nearing death, the swelling on his neck started to diffuse. Kosef J kept dabbing his forehead with a wet cloth, and in the rare moments the man regained consciousness, Kosef J would insistently remind him: 'You're free! You're free, understand?'

'Come on, give me a break!' the man would reply.

Yet an impassioned Kosef J carried on talking to him regardless. Something really major had happened in the life of the man with swollen throat. Had he, the man with swollen throat, realized what had happened in the course of the night? What was the man with swollen throat feeling? Was he feeling anything? No, the man with swollen throat wasn't feeling anything. And wasn't believing in anything either. No one was free. Yes, the two of them, Kosef J and the man with swollen throat, were free.

'Get out of here!' the man with swollen throat cried out, sounding borderline amused.

Oh no! How could the man with swollen throat not realize what had been going on? He didn't realize, because nothing was going on. How come nothing had been going on? Now that the man with swollen throat was nearing the end, he was no longer willing to be fooled. Kosef J had many years ahead of him, still, so he had reasons to allow himself to be fooled perhaps. He was still young and healthy. For him, there was a *point* in letting himself being fooled. Kosef J couldn't follow this. But there wasn't much to follow. And yet Kosef J wanted to understand. What, Kosef J didn't realize that he had been *bribed*? BRIBED? Yes, bribed. By whom? What for? Could it be that the man with swollen throat was already delirious?

'Give me a break, once and for all!' The man with swollen throat said yet again, and fell into a drowsy state.

Kosef J kept fretting in the cellar, waiting for the man with swollen throat to regain consciousness. Towards the evening, he tried to wake him up and make him swallow a few bread balls. But the man refused to swallow. He had clenched his jaws as if he'd given up on talking and eating.

On the tenth day, just as it came to lunchtime, the man opened his eyes and asked for some food. His voice was no longer trembling and his fingers were able to confidently grab the bread balls.

'I had a dream about all sorts of things that didn't make sense,' the man said as if he'd been woken up by these very dreams.

His gaze was clear, his face seemed serene and the man's entire being gave off a sense of restfulness, stability and calm. The man with a cheerful face came to visit the man with swollen throat. In fact, the man with swollen throat had turned into an almost normal person. The man with a cheerful face said a few encouraging words to the man who had just returned to normal. Then, the man with a cheerful face was followed by others. The man with a lisp gave a long speech to the man who had just returned to normal. The man with a darkened face came, too, and sat down quietly in a corner. The short and calm man only put in an appearance to address a few words to the man almost back to normal, and then turned to Kosef J. He had been very impressed with the way in which Kosef J had chaired the meeting.

'Really?' the latter replied, pleasantly surprised.

Yes, the short and calm man was of the opinion that Kosef J had demonstrated an incredible presence of mind, because *that* was one of the most difficult meetings they'd ever held. Every single intervention had turned out to be firm and precise. So events could have easily gone awry, but Kosef J had reigned them in every time and channelled them back to their usual, constructive and democratic path. Now they were about to decide over the issue of cauldrons because they were part of the same problem.

Kosef J knew nothing about the problem of cauldrons.

Cauldrons were no longer cleaned in the evening, as before. Rules had been changed. After the food had been dished out, Rozette would line up the cauldrons by the ovens. On the bottom and inner walls of cauldrons, however, as well as at the base of giant ladles the organic matter of leftover dinner would continue to be lying in wait. At times in very thick layers at that, enough to feed another ten if not fifteen people. Not to mention the hundreds of plates piled up unwashed in the kitchen overnight—adding these to the mix would raise the number of those who could be fed to up to twenty. In winter time and under the given circumstances, this particular winter being as harsh as it was, this source had simply become impossible to ignore.

Kosef J agreed. The source didn't appear negligible at all.

The only problem was Rozette. The short and calm man burst out in a loud laughter, pinched Kosef J on the cheek and winked. Kosef J responded with an idiotic smile.

The room had soon filled up with tired men, all turned livid with cold. Their shared breaths had started to warm the space up. Someone got ahead by telling about the hare they had caught a few days back. The traps lined up along the wall had finally proved to be useful. The cold would sooner or later drive the beasts out of their burrows. The men kept chattering and laughing. Due to the warm air the barrels had an even stronger smell of alcohol than usual. More and more tired and livid men turned up, and soon the room was packed with bodies. Following his conversation with the short and calm man, Kosef J found himself stuck in a corner, at some distance from the man who had almost returned to normal. When he tried to make his way towards the man he bashed into a quasi-compact mass, and didn't manage to break through this cluster of bodies that were basically preserving their body heat by sticking close to one another. The room was fighting for breath, akin to some giant beast coiled up on itself. Suddenly everyone got overwhelmed by a sense of elation. Words had become less clear, bordering on the vague, and gradually turned into babble, as if all mouths present had been trying to utter some pagan prayer. Bodies started to sway slowly, as if a wave-like movement was meant to accompany the incantation. Kosef J tried to take a look around but could only see the necks and temples of those glued to him. On his left, a man with cleft chin had closed his eyes and kept lifting his neck, as if he had been trying to elevate himself to the heavens. This giant beast was practically floating. Oblivion had slowly sneaked into his particles, and a gentle and pleasant sensation of numbness made him think that supreme goodness had finally come to life in his flesh.

The man nearly back to normal passed away during these illusory moments, unnoticed by anyone.

32

Winter settled into Kosef J's life like a hallucinogenic drug. It would be hard to say when and how he got to sleep with Rozette. As he'd wake up each morning, he'd continue entertaining the idea that days were simply lying ahead of him like a market stall from here he could take his pick. Yet, he'd always be confronted with a series of very precise duties, among them the one to sneak in to Rozette's after bedtime.

She'd wait for him curled up in the dark. She'd normally leave one of the electric ovens on, and he'd find her there, in the vicinity of that pleasantly warm breeze. In fact, he'd let himself be guided by the unique odour that the working oven would dissipate in the kitchen. He'd get closer and sit next to her in silence, letting himself imbibed with warmth and the smell of burnt potatoes. She'd place her forehead on his shoulders. He'd caress her gently on the cheeks, with two of his fingers, and she'd tremble with pleasure. He'd then start caressing her with his palm. At times, she'd ask, 'You've come?' and he'd respond, 'Yes, I have.' Sometimes she'd ask, 'Would you like a bite?' and most of the time he'd say yes. In case he said yes, she'd feed him in the dark. He enjoyed being fed in the dark because this way the food could always take him by surprise. She'd feed him in a very peculiar way, as if she'd be caressing him. He loved being fed and caressed at the same time. At the end she'd ask, 'OK?' and he'd respond, 'Yes, very much so.' Then she'd ask, 'Would you like some more?' and he'd say no. She'd stay glued to him and say, 'I'm so glad you're here,' and he'd say yes. He'd usually get sleepy after the meal, his entire body overcome by drowsiness, due to the heat and the dark. So he'd try to move things along a little faster. She'd enjoy being touched on her thigh, so he'd caress her thigh. In case she wanted to be caressed on the shoulders or neck or breasts she'd take his hand and place it on her shoulders or neck or breasts. He'd then take his time caressing her on the shoulders, neck or breasts. After a while she'd say, 'Let's,' and he'd undress her in no time. She'd lie on her back and hold on to the side of the electric oven with both hands. He'd be thrilled to be finally able to get started. She'd tremble at each and every touch and would break out in gushing sweat. Her body would be gradually covered in a very slippery film of sweat. She'd moan in panting desperation, and he'd be pleased because her panting acted as a clear indication that everything was going as it should. Her sweat would trickle across his skin, too. He could feel his shirt soaking with sweat, even his skin getting imbibed with her sweat. She'd climax in an extreme, almost suffocating orgasm and nearly lose consciousness. After each orgasm she'd remain in a state of prostration for up to an hour. All this time, he'd caress her gently, nearly falling asleep himself. This was the moment when those twenty men would sneak into the kitchen.

He'd never set eyes on them. He could have counted their shadows but never bothered. He could only hear them scraping off the food stuck to the inner walls of the cauldrons with their spoons and knives. No one would ever say a word. The men would eat in great haste, exercising self-control despite being famished. The unwashed plates would be passed on from hand to hand. Whenever Rozette would let out a moan, Kosef J would reassure her gently, 'Sleep, do sleep.'

The men would leave just as quietly as they had come. Kosef J would let out a sigh of relief once there was no more rustling or clanking noise to be heard in the kitchen. He'd feel overwhelmed by the sensation of duty fulfilled. He'd also stop caressing Rozette.

She'd soon wake up and fondly send him on his way, 'Come on, off you go now.' He'd plant a kiss on her forehead and stand up, then walk over to the dining hall to lie down there. He'd fall asleep at once.

33

As the weather went from bad to worse people got increasingly agitated and unpredictable. The prisoners got kitted out with warm winter outfits. Kosef J was following with envy the row of cheerful men buzzing in front of the clothing-supply room. For the duration of a day, the entire penal colony experienced the elation of having their clothes changed. The short, stocky and cheerful man was, however, transformed by this occasion into a short, ailing and sombre man. Each and every jacket and fur cap he brought out from the bowels of the clothing-supply room only deepened his wounds. He no longer dared to look people in the eye. With a trembling hand, he'd pass on their regulation equipment, grinding his teeth along the way. By the end of the day he had a gaunt face and red eyes, wide with fear, as if he'd been a witness to some terrible drama.

Kosef J was perplexed on this occasion, too. He was on the verge of desperation when he saw that even the guards and soldiers would receive their waterproof jackets and woollen socks and gloves. Discontent was surging in his soul, as if he was a child beaten up and unjustly driven away from home. He didn't have the guts to join he queue and thus try to obtain his dues, since he was unsure what his dues were. He decided to pay a visit to the short, stocky and cheerful man, now turned ailing and sombre.

'Have you seen all this? Have you?' The ailing and sombre man charged at him as he came in.

Kosef J could guess what the ailing and sombre man was hinting at and said yes.

'And what are your thoughts?' The short, ailing and sombre man asked, shaking his clenched fists.

Kosef J didn't want to reveal much, concerned that he might touch on a nerve. He simply said, 'What could they possible be?' and pulled a face in disgust. Seeing this indication of disgust, the man eased up a little, though he kept revolving round the room and kicking into the piles of uniforms brought back in return for the winter ones.

'Look at this mess!' The man cried out as he came to a halt in the middle of the room, arms akimbo.

Kosef J was unsure how to steer the conversation towards *his kit*. He simply said, 'The cold weather is coming,' but immediately realized that he'd made a major mistake. The short, ailing and sombre man exploded. Where had *they* come across this issue with the cold weather? Who had planted this business with the cold weather into *their* heads? How come *they* knew it all? Or, better still, how come *they* knew it all when it came to some matters but not others? Was Kosef J in a position to offer a satisfactory response to this question?

No, Kosef J was unable to respond to this question, but he was interested in finding out who did the short, ailing and sombre man mean when he said *they*?

Who did he mean? He meant *all* of them. Because all closed their eyes to something terrible, something that was unfolding right there, in front of their very eyes. Because everyone was complacent in *that* environment, in *that* disarray. Could *that* place be still called a penal colony? Could *those* people be called guards? Could the prisoners be still called prisoners? What kind of curse could have possibly been cast upon the management? What sort of underground pressures could make management tolerate such a state of affairs?

'What state of affairs?' Kosef J babbled.

The short, ailing and sombre man threw himself on the pile of summer gear. He was lying there head down, hands under his belly, looking like a man tormented by mangled entrails. Yes, underground pressure was so strong that it had engulfed even *the time for truth*. It was late now. Too late for truth to matter still. Everyone was waiting for the ultimate collapse, for both parties to collapse. No one could survive this collapse, since everything was already under the guise of dissolution. Jackets kept vanishing from the prison. Others wouldn't notice this because they were only interested in people. They only cared for the overall headcount to be always the same. But they failed to spot the jackets. They failed to see the KIT. They had no idea that every winter, for years on end, over half of the jackets would just vanish, although the number of prisoners stayed the same. Where would these people in jackets go to, and how come new people would take their places, people without jackets? Why would management over-look such an extraordinary loss of GOODS? To be fair, in spring when the prisoners would hand in their winter equipment, the jackets would also miraculously appear. But in what state! In what filth! How ragged and torn the lining would always be! Wasn't this enough of a warning? A warning for undeniable managerial agony, with as yet unforeseen consequences? Had he, Kosef J realized that *everything* was lost already?

After a few days of twisted discussions and hard bargaining, Kosef J managed to buy from the short man a cast-off jacket, with its lining all in tatters. Putting it on and checking himself out in the mirror, Kosef J was overwhelmed by a sense of embarrassement and injustice. He had never been so badly dressed or more confused. He almost wished he could return to his cell for at least three days, only to enjoy a few moments of peace.

Franz Hoss couldn't recall an uglier start to the winter, not in the last twenty years. Fabius claimed that seriously nasty winters tended to come around every seven years. Yes, Franz Hoss agreed to this view, but he hadn't quite seen such a start to the winter as this one. Kosef J, on the other hand, was of the opinion that all winters he had experienced while at the colony had been terrible.

'Well, this will be worse,' Franz Hoss observed.

Fabius couldn't agree with this. It wasn't the beginning of the winter that mattered. What really mattered was the middle and the end. Winters would get increasingly more terrible as they *drew out*.

'Well,' Franz Hoss noted, 'this one will be long and terrible.'

The old guard was more or less right. Frost had arrived earlier than usual, and because of the cold weather that exceeded regulation limits, prisoners were no longer taken out for work.

Night after night the two guards would warm up by drinking mulled wine in Rozette's kitchen. Kosef J would finish with the dishwashing in the dining hall and come over to join them.

'How's it going?' Franz Hoss would ask.

Kosef J would never be quite sure what this question really meant. He'd respond though, by saying, 'Thanks, well,' or 'How could it not?' or 'Well, how indeed?' The two guards would pour him some wine and ask him to tell them yet again about his audience with the colonel. Kosef J would tell them for the tenth, fifteenth or hundredth time how his meeting with the prison governor went. The two guards would start to re-examine every single moment of the meeting yet again. No one had seen the colonel for a good few weeks; Kosef J had been in fact the last person the colonel had spoken to. All orders arrived on small slips of paper, seemingly torn out of school books. It was obvious that something bad was going on. The colonel was angry. One could tell this from the short and sharp orders, too. Something had changed in the colonel's soul. After all, if the colonel had opted for that form of reclusion and loneliness, then it was obvious that loneliness could only be a response of some sort.

'Yes, but a response to what exactly?' Fabius tried to jog his memory. Franz Hoss carried on in a pensive mood and stared into the red mouth of the electric oven. The colonel stopped appearing in public. He was probably deeply marked by something that had happened at the colony. Something wasn't working properly at the colony. Something was rotten.

'Yes, but what?' Fabius wondered.

Franz Hoss didn't know what to say to this. Hadn't they, Fabius and Kosef, noticed that people had changed? Couldn't they see that people were no longer the same? A few good years had passed since he, Franz Hoss, was no longer keeping track of faces. He'd have never got them wrong in his youth. He'd know all prisoners both by appearance and number. Now, however, he'd only recall them by number. By number and only that, because *something* was going on with people's faces.

'Yes, but what?' Fabius continued to muse.

Franz Hoss didn't know how to answer this question either. He only knew that people would change face. They'd simply become someone else. He'd been seriously shocked by this at the beginning. It would regularly happen that in some cells, in place of *some* people *others* would turn up. In place of a young man, for instance, a much less young man would suddenly appear overnight, and in place of an elderly man, an even older one would at times turn up. Instead of a gaunt man with swollen eyes, another man would appear, all wrinkles and nearly blind. It took him a long time to speak to anyone about these oddities because he didn't have the courage. After all *numbers* were always the same and, in principle, nothing really bad happened. Also, he hadn't mentioned all this because he'd considered them mere hallucinations. But these hallucinations kept proliferating. There was something going on that went beyond what seemed to be mere hallucinations. Something bizarre that could potentially have serious consequences.

'Yes, but how serious?' Fabius cried out.

'I don't know,' Franz Hoss replied, defeated. 'I simply have no idea.'

Kosef J listened to the two old guards with an air of bewilderment and respect. He didn't dare to share his views although Franz Hoss and Fabius would ask him from time to time about his take on all these *events*. He didn't belive any of this. What could he possibly believe?

'Perhaps it's better this way,' Franz Hoss muttered and then started praising Kosef J: at least Kosef J would always

241

stay the same. Staying true to yourself was no mean feat, especially in such times of uncertainty.

Kosef J shrugged and modestly lowered his forehead.

'How about the colonel?' Fabius continued. 'What could possibly be on the colonel's mind? What could possibly reside in the soul of that man so loved by everyone?'

No one had any idea about what was going on in the colonel's soul. But the human soul as such had continued to remain a mystery, especially the soul of refined and delicate individuals. These have tended to remain a secret to all, and, in Franz Hoss's view, the soul of Kosef J was a mystery, too.

'When I think about the fact that you could have easily left, but stayed on to do what you are doing . . . ,' the old guard observed.

35

As they were heading down the cellar where all the rags were being kept, the short and calm man made the following comment: 'We are really lucky with you being as you are.'

A few days earlier Kosef J had noticed that the short, stocky and cheerful man had stored all the leftover materials from his endless adjustment and readjustment jobs in one of the damp corners in the basement. There were patches of all sizes and colours, collars, cuffs, epaulettes, bits of lining, iron-burnt rags, strips of fabric mangled by scissors in random moments of fury or impotence.

'Pure gold, the man with a cheerful face muttered as his expert eye started to check out the soft and fluffy pyramid.'

The odd metal button or buckle would occasionally gleam in the feeble lantern light. It was past midnight and, as an emotional Kosef J found himself in the firing line of grateful glances, the five men were building up courage to tackle this impressive mountain of rags.

The man with cleft chin was the first to jump in and start digging impatiently at the base of the pyramid, using both hands. He was trying to make his way towards the interior, as if some fur coat could have been awaiting him there. A skinny man with black teeth buried himself up to his neck in rags and then decided to move no further but stay there with his eyes closed as if he'd been enjoying a warm bath. He giggled a few times, then drew the air into his lungs and breathed out loudly, sounding like he'd been doing relaxation exercises.

The short and calm man slowly let himself down onto the floor, leaning against the cellar wall. He looked like someone hoping to contemplate from afar the fruit of this nocturnal expedition.

'See,' he said a little later in a sad voice to Kosef J, 'this is the great tragedy of poor democracies.'

The man with a cheerful face, who meanwhile had climbed to the top of the pyramid and lifted the lantern above his head, burst out in laughter. The man with cleft chin suddenly paused in his devouring battle with the rag mountain. What nonsense was the short and calm man going on about? What tragedy did he mean?

'Winter,' the short and calm man clarified, lifting a prophetic finger. 'Winter is the greatest tragedy of poor democracies.'

The skinny man with black teeth shuffled about in his new bed, which gave everyone the impression that the rag mountain had actually twitched. The man with a cheerful face sat astride at the very top of the mountain. He shoved his hand into the unknown, pulled out a fistful of rags and started to carefully study them in the lantern light.

The short and calm man carried on talking to Kosef J. Did he, Kosef J know that half of the members in the community had been sentenced to death?

'What the hell!' The man who'd shoved himself into the rag mountain mumbled.

'Yes indeed,' the short and calm man insisted. 'How many of us are here now? One, two, three, four, five . . . by March next year half of us will be dead.'

'This can't be,' the man with a cheerful face stepped in.

'Yes it can, everything's possible,' the short and calm man observed.

The man with cleft chin let out a victorious cry. He hadn't been toiling for nothing. He had found an untouched sleeve from a soldier's jacket and was now showing it to everyone: 'See? See?'

The man with a cheerful face had also pulled out a fistful of rags and then threw them behind him. He went on to rummage in the pile in this same indifferent way for a few times. The man with cleft chin, however, carried on toiling away vigorously. He believed in motion, effort, and the desperate straining of muscles. And in dignified tenacity. As he uttered the words 'dignified tenacity' he paused for a moment and held out his head through a little hole he had carved into the rag mountain. DIGNIFIED TENACITY! Sounds good.

'There's no dignity in the face of starvation,' the man at the top of the pyramid pointed out.

'Yep,' the skinny one concealed in the rags agreed.

The man with cleft chin had to sneeze twice in quick succession. This was caused by the dry and bitter whiff of the rag-innards turned inside out. How come there was no dignity in the face of starvation? Dignity was the only thing they had been left with, they the people who'd ensure at all costs that truth, the human sense of truth and, above all, DEMOCRACY was preserved.

'The democracy of hunger,' the man hidden by rags snarled.

The man with cleft chin fired up. So what? Was this a mean feat? No. They had already achieved what no one had done before. Their principles were perfect. They had managed to think through and select, from a motley heap much more diverse than the mound of patches, the perfect principles.

'There is no reasoning in the face of starvation,' the skinny man mumbled, hidden among the patches. He hadn't opened his eyes or changed his voice.

These words had hardened the man with cleft chin. Although he was just about to dig out a second jacket sleeve from the depths of the mountain, he gave up pulling at it and came to his feet.

'You're such a defeatist!' he screamed. 'What do you want us to do? Do you know what to do? Tell us then.'

'I do,' the man hidden among the rags replied in a calm voice. 'We need to break into the food storeroom.'

'Oh, no!' the short and calm man stepped in. 'Under no circumstances. Violence destroys democracy.'

'There you go!' The man with a cleft chin replied, sounding less tense.

The short and calm man opined that violence was the equivalent of suicide in a democracy. Violence was a monstrous eczema that devoured, one step at a time, hope and truth, illusion and certainty.

'Nonsense,' the skinny man noted. 'What matters is that we shoot the colonel.'

The colonel? No way. The colonel was the last man that needed shooting. If they ever had an ally *within*, this could only be the colonel.

'You know, Mr Kosef J has met colonel,' the short and calm man added.

They all turned their gaze towards Kosef J. The short and calm man took advantage of this distraction and grabbed the second jacket sleeve, the one the man with cleft chin had abandoned earlier.

'Is that right?' He asked Kosef J, coming closer to him and staring him in the eye.

'It is,' Kosef J replied.

'Impossible,' the man with cleft chin muttered.

The short and calm man smiled maliciously. What exactly did their freedom entail in fact? An illusion. And Kosef J's freedom? Another illusion. Illusions that, however, had a fairly high pricetag. Would you have wanted to enjoy the illusion of freedom? You had to pay then, even if not necessarily straightaway. At times, payment was due sooner, other times, later. It could even occur that meanwhile life *passed by*, and one thus avoided being made to pay. This didn't mean much, however. Someone, somewhere was keeping a tight watch. They'd know everything about your accounts, work out your dues, and follow you closely so you couldn't run away without paying first. But anyway, where exactly could you run?

'Right, Mr Kosef, where could you possibly run?' he pressed.

'Where indeed?' Kosef J babbled.

Ever since the short and calm man had started to ask him those nasty little questions that didn't even allow for a clear answer, he could no longer feel at ease. The triumphant expression he had displayed when leading them to the cellar had quickly disappeared from his face.

'This is what I'm asking too—where?' The short man recapped.

Kosef J had no time to respond because all of a sudden a scream, as if of a triumphant animal, resounded in the cellar. The man with a cheerful face stood up. They all looked at him somewhat edgily and with an envy that they no longer cared to hide. The man with a cheerful face was holding a winter cap in his hand. It was a nearly new rabbit fur cap, with ear flaps.

The man with cleft chin sighed and threw himself into his work in his hole. The short and calm man also got started at the task. He opened a sack and began to fill it with rags. The skinny man left his lair with an expression of deep discontent. He, too, grabbed a sack and started to stuff it with rags. Kosef J went up to the short and calm man and asked, 'Would you like me to hold your sack?' The short and calm man said, 'No, thanks.' After a while the man with a cheerful face announced, 'And that's that,' and the man with cleft chin added, 'I knew it.' The skinny man commented that 'This will never end, it will always be like this,' while the man with cleft chin noted, 'So what, if we are to bite the dust anyway . . . ' 'We have two options,' someone else intervened, 'either give ourselves up or fight them.'

36

The short and calm man was right. People had started to die as a result of the cold winter.

As the cluster of bodies would set in motion each morning, the most fragile fruits of democracy would stay behind, crouching on the floor. The bodies had to be buried and the gravediggers were selected through drawing lots. The frozen soil was a nightmare to crack open with their blunt pickaxes and spades. Each and every grave had to be painstakingly drawn out from the stubborn flesh of the earth. People had started to curse the dead, those alive hating those who had passed away. For weeks on end the living had been vigorously fighting against the dead.

One day one of the diggers got frostbite while digging a grave. A few days later he died, so, in turn, he also needed to be buried. Every single grave was driving the life force from the people digging it. No grave could be completed in less than half a day. When there were blizzards, finishing a grave started in the morning could take until late in the evening.

Another day one of the gravediggers died while actually digging a grave. He was buried next to the man whose grave he had been digging. The living had started to hate one another. Any one of them could instantly become the cause of immense suffering for all those around them.

Voices could be heard, voices raised against the dead. Why should the dead need to be buried? Couldn't they just be thrown into the abandoned pool or the colony's rubbish heap? No, came the answer. The dead could not be abandoned. Democracy would take care of its dead. Democracy couldn't abandon its dead because democracy would never abandon its people. It didn't matter whether these people were dead or alive.

Voices were raised anew. Dissatisfied and full of hate, these voices raised against the living, too. Wasn't dying a form of treason in itself, and weren't those who died traitors themselves? Wasn't everyone's duty in those terrible moments to carry on living? To simply live, in order not to coerce those around them to the drudgery of burials? One of these voices had completely gone berserk. Live, you wretches, the mad voice screamed, just live! Live, because no one is in the mood to bury you, fools that you are. It soon turned out that the mad voice itself was also dying.

All the same, the living had gathered on a few occasions to discuss the problem of the dead. Wouldn't it be more reasonable to deposit the dead somewhere until spring, so the soil can thaw a little? Nothing undignified would have happened to the dead if they had to wait until spring. Or until the end of the world, another voice, on the verge of going mad, howled. The voice on the brink of madness was restrained in no time. Only the lucid voices would talk. They moved on to taking a vote. Bizarre and incredible that this may seem, the majority demanded that the dead should be respected, despite everyone being fed up with digging graves. The graves continued to be dug by the living, for the dead. Moreover, some of the living died yet again in the process of digging these graves for the dead.

The living came together again. This time there were even more voices that sounded as if they were on the brink of madness. The voices on the brink of madness were demanding appalling things. Wouldn't it have been better to simply throw the dead onto the courtyard of the penal colony? Wouldn't it have been better for people to return, in a manner of speaking, to where they had come from? Nonsense, the lucid voices replied. We shall all die if we carry on like this, the voices on the brink of madness howled. Who had a stake in all these people dying? Dying continuously, digging or not digging graves, inside or outside graves? Nonsense, the lucid voices replied, no one had a stake in people dying. And yet, the voices on the brink of madness screamed, how come some people were drawn two or three times, and others not a single time? Wasn't drawing lots an absolutely idiotic principle? No, it wasn't, the lucid voices replied. Another vote was taken and yet again, the majority got to decide. The dead continued to be buried in deep individual graves. Moreover, it was also decided that burial places should be further away from where the living were based.

When the voices on the brink of madness seemed to outnumber the lucid voices, another gathering was held. The voices on the brink of madness had come unleashed like never before. The voices on the brink of madness felt that the truth hadn't been said before. So they started to say it. The truth was that something had slipped into the very heart of democracy. It wasn't yet known what that was, it could be a LIE, HATRED or THE ENEMY.

Otherwise, how could one provide an explanation for all this? Why in this world of almost perfect principles winter lasted longer than in other worlds, and why digging graves took longer than anywhere? The lucid voices got together in a corner and spoke confidentially for a while. Then they replied to the questions. Firstly, there were no other worlds beyond the two that everyone knew about. Secondly, what did the word *anywhere* mean? Thirdly, the dead had to be buried at all costs, because people had to be loved at all costs.

They took a vote, and beyond belief, the voices on the brink of madness lost again, although they were in considerably larger numbers.

37

The rag mountain was being gradually moved night after night, until the very last patch, thread and epaulette was taken away. People would now sleep immersing themselves into this mountain, breathing at the bottom of this pile of rags and making sure that the warm air coming out of their nostrils was directed towards the lower depths, in order to preserve the heat. They would no longer freeze to death, like before, though two or three elderly men choked to death instead. Their bodies were found two or three days later, huddled at the bottom. So the collective decided that rags had to be stirred on a daily basis to freshen up the air and also to find the dead bodies before they started to decompose.

The voices on the brink of madness continued to pose questions. These really insistent questions were asked with hate and repeated over and over again. *Time* had become the main object of hate for these voices. Time no longer flew as it should have. Why was time longer for some, and shorter for others? Why wasn't the time set aside for keeping watch shared more generously? Why was the watch time behind the garrison the shortest of all, that being the very place where the leftovers thrown out of the windows had become a major source of private property? Everyone was allowed to keep watch for so many minutes at an interval of so many days. Pure chance was ruling over these times of waiting, akin to a king's reign in a desert. The times set aside for *waiting* behind the colonel's rubbish crate had also become extremely rare and short. This was the second major source of private property. Spending time at the infirmary, however, was reduced the most. The list of those who had considered themselves to be ill soon included all members of the community. 'It's a shame, a huge shame,' the toothless man howled when he found himself replaced much earlier than he had expected. The white-haired man was only allowed to stay for two days, while the old man with shaven head found himself brought back in the course of his second night away. 'This isn't fair,' he hit out at all those who were prepared to listen to him. His heart would beat slowly, much more slowly than the heart of the others. He would beg everyone to listen, at least for a moment, to his heartbeat. 'This isn't a normal heart,' the man with shaven head would keep on whining for days. 'In a genuine democracy there should have been some regulation in place concerning those with slower hearts. I shall die, gentlemen, and no man alive would have me on their conscience,' he complained.

The voices on the brink of madness started to boo. In what sort of democracy would all people claim to be ill? Where were they heading? What was going on with the principle if all everyone wanted was to go to the infirmary? The principle remained the same as before, the lucid voices would respond. One of the most lucid voices even added: the principle had nothing to do with minor accidents. How come? the voices on the brink of madness yelled back. Their entire life pulsated around these very minor accidents. There really wasn't a way out of these minor acidents, a way to allow for both life and the principle to remain intact? The voice that had proved to be the most lucid responded again: *the principle* did not deal with *accidents*, the principle would make no concessions, the principle was one and indivisible. Those who wanted to smoke more cigarettes were free to become soldiers. Did anyone want to become a soldier? Did anyone want to betray the principle only to smoke more cigarettes? No, no one wanted anything like that, but wouldn't it be possible for the principle to stay intact and yet people be allowed to search for more cigarette butts? What nonsense, the most lucid voice declared. Shouldn't pure principle deserve any sacrifices? Did these people really fail to spot that there, in that filthy basement, mankind succeeded in preserving a thin layer of the absolute? Shouldn't the supreme ecstasy of floating on this thin layer deserve any sacrifices? Lo and behold, the human brain had emerged victorious after thousands of years of adverse history. Shouldn't this victory suffice on its own terms, was it necessary to mingle it with all the rubbish crates in the colony? Fine, one of the maddest voices roared, what is it in fact that you are really after, a victory of the dead? Could it be that the principle actually loathed life? Oh, no, that wasn't the case, the most lucid voice replied in a serious voice, however, it wasn't exactly normal for some people to be hiding penicillin. A riot of howls broke out. Who had been hiding penicillin, and why were they jumping from one thing to another? There was no jumping from one thing to another. The principle was keeping watch, and that was that. The toothless man had been hiding the penicillin. 'Me?' the toothless man howled. Yes, the lucid voices howled back in unsion. The toothless man had nicked ten bottles of penicillin from the infirmary. Sure, the very fact that he had managed to nick them was a major victory. But why had the toothless man hidden the bottles, and why would he keep them away from the others for over two weeks? Why hadn't he handed them over to the community as the principle required? Did he think that all the others, taken as a group, wouldn't be in need of penicillin? Who'd have the courage to speak in defence of the toothless man? Who'd have the courage to pretend that what the toothless man had done was a normal deed? Penicillin was on the list of things that needed to be declared and kept as the community's shared property. Right? What did the toothless man have to say? 'Me?!' the toothless man asked. Yes, you, the lucid voices howled and some of voices on the brink of madness joined them, too. Why had the toothless man trampled on everything, life, people, principle? Shouldn't this be called by its name, an abominable treason and a defiance of everyone else? Was the toothless man able to justify what he had done? 'Me?!' babbled the toothless man. Yes, you, more and more voices roared and the toothless man started to shake. The voices leashed out at him, and lodged themselves into his ears, brain and thoughts. 'To death with him,' a few voices yelled, comprising both some lucid ones and a few on the brink of madness. 'To death?' Kosef J mused without moving his lips, and starting to panic at the mere thought of what he had inside his pockets. 'Let's see the bottles,' an elderly man with an old-fashioned goatee whispered daringly. No one heard him though, because they had, all as one, jumped on the toothless man, clenching their fists.

38

When the frost thawed a little, the prisoners were brought out again for work. Hope was renewed among the escapees. Brains started to fret, and impatient voices demanded to move on to action. Democracy had to survive. This meant that provisionally it had to return to the cells. Democracy needed to have access to three meals a day and the 18 degrees Celsius guaranteed in prison cells. But how many people could return to their cells? And for how many people was this acually a *morally* acceptable choice? The voices discussed these matters at length. How many of them and who exactly would be chosen to be sent back *to the other side*? Being sent back wasn't easy. The prisoners would be working hard, so those chosen would need to be healthy. They started a list of volunteers. All members of the community put themselves on the list, as before. 'Shameful,' a few voices mumbled, 'how can it possibly occur in a democracy for all people to be sometimes ill, other times healthy?' The lucid voices opined that the number of people about to go to the other side shouldn't be over ten. Otherwise it could be too risky. The guards might start to suspect something. The community would also risk a lot if it were to lose too many of its members. Ten people going would also mean ten new, released individuals. Above all, however, these ten newly released people would represent uncertain human matter. Their integration had to be slow, they needed to be initiated into the free world. The community had no right to jeopardize its powers of assimilation. In short, ten people would suffice. Of course, these ten people would trigger other sets of ten, chosen in due course. Provided the frost didn't return, ten people could basically go to recuperate every so many days. And if those released were assimilated without glitches, the number of places available for recuperation could increase. To how many? To fifteen, twenty at most. One shouldn't overdo such things. The guards were perfidious, and could always lay on an ambush or suchlike.

For the first time the selection of those to be sent away was not by drawing lots. The more lucid voices felt that they deserved a reward. Democracy could afford to offer rewards. Some minds had pondered over this more than others and had thought about the glory and survival of democracy. It was proposed that ten of these minds that had totally given themselves over to the principle should be selected. A few voices on the brink of madness kept on hissing and clicking their tongues in discontent. The lucid voices snarled at the voices on the brink of madness. Why would the voices on the brink of madness keep hissing and whistling and snorting? They had no reason to despair. Sooner or later, everyone would make it to the recovery stage. The principle ensures access to RECOVERY for everyone. The fact that, at the moment, only the *first* ten people would make it to the place where everyone would get to in due course, shouldn't constitute a reason for animosity. 'Spite has nothing to do with the dignity of a free mind,' one of the most lucid voices concluded. 'Right?' the same voice asked around, and the ten minds lined up to re-enter their cells hastened to respond by squirting out the word YES.

39

Keeping watch was of the essence. Inquisitive eyes spread out everywhere and their task was to see everything. Whenever the prisoners would leave through the main prison gate, these eagle eyes would be present. At every bend in the road, there would be tens of such watchful eyes. Over each and every prisoner, and over each and every guard, a watchful eye would be hovering. Where would these prisoners actually go for work? Watchful eyes would know it all. Would the road lead through woods? These watchful eyes would be familiar with each and every tree on the way. Greedy as they were, these watchful eyes wouldn't miss a thing.

They couldn't afford to waste time. Kidnapping a prisoner and exchanging him with an escapee wasn't easy. After all, there were guards on the beat. There were also weapons. And there were the prisoners themselves. There was the open field where nothing could be attempted. The formation of prisoners would make their way in perfect order, and the workplaces would be under constant surveillance.

Not to mention that the prisoners themselves had turned into brutes. No one wanted to be exchanged during the winter. In recent years a certain resistance to being kidnapped in adverse weather conditions had been observed among prisoners. They wouldn't want to allow being kidnapped in bad weather. They would barely understand anything. They'd care about nothing. They'd organize themselves into groups to ensure mutual surveillance. There had even been embarrassing situations where some people basically would refuse to be released. They were like beasts who had been battling it out until their last breath.

By this point, the watchful eyes had started to clock the times for departure and arrival, for work and for breaks. They'd note all the times second by second, together with their relevant activities. Soon fortune decided to smile on the good. The woods near the town had almost entirely been cut down, and the prisoners were loading the wood into cargo carriers. All the timber depots were to be opened, and there were tens of such depots along the railway tracks. Thus the prisoners would spread out over a relatively large area. Consequently, the watchful eyes had spread out, too.

Night after night, the most lucid minds would make plans. The minds on the brink of madness would invariably say, 'It's great.' The lucid minds would come up with new plans all the time, mooting ingenious twists, real gems of the imagination and cunning. 'Let's get started once and for all,' the minds on the brink of madness would yell. The most lucid minds would give the minds on the brink of madness something very precise to do. This role, given to every mind on the brink of madness, was sabotage. The guards would essentially be shivering with cold all the time. They would also get bored easily. They'd blow hot air on their hands while stamping their feet. Some guards would carry small flasks with them, from which they'd take occasional sips of alcohol. It was easy to string along the guards. All the minds on the brink of madness had learnt what they needed to do to perfection.

The most lucid minds had prepared ropes and gags for those prisoners who were about to be released. One of the abandoned cellars was prepared in advance for their reception. A rota, covering at least a week of guarding duties, was put together, as the most lucid minds estimated that it would take about this long to *assimilate* the newcomers.

The watchful eyes had become increasingly impatient. Their minds would be thinking faster and faster, and the voices would turn more and more vicious. 'They are so fat,' the voices pointed out as the watchful eyes were checking out the prisoners taken out for work. 'Look at their cheeks,' the voices said. 'Look at their jaws, their chubby pink hands, their boots and jackets,' the voices continued to whisper. 'See how calm and quiet they are! They need to keep working really hard, following the orders of their guards,' the voices growled. 'They are basically animals, asleep on their feet. They seem to be ignorant of everything,' the voices continued. The most lucid voices added, 'It won't be easy with them—they won't accept freedom so lightly because they won't understand what it is.' They also noted that 'They are all brainwashed, so are basically a herd of cattle and a bunch of bread-eating machines. We have to be merciless with them.'

The first one to fall was a slim prisoner, with a high forehead. 'Oh no,' he thought when he found himself tied up, gagged and stripped of his jacket and boots.

'Pig,' the second said to himself.

'For heaven's sake, not again,' the third mused.

'What's this, what's this, what's this,' the fourth kept repeating for almost an hour.

'This isn't fair,' the fifth thought.

The sixth simply roared with laughter, even when he was being tied up, and continued laughing well after this job had been completed.

The seventh didn't think of anything because he had been knocked out by the blow he received on his neck.

'Finally,' the eight mused.

'They want to kill me,' the ninth thought to himself.

While the tenth did indeed die, choked by fear and the gag, only a few minutes after being thrown into the cellar where his mind was meant to be finally freed.

40

One of these days when Kosef J was returning from the bread factory, he noticed that Mr Bruno's beerhouse had gone. He looked around in anguish, wondering whether he hadn't lost his way by any chance. No, the surroundings were the same. Everything was in place, except for the beerhouse. On the site of the beerhouse, there was a layer of fresh soil, seemingly scattered about in haste, as if someone had wanted to cover up something shameful.

'They'll build a new one,' the elderly man with a short leg told him. It wasn't clear why he'd be keeping watch right at the middle of the intersection though.

A few days later, when Kosef J discovered that a whole row of houses had been demolished on the high street, the old man said the same thing: 'They'll build new ones.'

'Where?' Kosef J asked and the man with a short leg replied, 'Over there.' Since another five or six elderly men had also gathered in a cluster around him, he turned to them for confirmation. 'Right?' he asked, and old Adam replied for everyone, 'Of course, they'll build other ones.'

When the entire high street had turned into a strip of freshly scattered soil, Kosef J went up to the old men again. They were huddled up at the intersection, as before. 'Ha ha,' one of them started, and all the others followed him bursting out in laughter. Kosef J had no inkling as to what could have made these old men so cheerful. He wanted to ask them something but the old man with a short leg cut him short and said, 'They'll build others.'

'What?' Kosef J asked and the man replied, 'Another street.' 'When?' Kosef J asked and the man with a short leg turned to the others, as if he had wanted to consult them first.

'Soon,' the man replied seemingly for all of them, keeping, as usual, his hand on the shoulder of the person he was talking to.

As further houses kept being demolished, more and more elderly people would appear from nowhere and huddle up at the intersection. Kosef J would see them all the time, looking lively and cheerful, whispering to one another. He found out that a *new* town was being built next to theirs.

'A new town?' Kosef J cried out.

'Yes indeed,' old Adam replied again, 'a wonderful new and big town.'

Unfortunately, none of the old men was able to say in which part of the old town the new town was buing built. Kosef J asked them if one could see the new town from the old one. The old men had a little quarrel, all in whisper though. Some thought that the new town could be seen, and others that it couldn't. Kosef J was convinced that the old men had gone mad and for a few days he didn't ask them anything. Meanwhile a few other streets had disappeared, and the stone depot, the small archives and the fire station were demolished. The old men were now completely filling the intersection. In their much-too-large clothes, they looked from a distance like a colony of famished crabs emerged from underground and getting ready to besiege a chunk of meat.

'Is there anything to be seen?' Kosef J asked them in passing, the day after the excavation of the road.

The old men turned towards him, gazing cheerfully at him.

'Sometimes there is, sometimes there isn't,' an old man with a face shrivelled like a walnut kernel pointed out.

The entire group of elderly men broke out in a subtle yet gurgling laughter that really scared Kosef J. Still laughing, the men surrounded the bread cart and started to pat the horses. Their long bony fingers thrust deep into the horses' mane and skin, as if they had actually meant to reach all the way down to the blood. 'They are also building an astronomical observatory,' one of them pointed out. 'Everything can be seen at night-time,' another said. 'It's all very nice and spacious,' growled a third one. 'There are thousands of small squarish houses,' a few others whispered. 'Yes indeed,' one could hear the yearning of choking throats. 'We are ready,' a few mouths whistled. 'All we need is a sign,' the man with a short leg summed up.

The town looked like an animal that had been put through flames and had its skin scorched here and there. The old men would slowly emerge from all the cracks of this wounded town, and were crawling, as if for the first time, towards the light. They were appearing from everywhere in alarming, almost suffocating numbers. They would emerge from courtyards, half-demolished houses and buildings still standing, from basements that would only hold up the air above, and from behind remote walls.

The intersection was chock-a-block with elderly men and some of them had dispersed into former yards and foundations of houses now covered with soil. Kosef J felt more and more restless as he became aware of this fidgeting of hands and feet, contorted bodies and clashing canes. He would have liked to find another way to the bread factory, but he was unsure why. In addition, he also lacked the courage.

The brick wall around the bread factory was also demolished. The ovens now seemed sieged by an immense flat piece of land, and they appeared on the horizon akin to some bare outlines, a gathering of subtle and prudish mechanisms about to get covered in smoke. Kosef J felt sorry for the brick wall and felt worn down by a faint sadness for days on end. On his way back with the bread cart, he'd often take a few detours, hoping to make out the outline of the new town on the horizon, but he only came across an endless row of elderly men one morning, marching in an unknown direction.

41

When Kosef J told Franz Hoss and Fabius about the beer-house being demolished, they looked at him in disbelief. He then continued to bring them news of the demolished buildings and the chopping down of tress in the central park. The guards would listen to him with utter incredulity. The short, stocky and cheerful man had also spotted a dust cloud from the roof of his clothing-supply room, following which he kept repeating for days and days on end how he had discovered the dust cloud one morning, and how he found that the water tower *was* no longer there by the time the cloud had scattered.

'The tower, do you really mean the tower?' Fabius yelled, sounding rather frightened.

Yes, the tower indeed, the short, stocky and cheerful man confirmed. Then Kosef J came back with further news. The entire facade of the alcohol factory had collapsed overnight. The alcohol-filled barrels had been loaded onto lorries and driven away, somewhere unknown.

Rozette could overhear all this from behind the stacks of dirty dishes, and one night she burst out in tears. 'What the hell, the watchmakers as well?' 'Yes,' the short, stocky and cheerful man stressed, 'and the Pandolfi Mansion and the cadet school.'

'They'll build others,' Kosef J added, in the hope that this might calm Rozette a little.

'You really think they'll build others?' he quizzed Franz Hoss with a penetrating look.

It was obvious. Something bizarre was happening, something hovering about like a threat. The timber depots had been locked up for years, but now, lo and behold, they were being opened up, their contents loaded onto cargo trains and shipped out to all corners of the world. All those movements didn't seem to be normal. What would possibly become of the population? And the colonel, who had stopped leaving his house! Perhaps this was the reason why the colonel had refused to be seen in public. Perhaps the colonel had known about all this, and sick and disillusioned beyond repair that he was, he simply refused to show himself.

Kosef J told them about what was being said in town. About the new town that was being built in the vicinity of the old one.

'Nonsense,' Franz Hoss observed. 'Where exactly can you see a new town?'

The short, stocky and cheerful man also agreed that there was no trace of a new town anywhere on the horizon. Or at least, no such thing could be spotted from the roof of his clothing-supply room. Had Kosef J actually seen anything himself, from other roofs perhaps? No, Kosef J hadn't seen anything, from anywhere. Rozette, however, had seen something that, for her at least, could have a major significance. The labels on the pea crates had changed. They were no longer large and black, but small and blue.

After a few days of intense scrutiny, turning and twisting this information from all angles, Franz Hoss reached an initial conclusion. That was the last winter *they* were to spend *there*. Yet Fabius couldn't see the *connection* Franz Hoss had made with winter. What role did winter had to play here? So he asked him just that: 'What role did winter actually play here?'

'It did,' the old guard insisted.

The short, stocky and cheerful man seemed equally dissatisfied with Franz Hoss's conclusion. How come this was their last winter? So he told him just that: 'What you have just said is frankly unthinkable.'

'It is,' the old guard replied, sounding grumpy and withdrawn.

42

The lucid voices didn't take these items of news delivered by Kosef J too seriously. Kosef J tried several times to tell them about what was going on in town, and even about the guards being so out of their depths. Yet every time the lucid voices replied no. In case there was any disquiet in the air this could only come from *within* the community, because a few days earlier a man had gone missing.

The voices on the brink of madness didn't share Kosef J's concerns either. Sure, it wasn't great that such things were happening *out there*. Not to mention that irrespective of what was happening out there, these happenings would never benefit those *within*. Now, however, a man had gone missing. Nothing like this had happened before, or at least no one could recall anything of this sort to have ever happened. One of the free men had gone missing and nothing was known about him. The man hadn't left behind any signs, clues or words. The rag mountain had been thoroughly turned upside down, but he wasn't found in there. They had been looking for him in all the other abandoned cellars, in all the hollows that could have possibly sheltered a man, they had even broken the ice in the abandoned pool and looked from him underneath the layers of ice. They had searched for him in the snow, wherever the snow had been touched and gathered in heaps. They had searched for him in the cracks in the wall, after all he could have fallen into one of the rabbit traps himself. They had searched for him all around the colony, wherever the soil or the woods could have potentially concealed a frozen body.

In the end, it was Kosef J who found the missing man. Looking for a quiet and pleasant location to be alone with his thoughts, he had ventured into the apple orchard and his gaze fell on a withering corpse hanging from a tree. Kosef J was overwhelmed by such an intense shock that he burst out crying with hiccupps. The apple orchard had been his secret hideaway where he'd come once every month or so, to admire the sunset. Crying and unable to supress his hiccups, Kosef J ran to alert those in the committee that the missing man had in fact put an end to his days.

A horrible debate broke out at once within the free world. All the lucid voices started to yell as one that the suicidal man was in fact a *traitor* and an enemy of democracy. The lucid voices claimed that such a thing was unforgivable, in a democracy there is no such thing as suicide, one seeks other people's opinion, there is consultation, participation, etc. . . .

Kosef J was the only one unable to join the debate because he couldn't stop hiccupping and tears kept rolling down his cheeks. Something had entirely closed down in him, and he was suddenly unable to think, understand what he was being told or concentrate on the various tasks he had to carry out day in, day out. There was no way he could be sent out to bring bread or in a position to make love to Rozette. Kosef J would huddle up all day in the heap of rags, whimpering like a child.

Everyone was touched by what had happened to Kosef J. The suicidal man had been forgotten, in fact the committee had solemnly declared that the man hadn't actually existed. The reason for this was to prevent creating a precedent in *the zone of democracy*. Kosef J's situation, on the other hand, led to ardent debate.

Kosef J attended discussions without being able to focus on the meaning of the phrases uttered by all these people present in front of him. Various exclamations and reflections would reach his brain every now and then, such as: 'Democracy cannot allow itself to be ungrateful,' 'We must introduce a system of rewards, otherwise we fail,' 'People need time for recovery,' 'Let's not forget that it was him who had fed us all winter,' 'We have to send him away from the frontline *for a little while*,' 'People aren't destined just for work and fight, they also need moments of recreation, relaxation and entertainment. Having fun every now and then is not an anti-democratic concept.'

Perhaps in other circumstances Kosef J would have realized that the precarious state of his general and, in particular, mental health had generated in fact an ideological debate, and this would have been a source of immense pride for him. Now, however, he barely managed to stay put on a chair, with a confused look on his face and always nodding, as if he had been in agreement with absolutely everything that was being said. These head movements were in fact the only ones he was able to control, because he was actually trying to disguise his hiccupping and whining by means of these jerky head-based movements.

'We'll do the transfer tomorrow evening,' he could hear a voice, without also being able to feel the hand placed on his shoulder at the same time.

'This will do you good, you'll see,' another voice reassured him, while another hand was trying to gently wipe his tears away and make him blow his nose.

'You're still young, you'll recover swiftly, you'll see,' other blurred voices pointed out, displaying an unprecendent sense of communion for democracy.

Kosef J was almost entirely gone during the transfer. He was asked to keep as quiet as possible, and perhaps not to hiccup too loud. Apart from this, he was carried by four wiry men in a kind of labyrinth, and appeared rather patient as they had to wait hiding behind some crates for almost half the night, and was unable to understand why a man, for all intents and purposes seemingly locked away by the four men, might have wanted to protest.

Kosef J only came briefly to his senses when he realized that he was again back in cell number 50. An immense sensation of warmth overwhelmed him. At one point he heard a familiar clang and then a few swear words, which made him jump up because he had recognized them. When he also heard the overtly familiar creaking of the trolley, on which he *knew* that the breakfast trays would be brought along, Kosef J suddenly felt overwhelmed by a sense of gratitude. Yes, there was some *humanity* in this world, there was still hope. Kosef J became anxious only when he had to face the two old guards, Franz Hoss and Fabius. Yet these two simply looked through him, as if he were just a transparent frame, and this made Kosef J sigh with relief. He recalled that, at times, people were no other than mere *numbers*, and this realization finally put him at ease.

I'M

JOKING,
GENIUS!

Published in 2023 by Write Laugh Books
Rotorua, New Zealand

Text © Tom E. Moffatt, 2023

Illustrations © Paul Beavis, 2023

www.TomEMoffatt.com

ISBN 978-1-99-116177-2 (print)

ISBN 978-1-99-116178-9 (ebook)

A catalogue record for this book is available from the National
Library of New Zealand.

Cover design and illustrations: Paul Beavis
Developmental and copy editing: Vicki Arnott, Story Polisher
Proofreading: Marj Griffiths, Rainbow Resolutions
Print book and ebook design: Write Laugh

I'M JOKING, GENIUS!

★

TOM E. MOFFATT

★

ILLUSTRATED BY PAUL BEAVIS

For my sister, Helen,

who was always the clever one!

CONTENTS

CARESS THAT CRANIUM

Jokes are funny things!

You can sometimes hear an amazing joke with a unique setup and a brilliantly clever punchline... but it doesn't make you laugh. A smile, maybe. Perhaps some enthusiastic nodding. But no rolling about on the floor in hysterics.

Does that make it a terrible joke?

Or mean that you've got no sense of humour?

Not necessarily.

A joke doesn't have to make you wet yourself to qualify as a good joke. If it stretches your understanding and sizzles your synapses, it might be a big-brain joke. One that makes your mind more malleable and forces your brain onto its tippytoes before you can say, "I get it!"

And you never know... you may even let out a stream of laughter, instead of pee.

That was my aim with I'm Joking, Genius! I flushed the poo and bum sections in favour of more intellectual topics. And if I wrote a joke that was too simple, the rubbish bin beckoned.

That means these jokes are not for everybody. Anyone who hears rattling when they shake their head or smells burning when they count without using their fingers is not ready for this book. They might hurt themselves on its sharp corners.

YOU, on the other hand, are ready. You've been in training for years, stretching your vocabulary and following a strict diet of jokes. You've sharpened your wit and flexed your funny bone. You're ready to give your brain a workout, burning off some of that grey-flab. And you've come to the right place.

But you're not on your own. If you need a little support along the way, check out the glossary at the back of the book, where you'll find definitions of all underlined words. And if you still can't wrap your brain around a particular joke, ask an adult—or an expert in that field—to explain it to you.

Now, caress that cranium, genius... it's time for some big-brain jokes!

INTELLIGENCE JESTS

These Intelligence Jests will sharpen your intellect and turbo-charge your wit. So put on your thinking cap and get ready to laugh until your big brain hurts.

I'M JOKING, GENIUS!

What makes a criminal mastermind?

Lots of grey cells

What do you call a <u>rowdy altercation</u> of minds?

Cerebrawl

What's it called when you pay someone to reason for you?

Hire thinking

What do you call someone who makes sense when they talk out of their butt?

A geniarse

What do you call a child that needs caffeine to think?

Hyperintelligent

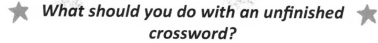

What should you do with an unfinished crossword?

Save it for a brainy day

What do you call a group of clever men?

Intelligents

I'M JOKING, GENIUS!

MAN: *How do you get into the <u>Mensa</u> building?*

WOMAN: I Queue

INTELLIGENCE JESTS

Why was the Nokia <u>barred</u> from the smart phone conference?

It wasn't apped

What's it called when your parents give you intelligence?

Gifted

What's the pass grade in astronomy?

A star

What do you need if an issue is not black or white?

Grey matter

What do you call a Mac with AI?

One smart Apple

I'M JOKING, GENIUS!

What would make the alphabet excessively intelligent?

Two Ys

What's the wisest thing to plant in your garden?

Sage

Why did the quiz show contestant sit on a <u>whetstone</u>?

To stay sharp

What do you call a hippie at University?

A high achiever

Why didn't Shakespeare go to the pub?

He was <u>bard</u>

What do you call a person who's a fraction smarter than you?

Too clever by half

What did the brain do when its body died?

It joined a think tank

FUNNY BY NATURE

Nature lovers... it's
time to branch out and
explore the wild side of
humour. Stroll through these
naturally funny jokes and prepare
to chuckle like a babbling brook.

I'M JOKING, GENIUS!

When does nature bounce back?
Spring

 ### What did the grey rock say to the green rock?
I'm lichen your colour!

What do you get if your feet are stuck in the mud?
A face plant

How should you talk to plants?
With flowery language

What did the driver say to the tree that knocked her wing mirror off?
Eucalyptus

FUNNY BY NATURE

How do clouds act like royalty?

By raining over the land.

I'M JOKING, GENIUS!

How did the mountain know what was on the other side?

It had a peak

Which trees bounce back quickest after a forest fire?

Rubber trees

FUNNY BY NATURE

☆ **How would dolphins grow on trees?**

In a pod

Which tree looks like a genius? (Or you could say an idiot, if you wanted to be mean!)

Yew

★ **Which tree gets ill most often?** ★

A sycamore

What do you call a plant growing in your hand?

A palm tree

How many bits of pollen does a flower need to pollinate?

Eight

I'M JOKING, GENIUS!

What happens if you put a seed in the barrel of a gun?

It won't shoot

Why do people laugh more in mountainous regions?

They're hill areas

Which flowers should you buy for nervous people?

Chew-lips

What delivers baby plants?

A stalk

What has fur and barks, but isn't a dog?

Fir trees

24

FUNNY BY NATURE

What has pincers and grows on trees?

Crabapples

What do you call a dead pine tree?

A nevergreen

CONVIVIAL CHEMISTRY

If a lab coat is your favourite item of clothing and you've got a poster of the periodic table above your bed, these chemistry jokes are for you. And they're a great way to bond with your fellow science nerds... just be sure to test their reactions!

I'M JOKING, GENIUS!

Where do scientists get their toothpaste?

From a test tube

What did the Hawaiian say when creating a metal out of Hahnium?

Alloy Ha

CONVIVIAL CHEMISTRY

What's it called when something can't be solved with chemistry?

A chemystery

★ **How do you make an atomic bum?** ★

By splitting a nuclearse

Why did the chemist often eat dinner on his lap?

He only had a periodic table

Yesterday I combined Fluorine, Uranium and Nitrogen. It was FUN.

What do you get if you cross 007 with H20?

A Hydrogen bond

I'M JOKING, GENIUS!

I watched a great movie about chemistry. It was un<u>miscible</u>.

 Why did the ion keep complaining?

It found it hard to stay positive

What do you call a cat that sets off the other cats in the neighbourhood?

A <u>catalyst</u>

Why was the liquid poured down the sink?

It failed its <u>litmus test</u>

What did the scientist say when she was offered some Sodium?

Na

What do you get when the King farts?

Noble gas

 Who made that balloon go on the ceiling?

He did!

I'M JOKING, GENIUS!

What's the best way to fail a chemistry test?

Get Absolute Zero

Why did the scientist hold a periodic table over her head during a storm?

She was braving the elements

What did the chemist do in the orchestra?

He was the conductor

What's a scientist's favourite tree?

Chemistry

What do you call a chemist who's often on his hands and knees?

A periodic table

> *What's it called when a substance is surrounded by bullocks?*
>
> Oxidation

SCI-FI ESCAPADES

Buckle up and embrace
your inner geek as we explore
the final frontier of humour. And
don't forget to share them with your
nerdiest buddies, now... or in the future.

I'M JOKING, GENIUS!

What do you call someone with one hand in the future?

A future-wrist

Where do knees graze?

On a force field

What's another name for a robotic arm?

A hand droid

Why did the child drink a bottle of coke before getting into the hover-car?

To go into <u>hyperdrive</u>

What's it called when all humans are wiped out and only their mouths remain?

The <u>epoch</u> o' lips

SCI-FI ESCAPADES

What's it called when you go horse riding with an alien?

A close in-canter

Why do clones' legs all look the same?

They have ripped genes

I'M JOKING, GENIUS!

What do you call a person who's always annoyed?

A humanoid

Where can feet live in harmony?

Utoepia

SCI-FI ESCAPADES

What's it called when technology gets in the way of progress?

Science Friction

Why are ants so light?

Anty gravity

 ### What do you call a machine served in a split bun?

A cyburger

How do groups of birds time travel?

With flocks capacitors

I'M JOKING, GENIUS!

What's an EOU computer?

One without AI

How do you make robots more human-like?

With Artificial Stupidity

What do you call a mechanical bottom?

A robutt

What do you say to clones who are upset?

You look like you're beside yourself

Why did the astronaut stick herself to the ceiling in protest?

She was anti-gravity

SCI-FI ESCAPADES

 How do you freeze tears?

With <u>cryogenics</u>

Why did the alien climb into a teacup?

It couldn't find its saucer

INSTRUMENTS OF LAUGHTER

Whether you're a musical genius or are still struggling with the recorder, this section has all the jokes you need to hit the right note with your audience.

I'M JOKING, GENIUS!

What does a guitar wear to cover its frets?

A G-string

Which instrument can't sit still?

A fiddle

 What do you call a hollow branch that still has termites inside?

A <u>didgeridon't</u>

What's the best instrument to accompany a mouse?

A keyboard

Why did the musician always lose sack races?

He kept playing the sax

INSTRUMENTS OF LAUGHTER

What should you say to a worried guitar?

Don't fret

What's brown and can be found at the bottom of a piano?

A piano stool

What's a dog's favourite instrument?

The trombone

Which instrument is Joe not allowed to play?

The banjo

INSTRUMENTS OF LAUGHTER

What happens when you go back to drums after a long break?

There are repercussions

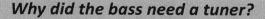

Why did the bass need a tuner?

Its scales were out

 What instrument should you play before bed?

A tuba toothpaste

What did the drum say when it lost the race?

You beat me

How do you play a razor blade?

In B sharp

I'M JOKING, GENIUS!

What do you call musical instruments living on the streets?

'Oboes

What instrument do surgeons play?

Organs

What do you call a piano that costs one thousand dollars?

A grand piano

How do you play a pencil?

By making notes

What's a burglar's favourite instrument?

The lute

INSTRUMENTS OF LAUGHTER

Why did the musician get struck by lightning?

He was a conductor

WORDY WISECRACKS

If you're a grammar nerd or a lover of
language, this section will make you
LOL. Otherwise, grab a dictionary
and get ready to expand your
linguistic horizons.

I'M JOKING, GENIUS!

Why is it easy to understand a pilot?

They speak in plane English

 Who can spell everything and anything?

A Langwitch

We tried to steal their dictionary but they-saw-us.

Why did the peach join in with the nouns, verbs and adjectives?

It was a part of speech

What happened to the word that broke the law?

It got a long sentence

WORDY WISECRACKS

Why was the theatre stage made of dictionaries?

It was a play on words

Why do you usually hear verbs before nouns?

Actions speak louder than words

I'M JOKING, GENIUS!

Why is it difficult to write about
Christmas dress-up parties?

There are too many <u>clauses</u>

*My car can't talk, but it goes without
saying.*

WORDY WISECRACKS

**Why did the metaphor build a statue
out of words?**

It was a figure of speech

**What has the lucky verb received for its
birthday?**

The present perfect

**Five verbs entered a room. One gallops.
One slithered. Two were dawdling and
one had been waiting.
It was a tense situation.**

 Why can't you understand a butcher?

They mince their words

I'M JOKING, GENIUS!

How do you get hold of a unit of sound?

Phoneme

What did the thesaurus buy from the bakery?

A synonym roll

Why did the boy stare at a dictionary?

He was told to watch his words

★ **How do words travel?** ★

By vo-Cab

What would smile if it only had one eye?

A simile

WORDY WISECRACKS

Where do you go to get money, cash, dough or bucks?

A word bank

Viruses always change their point of view. They start off in first person, then go to second and third person. Then they become <u>omnipresent</u>.

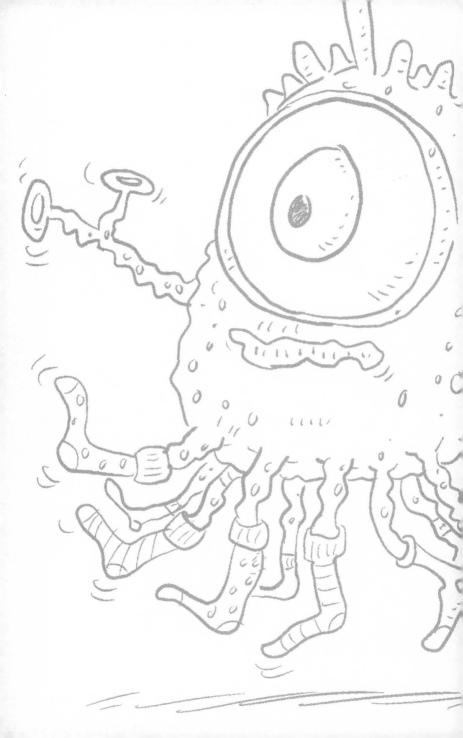

ALIEN ANTICS

Jokes—like the aliens
in books and movies—come
in all shapes and sizes. Long, short,
silly, funny, decidedly unfunny. This
section has giggles for everyone, whether
you believe in little green men or not.

I'M JOKING, GENIUS!

What's it called when a creature from outer space implodes?

An alien inversion

How do you greet a friendly alien?

Give him a high four

What do you call an alien spaceship that crash-lands?

A UO

How do you know when an alien has been to the toilet?

It wipes its noses

What would gigantic spiders from outer space love about Earth?

The World Wide Web

ALIEN ANTICS

How can you tell if there's an alien under your bed?

Your nose touches the ceiling

 What do you call a creature from outer space that stings and collects honey?

An alien beeing

I'M JOKING, GENIUS!

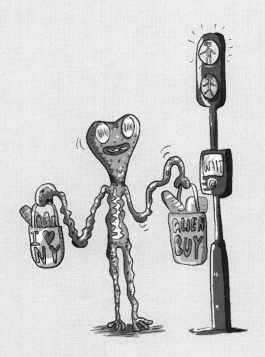

Why did the alien cross the road?

To get to the other little green man

★ **When is an alien hungry?** ★

While you're still in its mouth

ALIEN ANTICS

 What did the alien fish say?

Take me to your litre

How can you tell if your teacher is an alien?

It smiles

What should you do after an alien shakes your hand?

Ask for your arm back

How do you know when you're playing football with an alien?

The ball growls

What do you say when an alien stresses out?

Keep your hats on

I'M JOKING, GENIUS!

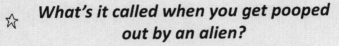

What's it called when you get pooped out by an alien?

A close encounter of the turd kind

Why are aliens good at solving problems?

Two heads are better than one

How can you tell if your best friend is an alien?

Count his heads

What do you call an alien that escapes captivity?

An aliout

How does an alien make you laugh?

With ten-tickles

ALIEN ANTICS

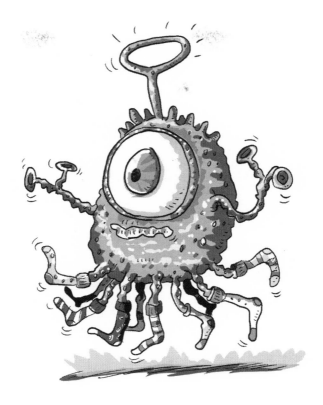

How do you know when an alien has borrowed your socks?

You don't have any left

MUM MUMMERY

Mothers bring an awful lot to the table, such as love, hugs, and chicken pie, but they often lack good quality mum jokes. And here's the remedy! A bunch of mum-related howlers to enlighten, cheer up, and annoy your mother.

I'M JOKING, GENIUS!

What do you call a mother who leaves home?

Margot

CHILD: Why do I need a needle and thread?

MOTHER: Because I said sew!

Why did the mum take her baby boy to the beach?

To get a son-tan

What do you get if you cross Mumma and Dadda?

Madder

Where does AI get its personality traits?

From its motherboard

MUM MUMMERY

My mum just became a <u>barrister</u>, so now she's also my mother-in-law.

 What did the mum say to her baby before it was born?

Tidy your womb

I'M JOKING, GENIUS!

What did the boy say when stuffed into his mum's pocket?

That's smothering

Why was Mother Monster worried about her kids?

They were getting too much Scream Time

MUM MUMMERY

 What did mummy poo say to baby poo that wouldn't stop running?

You're <u>a cute diarrhoea</u>

Where did the baby aliens run to?

Their mother ship

Why did the mum expect Mother's day cards from all her children?

She was on a mother planet

What do you call ten mums in the back of a truck?

The mother load

How do all mums understand each other?

By speaking their mother tongue

I'M JOKING, GENIUS!

When does Mum cook chicken?

When she's in a fowl mood

How do you know your mother can keep a secret?

Mum's the word

Where should you go for the best interest rates?

The Bank of Mum

MUM MUMMERY

★ *What did the baby sheep say to its* ★
mummy?

I love ewe

What do you call a naked mum?

Mother Naturist

What did the baby ice-cream say to its mummy?

Lick at me!

CURIOUS CREATURES

Move over
cats and dogs...
in this section, we're
exploring the furry
corners of the animal
kingdom. If you know
someone who loves all
animals, regardless of how
quirky or obscure, these curious
creature jokes are for them.

I'M JOKING, GENIUS!

What's the best way to cook alligator meat?

In a croc pot

How does a bison fly?

With buffalo wings

What did the girl lose when she made an anagram for panthers?

Her pants

How do you make a racing dog go faster?

Whippet

What's it called when a <u>marsupial</u> jumps to the front of a queue?

Kangarood

CURIOUS CREATURES

What did the waiter say when a duckbill platypus came to his restaurant?

You have an outstanding bill

What do you call a big bird with a rubber neck?

An ostretch

I'M JOKING, GENIUS!

What do you call wild cats in a chain?

Lynx

How does a duck make you laugh?

By quacking a joke

What weighs three tonnes and loves cheese?

A hippopotamouse

CURIOUS CREATURES

Why did the thief visit a goose farm?

To take a gander

What do you get if you cross a pig with a Christmas tree?

A porky-pine

Which mammal can fly through circus hoops?

An acrobat

I'M JOKING, GENIUS!

What do you say when you eat a bad steak at the top of a mountain?

Yak

How do Peruvians know when danger is near?

A llama bells ring

Which is the coolest rodent?

A chinchiller

Why did the chameleon go green?

It was worried about the environment

What do you get if you cross a bird and a cow?

An emoo

CURIOUS CREATURES

What do you call an ant that can use a spreadsheet?

Excelant

What happened when Frog's car broke down?

It got Toad

FUNNY BOOK TITLES

STUDYING NATURE
BY THERESA GREEN

FALLING OFF A CLIFF
BY EILEEN DOVER

FEEDING A DOG
BY NORA BONE

Books and intelligence go together like keys and locks. You can't have one without the other. But the key to a best-selling book is a clever title... especially if you have a silly name like these jokers.

I'M JOKING, GENIUS!

It's a Draw
By Eve N. Stevens

Old and Decrepit
By Jerry Attrix

Shake it up, Baby
By Tristan Showt

You're so Lucky
By Landon Yafeet

Avert Your Eyes
By Luca Waye

Find the Best Deal

By Hunter Round

Healthy Hens

By Leia Negg

Enormous Snakes

By Anna Konder

Not What I expected

By Sir Prizing

FUNNY BOOK TITLES

How to be Funny

By Joe King

I've Been Through it All

By Helen Back

No More Debt

By Bill Spade

A Tight Squeeze

By Justin Side

The Perfect Fit

By Taylor Maid

I'M JOKING, GENIUS!

 ### *It's a Monster*

By Frank N. Stein

It Feels Like Summer

By Sonny Spell

Game Over

By U. R. Dunn

 ### *Becoming a Butterfly*

By Chris Ellis

Not Today

By Tom Morrow

Human-Powered Vehicles

By Rick Shore

GREEK GAGS

If you're a history buff, this collection of Ancient Greek jokes will light your torch and satisfy your thirst for knowledge.

I'M JOKING, GENIUS!

 What do you call a Greek mountain cat?

Olympuss

How should you defeat Cyclops?

With an eye for an eye

What do you call a collection of ancient Greek facial hair?

A MOsaic

How do you learn about Ancient Greek art?

With artifacts

Who stopped the spread of cheesy jokes in Ancient Greece?

Alexander the Grater

GREEK GAGS

What makes some yoghurt Greek?

It's culture

Who is the Greek God of children's books?

Dr Zeus

I'M JOKING, GENIUS!

What was the first booger flicking contest called?

The olympicks

Which Greek philosopher gave society warmer feet?

Sockrates

What happened when Zeus threw a lightning bolt at mankind?

It mythed

GREEK GAGS

 What history do butterflies study?

Greek Mothology

What did King Midas give his servants when they left his employment?

A golden handshake

Where should you file stories about Greek Gods?

Under mythellaneous

What should you say to an ancient Greek with a wooden horse?

Nice Troy!

Which ancient Greek had the most statues?

Medusa

I'M JOKING, GENIUS!

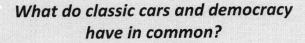

What do classic cars and democracy have in common?

Ancient grease

Why did the ancient Greeks use spreadsheets?

They loved columns

What did ancient Greek farmers grow?

A-crop-of-leaks

★ **How did the Ancient Greeks serve food for thought?** ★

On a plato

GREEK GAGS

How did Greek children explore the labyrinths?

On a minor tour

BEVERAGE BANTER

Thirsty for more giggles? Pull up a
chair and join me for a round of
delicious drink jokes, which
will have you sipping and
laughing at the same time.
Just try not to spray liquid
out of your nostrils.

I'M JOKING, GENIUS!

 Why did the tea-bag panic?

It was in hot water

What did mommy grape say to baby grape?

Don't whine

How do rulers like their whisky?

Straight

What do you call a dog that drinks yogurt?

Lassie

Where do aliens keep their teacups?

On their saucer

BEVERAGE BANTER

What happened to the naughty coffee bean?

It got grounded

 Why do people make fizzy drinks?

So da water tastes better

I'M JOKING, GENIUS!

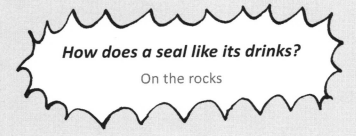

How does a seal like its drinks?

On the rocks

BEVERAGE BANTER

What did the annoying guy get at the party?

A punch

What's it called when you cure someone with citrus fruit?

Lemon aid

What do you call a kitten in a coffee cup?

A fluffy

Why did the glass get left behind?

It ran out of juice

 ### What's the most charming drink?

A smoothie

I'M JOKING, GENIUS!

What do you call a glass full of feathers?

A cocktail

What drink can you make from eucalyptus trees?

Coca Koala

Why did the lady rush up the mountain with a thermos flask?

To have High Tea

What do you call the bit of tea that you don't drink?

Tea leaves

What do you call flat Sprite?

Sprong

BEVERAGE BANTER

Where does the Enter key go for a drink?

The space bar

Why did the banana go to Saudi Arabia?

To become a <u>Sheikh</u>

FAMILY FROLICS

They say
that families that
laugh together, stay together.
So, gather your loved ones and get
them giggling with this family-focussed fun.

I'M JOKING, GENIUS!

What's it called when you're forced to take your dad out for dinner?

A <u>mandate</u>

Where do you keep the key to your family?

In your genes

What do you call three clumsy siblings?

Triplets

When should you play happy families?

When you're elated

What do you call your dad's goofy brother?

Your uncool

FAMILY FROLICS

Why was Isaac Newton just like his father?

The apple didn't fall far from the tree

 STRANGER: *I am your mother's sister.*

GIRL: You aunt!

I'M JOKING, GENIUS!

What did the young cheese say when it saw a pizza?

It's Grate Granddad!

Is that your father lying at the front door?

No, it's my step dad

FAMILY FROLICS

 Which trees have more dead branches than live ones?

Family trees

My uncle moved to Timbuktu. Now he's a distant relative.

What did the little bubble call the big bubble?

Pop

What do you call a sibling from hundreds of years ago?

Ansister

 My little brother got a chainsaw for Christmas. Now I have two half-brothers.

I'M JOKING, GENIUS!

What do you call a mum, a dad and two kids wrapped in cellophane?

A family pack

Who is a PC married to?

His Wi-Fi

★ *What's it called when your dad falls asleep on your golf ball?* ★

Below Pa

Hereditary food poisoning: runs in the family

FAMILY FROLICS

What did the daddy poo say before being separated from his child?

I'll meet you at the bottom

What did the baby do at the amusement park?

A big diaper

SILLY STAR WARS

Here's a section for
all the Star Wars fans in the
galaxy. If you've not seen the
movies yet, you should watch
them first. For everyone else...
may the laughs be with you,
always.

I'M JOKING, GENIUS!

What do you call a night that isn't dark?

A Jedi Knight

Why is BB8 the most useful droid?

It's always around

What did Obi-Wan Kenobi say when Luke ate with his hands?

Use the fork, Luke

Why did Commander Snoke's pizza arrive on time?

He made the first order

What was Baby Spoon's favourite movie?

Stir Wars

SILLY STAR WARS

How does a Jedi open a locked door?

By using force

How does the small furry creature travel through the forest?

E-walks

I'M JOKING, GENIUS!

Why did Han Solo refuse Wookiee meat?

It was Chewie

 Where does the Dark Side go shopping?

Darth Mall

SILLY STAR WARS

Why was baby Ben Solo safe from the dark side?

He had a protective Leia

You're a droid.

Am not

R2

What did little Ben Kenobi say when he first saw a Jedi?

I'll be one

Who is the silliest Star Wars character?

Daft Vader

Why is it easy to break through the rebel alliance?

It only has one Leia

119

I'M JOKING, GENIUS!

Why do young Jedi need a boat?

So they can learn to paddle-one

What do you say to a Jedi who's eating baked beans?

May the farts be with you

Why did Boba Fett search for chocolate coated coconut?

He was a Bounty hunter

What do you say to a dog on the dark side of the road?

Sith

 ### Why was the storm trooper late for work?

He couldn't decide what to wear

SILLY STAR WARS

Why was Darth Vader late for work?

He could only find one black sock

GEOMETRIC JAPES

If you're a maths enthusiast,
you'll love these Geometric Japes.
Everyone else needs to come at it
from a different angle and get into shape.

I'M JOKING, GENIUS!

What's it called when gravestones are not mirror images of each other?

A cemetery

Why did the straight line lie down?

It was out of shape

What happened when one rectangle landed on top of another rectangle?

They became cross

Why did the lady put an exercise bike inside a large cube?

So she could get into shape

What did the square say to the rectangle?

I'm just a regular guy

GEOMETRIC JAPES

What shape do you get when a parrot flies through a window?

A polly-gone

Which shape kisses?

Ellipse

 When your grandmother dies, what shape is left in your heart?

A nanagon

How do mathematicians hit the dance floor?

Throwing some shapes

Which knight was only allowed at the edge of the round table?

Sir Cumference

What did the other shapes say when the pyramid went off to reflect?

Bipyramid

GEOMETRIC JAPES

Why did the photographer stop shooting triangles?

She could never find the right angle

 ### Why did the line stop making shapes?

It couldn't see the point

I took the wrong kind of compass on my hike and we kept going round in circles!

I'M JOKING, GENIUS!

What happened to the unfit ice-cream?

It got licked into shape

What do you call a small furry shape with three sides?

Acute Triangle

What do you call a shape that's only round for the warmer parts of the year?

A summer-circle

Who makes shapes at the circus?

A trapezium artist

What happened to the red light that broke the laws of physics?

It got sent to prism

GEOMETRIC JAPES

What did Shakespeare say when writing a play about shapes?

2D or not 2D? That is the question.

COOKING CAPERS

Spice up mealtimes
by sharing these delicious
jokes with your friends and family.

I'M JOKING, GENIUS!

What do mathematicians like to cook?

Pi

How do chefs take their cooking instructions?

With a pinch of salt

What do you call main courses that you eat in front of the TV?

On trays

When should you not eat three loaves of bread at once?

When you're glutton free

What's it called when ants eat the things you need to make a cake?

Ingreedyants

COOKING CAPERS

Why did the chef take some meat to the doctors?

To get it cured

 What did the chef do to the naughty lamb?

Gave it a grilling

I'M JOKING, GENIUS!

What did the chief do when he lost an eye?

He became a chef

Which cannibal is in charge of cooking eyeballs?

The head chef

COOKING CAPERS

What do you say to a slow chef?

Chop chop

How do horses order their food?

À la cart

What did the carrot say to the chef's knife?

You're looking sharp

Why was the chef kicked out of his flat-share?

He kept poaching everyone's food

 ### Why did the chef need a sewing kit?

To dress the salad

I'M JOKING, GENIUS!

What do you call a cooking pot that doesn't age?

A Peter Pan

When is a carrot unlucky?

When it's diced

What did the kitchen utensil have before his wedding?

A spatula party

Why didn't the cheese like the recipe?

It had seen grater

What does a chef become while the food is cooking?

A waiter

COOKING CAPERS

What do you call a monk who falls down a well?

A deep fryer

COMMON NAME COMEDY

This section takes everyday names and turns them into extraordinary jokes. Bonus laughs if you can find your own name—or that of a family member—among the collection.

I'M JOKING, GENIUS!

What do you call a girl who sets fire to a bank loan?

Bernadette

What do you call a noisy lioness?

Aurora

What do you call a boy lying across a river?

Adam

What do you call a boy who doesn't wear underpants?

Nicholas

What do you call a guy with ash in his pockets?

Ern

COMMON NAME COMEDY

What do you call a girl who's not as kind as you?

Mina

What do you call a boy with big eyes?

Seymore

I'M JOKING, GENIUS!

What do you call a short pirate?

Arlo

What do you call a boy who shrinks a little every day?

Peter

COMMON NAME COMEDY

 What do you call a lady who looks after animals?

Yvette

What do you call a boy who steals?

Rob

What do you call a boy with small plaits in his hair?

Brady

What do you call a girl sitting cross-legged on your head?

Hattie

What do you call a boy with a fresh haircut?

Shaun

I'M JOKING, GENIUS!

What do you call a boy who breathes out a big puff of air?

Si

What do you call a girl who gambles?

Bet

What do you call a boy who only travels by bike?

Ryder

What do you call a boy who can't count to two?

Juan

What do you call the boy who defeats you?

Victor

What do you call a man lying on a barbeque?

Cole

HUMOR USA

Between the
Statue of Liberty
and the Golden Gate
Bridge, there is plenty
of room for a few jokes.
Get your map out... it's
time for a comedy tour
of the USA, without
leaving your couch.

I'M JOKING, GENIUS!

What's the quickest way into the USA?

The American Express

Where's the best place to store precious jokes?

Fort Knock-Knox

What do you call someone who's not allowed to live in the USA?

American't

Which American landmark really sucks?

The Hoover Damn

 Where does the Society of American Grandmothers (SAG) meet?

Gran Central Station

HUMOR USA

What's the busiest place in America?

Mount Rushmore

Where do sponsors' logos go at the end of the season?

New Jersey

Where does stationary go on vacation?

Pencilvania

I'M JOKING, GENIUS!

Where did the egg go on vacation?

New Yolk

★ **How do you get to the White House on** ★
Black Friday?

By Greyhound bus

HUMOR USA

MAN: *I used to live in North Carolina.*

WOMAN: Raleigh?

MAN: *Yeah... don't you believe me?*

Where did the worm go to make its fortune?

The Big Apple

 Why is air conditioning popular in Washington?

Everyone loves ACDC

Where do the International Butchers' Board (IBB) hold their annual meating?

The United Steaks of America

I'M JOKING, GENIUS!

Many state abbreviations are hard to remember, but Oklahoma's OK.

Did you drive to Wisconsin?

No, Me-walkie

Where did the boat full of ladies disembark?

She-cargo

Does your mom know where Anchorage is?

Alaska

Why did the ice cube jump into the Mississippi river?

It wanted to change states

What's an American vampire's favourite day of the year?

Fangs Giving

NURSERY RHYME JOKES

Nursery
rhymes play
an important part
in the development
of little brains. So, let's
see how your big brain copes
with these nursery rhyme jokes!

I'M JOKING, GENIUS!

Why did the criminal do the Hokey Pokey?

To turn himself around

Who took my cat away from me?

Kitten-Eyed Joe

What did Little Miss Muffett do after marrying Tom Thumb?

She sat on her bum

Why did the sailor go to the city city city?

To see see see a speech therapist

My favourite nursery rhyme is about body parts. It's head and shoulders above the rest!

NURSERY RHYME JOKES

Where does Goosey Goosey Gander go to the toilet?

In the lady's chamber pot

What do you sing at a snowman's birthday?

Freeze a jolly good fellow

I'M JOKING, GENIUS!

What did Alice the camel do when they stopped playing her song?

She got the hump

Why were there two hot-cross buns down the toilet?

Someone spent a penny

NURSERY RHYME JOKES

☆ **What did this little piggy do in the** ☆
bathroom?

Wee, wee, wee

Where did the mouse moor its boat?

In the hickory, dickory, dock

Why did the boy feed laxatives to the
three blind mice?

To see how they run

 What vowels does old Macdonald
know?

E, I, E, I, O

I'M JOKING, GENIUS!

Why was Humpty Dumpty happy come Winter?

He had a great Fall

What happened when the mouse left matches lying around?

The clock struck one

Why did This Old Man move to the top of a Hill?

He was fed up with rolling home

What do you get if you put a firecracker down the waterspout?

Itsy bits of spider

Where should ewe go for a haircut?

Barber Blacksheep

NURSERY RHYME JOKES

★ **What instrument did the piper's son play?** ★

The Tom Tom

Why did Bingo shout "Bingo"?

Because he won the game-o.

DOCTOR-DOCTOR JOKES

If you're a wannabe medical student, this section is just what the doctor ordered.

I'M JOKING, GENIUS!

Doctor, Doctor, why is everyone in the waiting room dressed in see-through clothes?

I'm sorry... my patients are wearing thin

Doctor, doctor, I'm inflating like a balloon!

Pop yourself on the bed

Doctor, Doctor, I keep falling down the same water hole.

You clearly can't see that well.

Doctor, Doctor, I feel like a piece of lost baggage.

Sorry, this is not my case.

DOCTOR-DOCTOR JOKES

Doctor, Doctor, a loading icon has appeared on my forehead.

Ah yes... it's good that you're showing progress.

 Doctor, Doctor, I think I want to marry you!

If you still feel the same way later, give me a ring.

Doctor, doctor, I think I'm turning into a small bucket.

You do look like you're a little pail.

Doctor, Doctor, my invisibility is wearing off.

I'll be able to see you in a few minutes.

★ **Doctor, Doctor, I've been told I'm due in court in five minutes.** ★

Let me just check your <u>hearing</u>.

DOCTOR-DOCTOR JOKES

 Doctor, Doctor, I can only turn my head in one direction.

I thought you didn't look right.

Doctor, doctor, my fingers are numb.

I guess you're not feeling well?

Doctor, Doctor, what did you see when you looked in my mouth?

I sore throat.

Doctor, Doctor, eggs keep falling out of me and breaking on the floor.

Try laying low for a few days.

Doctor, Doctor, I keep getting stung by the same vicious insect.

Yes, there's a nasty bug going round.

I'M JOKING, GENIUS!

Doctor, Doctor, do you have anything for bad breath?

Try eating some dog poo

Doctor, Doctor, I've painted my face green and written STOP on my forehead.

That's not a good sign.

Doctor, Doctor, I don't fit inside my filing cabinet anymore.

Come this way and I'll get you sorted.

Doctor, Doctor, I've got a strawberry stuck in my throat.

I can give you some cream for that.

DOCTOR-DOCTOR JOKES

Doctor, Doctor, I can't seem to tell the truth.

Lie here, please.

Doctor, Doctor, my neck is sore from carrying all these clocks on my head.

You need to take some time off.

NUMBER MUMBO JUMBO

Looking for a way to make Maths more fun? Laugh and learn at the same time with this number-crunching humour.

I'M JOKING, GENIUS!

What should you do with two lines side-by-side?

Treat them as equals

Why did 4 bully 3 and 5?

It was mean

What did X say to the number 10?

When in Rome

What's it called when someone doesn't learn to count?

A cardinal sin

What did the baker say to the butcher when he was one short?

Dozen matter

NUMBER MUMBO JUMBO

How do you measure how far an insect crawls on you?

In feet and itches

What do you call a box that subtracts small parts of a whole?

A takeaway container

I'M JOKING, GENIUS!

What do you call 3 apes, 7 monkeys and 11 orangutans?

Primate numbers

Where does a number go to buy spare parts?

A decimall

NUMBER MUMBO JUMBO

What did the formula wear to cover its chest?

An algeBRA

 Why did 12 carefully consider 3 and 6?

They were both important factors

I might mend my broken abacus, but I wouldn't count on it.

Why didn't Six go camping?

Because Seven ate nine tents!

What did the even number say when he misplaced a digit?

That's odd

I'M JOKING, GENIUS!

What's it called when nothing adds up?

A total disaster

 ## How does 2 feel about 1 and 3?

Average

What did Simple Simon say to his Fingers?

I am counting on you

What did 4, 6 and 8 say when 5 told a joke?

That's not even funny

NUMBER MUMBO JUMBO

What do dairy farmers use to count their herds?

A cowculator

 Why did the old man stop reading decimal numbers?

He couldn't see the point

GARDEN GAMBOL

Like plants, intelligence comes in many varieties. If you're a genius in the garden, dig into this fresh collection of jokes, weeding out the best ones to share with your garden gnomes.

I'M JOKING, GENIUS!

What can you use to pay for gardening work?

A <u>hedge fund</u>

How do you get a message to your garden?

By fence post

When is gardening easy?

When it's a bed of roses

What do picking your nose and gardening have in common?

Green fingers

Do you have any dandelions in your garden?

No, but I've got a big fancy cat

GARDEN GAMBOL

★ *What should you put on your veggie garden to help Brussel sprouts grow?* ★

Fartilizer

Why did the leaf collector love his job?

He was raking it in

I'M JOKING, GENIUS!

 How do you select the best garden fence?

Picket

What do you call a watering can with a hole in the bottom?

A watering can't

Where did the boy sleep when he was locked out of his house?

In the flower bed

GARDEN GAMBOL

What do you get when seedlings fart?

Greenhouse gases

When are grass seeds unhappy?

When they're for lawn

What's the most prestigious award for veggie gardeners?

The Nobel Peas Prize

 Why did the boy bury his pants in the garden?

They were soiled

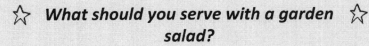

I'M JOKING, GENIUS!

☆ **What should you serve with a garden salad?** ☆

Wood chips

Why did the gardener place a piece of dried fruit in a tree?

It needed a prune

What should you do if you want to give up gardening?

Throw in the trowel

Where did Adam and Eve get cheese?

The garden of Edam

What do noses and fruit have in common?

They both need picking

GARDEN GAMBOL

My cat's a terrible decision maker. She's always sitting on the fence.

VIKING VAGARY

If you wear a
horned helmet to
raid the fridge, this
section is for you.
Pillage your way through
these hilarious jokes and let
laughter be your battle cry.

I'M JOKING, GENIUS!

What were Viking boats like in low winds?

Oar full

Which symbol appears in most Viking comics?

Asterisks

What did Vikings take to feel better?

Pillage

VIKING VAGARY

What do you call someone who was scared of being raided?

A Viking Worrier

★ **How does Thor protect the realms?** ★

<u>As guard</u>

Why didn't Vikings keep their boats for long?

They were always for sail

I'M JOKING, GENIUS!

How did villagers feel when they saw Vikings?

Plunder-struck

What did Vikings do with bugs?

Raid them

What do modern-day Vikings do when they are hungry?

Raid the fridge

VIKING VAGARY

Why did the Viking Scribe cry?

His life's work was in runes

What music did Vikings listen to?

Ragnorok'n'roll

 ### Why did the wind keep the Vikings awake?

It kept blowing their horns

What do you call a Viking that loses both eyes?

A Vkng

Who was the Norse God of Spring?

Thaw

I'M JOKING, GENIUS!

Why did Vikings grow big beards?

It was Baltic!

How did Vikings send messages?

By Norse code

Why weren't the Vikings ruled by women?

Because that would have made them Viqueens

How do you greet a Viking God?

Valhallo!

VIKING VAGARY

What did Vikings do when they were dead tired?

Burn their beds

⭐ *Why were there no Vikings called Ruth?* ⭐

Because they were Ruthless

CHEESY JOKES

Whether you're a fan of Brie, Cheddar or Gouda, this collection of Cheesy Jokes will fill your cracker and tickle your taste buds.

I'M JOKING, GENIUS!

★ What did Sherlock Holmes say when he found a cheesy clue? ★

Emmental, my dear Watson.

What do you get if you feed cheese to cows?

Extra manure cheddar

What does cheese say when you take its photo?

Humans

CHEESY JOKES

What do you call melted cheese that you shouldn't eat?

A fondon't

What did Mummy Koala say to Baby Koala when it was time for some cheese?

Come-on-bear

Which cheese can block a river?

Edam

What do you call cheese that you can write on?

A diary product

Why did baby blue cheese look just like its dad?

They were from the same mould

197

I'M JOKING, GENIUS!

What did the English Cheddar say to the Camembert?

Where are you <u>fromage</u>?

What happened to the cream on its first day in the cheese factory?

It got the sack

Who runs a dairy factory?

The big cheese

CHEESY JOKES

Why did the piece of cheddar get sent to its room?

For being immature

What did the curd say when it turned into cheese?

No <u>whey</u>!

I'M JOKING, GENIUS!

Where can you find baby cheeses?

In a cheese manger

★ **Why did the priest give swiss cheese to her congregation?** ★

It was holy

What did the cheese say when it arrived at the party?

This is a fun do

What's the difference between cheese and cheesy feet?

Cheeses lactose

Why did the cheese maker keep his hand in the fridge?

He was feeling blue

CHEESY JOKES

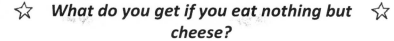

☆ *What do you get if you eat nothing but cheese?* ☆

Cheese bored

What did the police officer say when he caught someone stealing soft cheeses?

Spread 'em

TINY TALES

To celebrate its
tenth anniversary, The
Alliance of Independent
Authors held a ten-word story
competition. I didn't even know
ten-word stories were a thing, but I
wrote one and it came runner-up in the
contest. That gave me the genius idea
to write twenty Tiny Tales for this book.

I'M JOKING, GENIUS!

 Astronaut announces birth of healthy baby boy. Weight: 0lbs.

The babysitter's sitting, arms tied behind his back.

King Cloud's reign ends in rain.

You're under arrest, so please undo these handcuffs.

He punches that annoying face, cracking both knuckles and mirror.

TINY TALES

Princess needed for Happily Ever After.
Must enjoy space travel.

The alien explores the strange planet,
missing her home... Earth.

The bully dangles from the bridge, Mum
holding his ankles.

Sorry I'm late for Monster-Maths... my
homework ate my dog.

Pass, catch. Tears for years. Pass, catch.
Win the match.

I'M JOKING, GENIUS!

The Tree Sprout leaves when the tree sprouts leaves.

Big hand holds small hand. Bigger hand holds old hand.

Walking back home. Same feet, different shoes.

The auctioneer recognises forgery as the detective wins the bid.

Tooth Fairy steals fifty dollars; compensation for the fake tooth.

Zombie doctor searches for a pulse, then declares herself deceased.

Dragon slayer slips in wet bathroom and breaks his neck.

TINY TALES

The sky isn't falling. The ground is rising.

Brave warrior admits defeat after only two days teaching kindergarten.

Kevin waits outside the principal's office, regretting becoming a teacher.

Now have a go at writing your own teeny stories in ten words or less! You just need to choose a character, then add some action or a problem. And can you give it a clever twist?

READERS' FAVOURITES

Want in on the action?
Next time you crack up at a
clever punchline or a genius one-
liner, jot it down and send it to me.

I'll include the funniest ones in the
Readers' Favourite section of my
next joke book. Here are some of
the jokes that have recently
tickled my inbox (and my
funny bone!):

I'M JOKING, GENIUS!

★ **What's the difference between ignorance and apathy?** ★

I don't know and I don't care.

Olivia, age 15
Oxford, UK

Why did the frog take the bus to work today?

His car got toad away

Annabelle, age 10
Auckland, New Zealand

What has to be broken before it is celebrated?

A world record!

Sadie
Bulls, New Zealand

 Why did the hand cross the road?

To get to the second-hand shop

Nathan
Palmerston North, New Zealand

Why was the football pitch a triangle?

Because someone took a corner

Samuel
Palmerston North, New Zealand

I'M JOKING, GENIUS!

What did the fish say when he swam into a wall?

Dam!

Lacey, age 10
Auckland, New Zealand

If you put a picture of yourself inside a locket, you would be independent.

Jacob, age 15
North Carolina, USA

Why didn't the skeleton go to the dance?

Because it had nobody to go with

Lucy B.
Bulls, New Zealand

I went to the bank and a lady there asked me to help check her balance, so I pushed her over.

Kahli-Rae, age 11
Dannevirke, New Zealand

READERS' FAVOURITES

 ☆ **What do you call a person with no body and no nose?** ☆

Nobody knows

Bodie John, age 12
Melbourne, Australia

Why did the scarecrow get a promotion?

For being outstanding in his field.

Joshua
Auckland, New Zealand

213

I'M JOKING, GENIUS!

What did the ocean say to the pirate?

Nothing, it just waved

Anja and Marshall, ages 11 and 10
Bulls, New Zealand

Why do we tell actors to break a leg?

Because every play needs a cast

Joey, age 13
Dannevirke, New Zealand

What did the intelligent fish say to the riverbed?

You need to learn how to reed

Aidan
Whanganui, New Zealand

Have you heard of the band 623MB?

They haven't done a gig yet

James C.
Ohope, New Zealand

READERS' FAVOURITES

What did Santa say while gardening?

Hoe Hoe Hoe

William
Whanganui, New Zealand

Which pharaoh farts a lot?

Tooting Khamun

Lloyd Kendall, age 8
Palmerston North

I'M JOKING, GENIUS!

Why did the potato cross the road?

To get to the other sides!

Wil, age 11
Tamaki Makaurau

What did Luke Skywalker say to the geologist?

May the quartz be with you.

Atticus Wood, age 9
Dunedin, New Zealand

 What lies at the bottom of the ocean and twitches?

A nervous wreck

Zoe C, age 13
Brisbane, Australia

THAT'S ALL, FOLKS

Congratulations! You've made it to the end of the book.

You really are a genius.

But if you're feeling glum because the jokes are over, don't worry! You can always use that big brain of yours to start again from the beginning and make up some clever punchlines of your own. Or you could check out the other books in the series... *I'm Joking* and *I'm Seriously Joking*.

There won't be any more collections of big-brain jokes, but there will definitely be more jokes. I haven't yet found a switch in my brain that can turn them off. Next up is an entire book filled with original Knock-Knock Jokes.

I'M JOKING, GENIUS!

And after that... pranks. Lots and lots of pranks.

Plus, my *You're Joking* series is not yet complete. After the success of *Become an Expert Joke-Teller* and *Create Your Own Knock-Knock Jokes*, I'm preparing to assemble the definitive joke-writing guide. But it's a very big topic. HUGE, in fact. So, I need to clear some space in my brain first by getting rid of a few chapter book ideas that have been hanging around, begging to be written.

To find out when new books come out and to stay up-to-date on my latest news, subscribe to my Joke-Stars' mailing list at:

www.TomEMoffatt.com/keepjoking/

THAT'S ALL, FOLKS

Plus, you'll receive ten brand-new jokes in your inbox every month, along with other freebies and goodies.

Also, check out the latest animated joke collections on my YouTube channel:

@writelaugh

But most importantly, continue exercising that Big Brain of yours. And keep on joking.

ALSO BY TOM E. MOFFATT

MY JOKINGDOM - FREE EBOOK

I'm joking. You're joking. Everyone's joking in Tom E. Moffatt's Jokingdom.

Learn how to tell jokes, how to write knock-knock jokes and create your own hilarious howlers. Collect original jokes along the way and discover how to store them for future joke-telling sessions.

This FREE eBook takes you on a tour of Tom E. Moffatt's world of jokes. So, don your jester's hat and download it now.

www.TomEMoffatt.com/Jokingdom/

I'M JOKING
&
I'M SERIOUSLY JOKING

Still hungry for more?

Fill yourself up with over one thousand original jokes for kids in *I'm Joking* & *I'm Seriously Joking.*

From barking mad dog jokes to stinky poo gags, these jokes are so fresh and funny that people will think you made them up yourself. Which is fine, as long as you remember to buy me a doughnut when you're a world-famous comedian.

YOU'RE JOKING - VOLUME 1

BECOME AN EXPERT JOKE-TELLER

Tired of no one laughing at your jokes?

You don't have to be.

Joke-telling is a skill, like playing the piano or juggling live hedgehogs.

This book teaches you that skill using easy-to-follow instructions and simple exercises. With 101 hilarious jokes (and lots of practice), you'll soon get the laughter and applause you deserve, without ever needing to juggle hedgehogs.

YOU'RE JOKING - VOLUME 2

CREATE YOUR OWN
KNOCK-KNOCK JOKES

Want to knock bad jokes on the head?

Learn everything there is to know about knock-knock jokes, from their history and types, to crafting your own knock-out punchlines.

Packed full of tips, prompts and 100+ hilarious examples, this book gives you the tools you need to create thousands of your own jokes. With easy-to-follow exercises (and plenty of practice!), you'll become so funny your friends will be knocking your door down for more jokes.

223

THE JOKE COLLECTOR'S NOTEBOOK

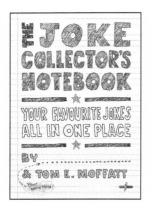

Need somewhere to store your favourite jokes?

Jot them down in T*he Joke Collector's Notebook*, complete with 100 illustrated jokes, fun challenges, and handy tips on finding and telling jokes.

For a FREE Word document version, go to:

www.TomEMoffatt.com/notebook/

BONKERS SHORT STORIES

VOLUME 1:
MIND-SWAPPING MADNESS

A boy in a fly's body.

A toad waiting to be kissed.

Horses that know Morse code and aliens who hijack children's bodies. Has everyone gone completely bonkers?

VOLUME 2:
BODY-HOPPING HYSTERICS

Not all superpowers are a good thing.

Especially NOT if your mum has them. Or if they're fuelled by embarrassment. And what if you can't find your way back home?

VOLUME 3:
MIX-UP MAYHEM

Teleporting your mind across the Solar System.

Strangers using your body while you sleep. Underage time-travellers and remote-controlled baby-sitting devices. What could possibly go wrong?

ABOUT THE AUTHOR

Tom E. Moffatt does not consider himself big-brained or clever, although, he has always surrounded himself with clever people. At both primary and secondary school, all his friends were extremely smart.  Unfortunately, this did not rub off on Tom or his grades.

It wasn't until university that Tom was diagnosed with dyslexia and finally given some learning support. But by then, he'd already devised many coping strategies, one of which was humour.

After a string of brain-shrinking jobs, Tom became a primary school teacher and travelled the world teaching kids to read and write, and sharing his love of books. When he eventually found the courage to write his own ideas down, his first book, Barking Mad, won two national awards. No one was more surprised than Tom, except perhaps his High School English Teacher. He has since published multiple books for kids, including several joke and short story collections.

He lives in Rotorua, New Zealand, with his wife, three daughters, and cat, all of whom are much cleverer than he is.

GLOSSARY

Absolute Zero: The lowest possible temperature (or score!).

A cemetery: A cemetery is a burial ground or graveyard, whereas asymmetry is when two halves of something are NOT symmetrical/mirror images of each other.

Acropolis: A 'high city' with fortified walls in Greece, such as the Acropolis of Athens. I'm sure you'd find lots of leaks there, too. Of both varieties.

Acute diarrhoea: Acute means very serious or severe and diarrhoea (or diarrhea) is runny poos. When you put the two together, the result is the opposite of cute.

À la carte: This literally means by the menu and refers to ordering off a menu where each dish is individually priced. Alternatives would be a set menu, an all-you-can-eat buffet, or off the back of a cart... which is how a horse might eat.

Asgard: The realms where the Viking gods lived, including Valhalla—the home of Odin—and

Thrudheim—the realm of Thor. It was said to be connected to Earth (Midgard) by a burning rainbow bridge. Pretty cool, huh?

Bard: A person who wrote epic poems. Also, Shakespeare was known as The Bard, possibly because he was so epic.

Barred: To be blocked from doing something, as though there were bars in the way. Steel bars, though. Not the kind where drinks are served. Although, it is possible to be barred from a bar.

Barrister: A lawyer in the higher courts, often seen wearing a funny white wig.

Bipyramid: Two identical pyramids base-to-base.

Cardinal: Cardinal numbers tell you how many of something there are, such as 3, 9, and 77. By contrast, ordinal numbers tell you what order things come in, such as 1st, 2nd or 99th. Cardinals are also high-ranking members of the Catholic Church, and a cardinal sin is something that everyone strongly disapproves of.

Catalyst: Something that causes a reaction without being affected itself. It has nothing to do with cats.

Clauses: A clause is a group of words that contains a verb, so a long sentence may have many clauses. As would a Christmas dress-up party.

Conductor: The conductor is the person who stands in front of the orchestra, waving their hands around and directing the music. It is also anything that conducts heat, sound, or in the case of this joke... electricity.

Cryogenics: The science of how things are affected at very low temperatures. Sniff, sniff.

Didgeridoo: An Aboriginal wind instrument that you blow into with vibrating lips. Didgeridoos are traditionally made from branches of eucalyptus trees that have been hollowed out by termites.

Epoch: A long period of time. Epoch o' lips refers to the apocalypse, which is the total destruction of the world.

Flux Capacitor: The technology that enabled Marty and Doc to time travel in the movie Back to the Future.

Fromage: The French word for cheese.

Gander: A gander is a male goose. But to take a gander means to have a look at something.

Golden Handshake: The chunk of money that someone is given when they leave their employment. However, since everything that King Midas touched turned to gold, a 'golden handshake' might be the last thing they got.

Hearing: This is obviously what your ears are for, but a hearing can also be an official meeting where you present evidence and arguments about your case, often held in a court or a private meeting room.

Hedge fund: A high-risk investment scheme that has nothing to do with hedges.

Helium (He): A light gas that is often used to help party balloons escape from parties.

Hereditary: Characteristics passed down from parent to child through their genes. Or in the case of food poisoning, through their jeans.

Hyperdrive: A science fiction term for anything that can power a vehicle faster than the speed of light. Hyper also means unusually energetic or hyperactive, such as a child who's had too much caffeine.

Labyrinth: A complex network of pathways, like a maze. Also, a cool movie from the 1980s that starred David Bowie.

Litmus test: When you use a piece of litmus paper to find out if a liquid is acidic or alkaline.

Mandate: A command or order to do something.

Marsupial: A mammal whose babies are carried in a pouch on the mother's belly, such as kangaroos, wallabies and opossums.

Medusa: A mythological woman with snakes for hair. She was said to be so hideous that looking into her eyes would turn you to stone.

Mensa: An organisation for people with very high IQs. If you make it to the end of this book, you've got what it takes to join.

Minotaur: A mythological creature with the head of a bull and the body of a man that lived in the labyrinth in Crete. A minor refers to someone who is less than eighteen years old, and therefore legally a child.

Miscible: Can be mixed together. If something can't be mixed together, it is immiscible. However, some blockbuster movies are unmissable.

Omnipresent: Present everywhere at once, like God, air and dad jokes.

Rowdy Altercation: Rowdy means rough and disorderly, and an altercation is an angry or heated argument. The two together may very well turn into a brawl, a rough and angry fight. Cerebrawl is a play on cerebral, which means relating to the brain.

Sheikh: A sheikh (pronounced shake) is a male Arab leader or ruler.

Utopia: A perfect place or society. Therefore, utoepia would be the perfect place for feet.

Valhalla: See Asgard.

Whetstone: A stone used for sharpening knives and other tools. Many whetstones need to be wet (not whet?) before use.

Whey: Cheese is made by intentionally curdling milk. The lumpy part that eventually makes up the cheese is called curd. Whey is the thin watery liquid that gets taken away (or awhey!).